RICK PARTLOW

DROP TROOPER BOOK THREE

DANGER CLOSE

DANGER CLOSE

©2020 RICK PARTLOW

Aethon Books
PO Box 121515
Fort Worth TX, 76108
www.aethonbooks.com

Print and eBook formatting, and cover design by Steve Beaulieu.

Published by Aethon Books LLC.

Aethon Books is not responsible for websites (or their content) that are not owned by the publisher.

WHAT'S NEXT IN THE SERIES?

CONTACT FRONT
KINETIC STRIKE
DANGER CLOSE
DIRECT FIRE

1

[1]

"You don't belong here," Josip Brena snapped, and I knew he was talking to me.

Major Brena was a big man, tall and broad across the shoulders, his hair buzzed as close to his scalp as it could be without being shaved bald. His uniform was pressed until the edges seemed sharp enough to slice flesh and his eyes were dark pools of accusatory black fire. He paced across the front of the formation and I didn't follow his movements, staring straight ahead, blinking at the sweat as it dripped into my eyes. Summer in Tartarus was brutal, Brena only slightly less so.

"Someone has lied to you," Brena went on, his voice grating, gravelly. "Somewhere in your chain of command, someone has told you that you are special."

His voice trailed off like a star redshifting as it traveled away from a telescope as he went all the way down the line of Officers Candidate School cadets, all of us braced at attention and frozen in place, not even daring to look at him.

"They told you that you deserve to be officers in the Commonwealth Fleet Marine Corps. This is a lie. None of you deserve a damned thing."

Blueshifting now, coming back toward me. Back into my peripheral vision, a dark shape, a shark swimming in the shallows where I waded, then right in front of me in startling clarity, his chest in front of my face. I glanced upwards at his interface jacks, feeling like I could stare through them into the darkness of his mind.

As if he'd noticed me looking at his temples, he jabbed a finger toward his chest, to the dark cloverleaf symbol there.

"Do you see this, cadet...." He paused and I knew he was checking the name tape on my uniform. "...Cadet Alvarez? Do you know what this is?"

I knew how to answer. That much had been made clear to us by the NCOs screaming at us as we came off the busses from the spaceport, duffle bags dragging us down.

"Sir, yes, sir!" I bellowed as loud as I could, able to keep my voice from breaking with the volume by a trick I'd learned at NCO school. *Shit. Was that less than a year ago?* "It's a major's rank, sir!"

I tried to look past him, tried to avoid meeting his eyes. The training barracks were a sickly yellow tone behind him, the ground a sandstone red, baked in the heat just as we were, and I wondered that even the northernmost continent on Inferno was considered habitable.

"You're damned right it is, Alvarez!"

What the hell did I do to attract his attention? Other than being first in the training company alphabetically.

"Do you know how I got this rank, cadet?" I thought for a panicked moment that he actually wanted me to answer the question and I had no idea which answer he was fishing for, whether hard work, intelligence, breeding, luck, or superior personal hygiene. Luckily, he finished the thought on his own. "I earned my commission as an officer in the Marine Corps the way my father did, and his father before him! I applied to the

4

Service Academy, met their criteria, spent four years working my ass off physically and mentally and graduated with honors!"

He passed on from me and I sagged just slightly, feeling as if I might keel over from the relief.

"And how am I rewarded for this effort?" he went on, his volume increasing along with the outrage in his tone. "How are all of us rewarded, a line of men and women going back a hundred and fifty years? We're told that, due to the needs of the service, the Corps is instituting this clown show! Officers Candidate School my hairy, rounded ass! Sixteen weeks to teach a gaggle of enlisted and junior NCOs what it took me four *years* to learn!"

Which was bullshit, of course. The Academy didn't just teach students how to be officers. It was a college, teaching history, advanced math, science, literature, engineering. It awarded a degree right alongside the gold bar.

Off to my right, someone collapsed, a victim of the heat, or maybe of locking their knees at attention. No one moved to help them.

"It's a fool's errand. But orders are orders. And I've decided that the best way for me to protect the institution of the Marine officer's corps is to do my best to make sure anyone who graduates from this course is worthy. Which means most of you will be returning back to your units with your tails between your legs." I couldn't see his sneer but I could sure as hell hear it. "Which should be about ninety percent of you." He sniffed, and I thought if he were an NCO, he might have spat. "Platoon trainers, take charge of your units. Get this gaggle of wannabes out of my sight."

The usual procedure for a formation like this would have been to call us to attention to turn us over to our officers, but Brena had never called us to parade rest in the first place, so we'd spent the whole twenty minutes of his rambling introduction braced and dying slowly of heat prostration. My own vision was beginning to haze over and I barely noticed when the smaller figure moved out in front of our platoon.

"Platoon," the younger man barked, his voice higher-pitched and more pleasant than Brena's, "at ease."

The breath went out of me in a whoosh as my shoulders relaxed and I stepped into a wider stance, hands clasping behind my back. It was a small motion, but it made me feel as if I'd dived into a swimming pool of cold water by comparison. I was able to take a better look at the man standing before us. He was about my age, maybe a couple years older, probably no more than a year and a half out of the Academy himself, though certainly no less full of himself for all that. His face was lean and sharp-edged and pale, his eyes a dusty brown.

"I am Lt. Manzer," he told us, his tone stiff and awkward, like he wasn't at all used to addressing trainees. I wondered if we were his first class. "I will be your training officer for your entire OCS class, unless you're recycled. Besides the classes you'll be taking in the regular, organized instruction, I'll be teaching lessons on a platoon level after training is over for the day. You will be tested on these lessons, so please treat them as just as important as your classroom education. If you have any problems or questions for me, you need to go through your training NCO, Gunny Reznick."

Yeah, and I was so sure the Gunny would pass our concerns on to the Lieutenant rather than telling us to stuff them up our ass. Maybe the LT thought he was talking to a bunch of E-1 privates.

"I'll turn you over to the Gunny now and she will get you settled into your barracks." Manzer came to attention. "Platoon!" We all snapped to parade rest at the preparatory command, though it had been quite a while since I'd used drill and ceremony for anything but a memorial for the dead. "Attention!"

Gunny Reznik was as tall as Manzer and probably had bigger arms and I got the impression of a little boy playing soldier with his mother when she saluted him and he returned it, turning the platoon over to her. Whatever matronly feelings she might have had for the LT, Reznick quite obviously didn't harbor any such good intentions toward us cadets, given the scowl twisting her features when she faced us.

"Do you worthless motherfucking officer wannabes see that big pile of shit?" she bellowed, pointing off to the side. I didn't look because turning while standing at attention would have gotten me dropped for about a million pushups, but I knew she was indicating the huge stack of duffle bags off to the right of the barracks. It was where they'd told us to drop our bags when we got off the bus, but that didn't mean we weren't going to get ragged out about it.

"Yes, Gunnery Sergeant!" The reply wasn't the antiphonal gaggle I'd heard in Boot Camp or even the slightly deeper and more organized response of NCO school. We were all combat vets, none of us lower than a corporal and most of us buck sergeants like me. The response was sharp, a chorus of professionals.

"Un-fuck this shit," Reznick said forcefully and eloquently in the way only a gunny can, "and get it put away in your barracks in half an hour or you'll be using your extra underwear to brush the fucking dirt off the sidewalk! Go! Now! Fall out, you sorry fucks!"

I ran because it was what she wanted, and I was pleasantly surprised to see everyone else in my platoon doing likewise with the same amount of purpose and alacrity.

"Don't bother searching for your own bag!" I yelled over the murmurs and confusion as we reached the pile. "Just grab one and take it inside! Quick!"

I knew I wouldn't be the only one to think of it, but all it would take is one or two of us not getting the idea and arguing with someone else about it and we'd lose time we didn't have. Maybe they'd think I was a bossy know-it-all, but I could live with it if it meant getting through this stupid bullshit as quickly and painlessly as possible. I grabbed a duffle bag and sprinted for the barracks.

The barracks were exactly like every training barracks I'd ever seen in my time in the Marines from basic training to Armor school to NCO school, just one rack of bunks after another, a polished, white tile floor and white, plaster walls. Stairs in the near corner led to the second floor, where the females would sleep, making things complicated and harder to coordinate, but that was the military. If they didn't put us on different floors, we'd *obviously* be having sex in our bunks after lights out.

At least it was air conditioned. Not *well*, but air conditioned.

I didn't look at the name stenciled on the duffle bag I'd grabbed until I'd dumped it at the foot of a random, unoccupied bunk. It read F. Kodjoe and I started looking around at the other Marines as they filed into the barracks, sweat beading off brows and staining armpits.

"Kodjoe!" I yelled. "Got a bag here for Kodjoe!"

"That's me!" The man was tall and lanky, his head shaven. "Freddy." He grabbed the bag and started unpacking the clothes, quickly and efficiently. "Thanks man."

"Cam," I supplied.

"Alvarez!"

I looked around and saw a woman with short, blond hair

and broad, open features holding my duffle out with one hand like it weighed nothing.

"That's me." I weaved between a cluster of other Marines and grabbed the bag from her. "Thanks."

I didn't feel like looking for another bunk and I already knew Freddy's name, so I took the bag back to where I'd left him and tossed it on the top bunk, claiming it as my own.

"Is it okay if I take this one?" I asked, being polite.

"Long as you don't snore," he told me, laughing softly, not looking away from the footlocker where he was neatly folding his gear. "Where you from, Cam?"

"Trans Angeles." I unzipped the bag and dumped everything on the bunk. I'd packed it in the order I was going to stow it, this not being my first rodeo, and I began sticking them very carefully into the second footlocker. Actually, I was from Mexico originally, but that was a long story I didn't feel like getting into right now. "You?"

"Lagos, Nigeria. Africa," he added, in case I hadn't heard of it. It was only the largest city on the whole continent, the only megacity constructed there after the Sino-Russian War.

Okay, to be fair, I *hadn't* known any of that until I took the educational supplements required before I attended OCS.

"Trans Angeles is a big place," he mused, folding his duffle and laying it in the compartment at the bottom of the footlocker. "Bigger than Lagos by about half, I think I heard. A place that big has got to be crazy. Did you like it there?"

"Not particularly," I admitted. "I mean, I'm here, right?" I gestured out toward Inferno in general. "What about you? Is this hellhole nicer than Lagos or are you a patriot?"

"Lagos is beautiful," he assured me. He seemed a little wistful as he shut the footlocker. "My school used to take us out of the city on field trips to the nature preserves. I got to see elephants, giraffes, even lions. But there's a war and someone has to fight it, you know?"

"A patriot, then," I decided, finishing up and shoving my footlocker back under the bunk before I popped back up. "I don't know which of us is in worse shape, you for believing that bullshit and leaving everything you loved to fight a war dozens of light-years from home, or me for thinking it's bullshit but being here right alongside you."

"If you don't believe in it," he said, frowning, "then why are you here?"

"In the Corps?" I shrugged. "It was either the Marines or a long stretch in punitive hibernation. In officer's training?" I rubbed a hand over my eyes. "I've been asking myself the same thing. Maybe it's just that I was the best of what was left."

I shook my head and checked around the rest of the floor, looking for anyone else who might need a hand. Everyone seemed to be squared away so I cruised by each of the bunks and checked the tightness of the sheets in case the Gunny was going to be a real dick and blame us for poorly-made beds when we hadn't even slept in them yet. Which was always a possibility. I never underestimated the ability of training NCOs to be dicks.

And right on time...

"At ease!" someone bellowed, and I knew right away the Gunny had walked in. If it had been an officer, they would have called us to attention, but an NCO rated an at ease.

Everyone shut up and turned toward Reznick as she stalked into the barracks about five minutes too early. She seemed disappointed not to find everything disjointed and shambolic and I wondered what these people were expecting. This wasn't Boot Camp.

Gunny Reznick walked past me, hands behind her back, dark eyes scanning everyone carefully, as if searching out some flaw she could latch onto. She made it halfway into the barracks before she turned and faced back my way.

"Well, you turds have proven you can follow orders, which I suppose is a testament to the training you've had to this point. Let's see if you can work together as well as you work separately. Females!" she bellowed loud enough to carry up the stairs. "Get down here now!"

She hadn't checked their floor, which might mean she planned to be harder on the males or might mean this place was being monitored with security cameras and she knew what she was going to find before she even set foot in the barracks. I wasn't crazy about either possibility.

The women tromped down the stairs in a ragged line but formed up neatly at the foot, awaiting her orders.

"I'm going to give you your squad assignment," Reznick announced, pulling a tablet out of her thigh pocket and unfolding it. "After you receive this assignment, you will have thirty minutes to decide squad leaders, platoon sergeant, and a platoon leader for this phase of training. If whoever you pick fucks up, you *all* get punished, so choose wisely." Her eyes went to the tablet. "Listen up! First squad, Taylor...."

I didn't really pay attention to the other squads since there was no way I was going to remember them without writing this down. Until she got to Third squad and I was the fourth name mentioned. Even then, I didn't try to memorize the others yet, just waited until she was done and snapped the tablet shut with an impatient finality. I was gratified when Freddy was on the list. It would have been inconvenient to have someone from another squad as a bunkmate and one of us would likely have had to move.

"That's it! Thirty minutes! When I get back, the platoon leader had best be reporting to me!"

"Third squad over here!" I said, raising a hand and stepping back towards my bunk. Again, I hated being the one to take charge, but I couldn't take the chance no one else would.

The others began separating while nine more people crowded in around me and Freddy. Five males, five females, and I thought the other squads seemed evenly divided too. There wasn't time for more than first impressions and snap judgements and we'd all have to hope those were enough to make our decision.

"I'm Cam Alvarez," I told them, then nodded to Freddy and he introduced himself.

"Bethany Chang." That was the blond who'd thrown me my bag. She eyed me suspiciously, as if she didn't trust anyone else to handle anything so complicated as introductions.

"Xavier Horan." Not bald but with the sides of his head shaved back to keep the curly black hair clear of his interface jacks.. His eyes were blue and steady, the set of his jaw strong. Everything about him gave an impression of solid, soft-spoken reliability, but I had the instant impression that he was a follower, not a leader.

"Trey Thompson." Tall, rangy, powerful. Brown hair in a flattop, blue eyes clear and piercing and somehow accusatory.

"Emily Harris." Dark eyes and hair just long enough that it took me a second to tell she had to be Recon. Medium height, medium build, nondescript, average. What you'd get if someone went to a rack in the supply room and asked for Fleet Marine, Drop Trooper, Female, one each.

"I'm Corporal Lea Pineda," a short, dark-haired younger woman piped up with more enthusiasm than I would have had after the last couple of hours of this place.

"You're *Cadet* Pineda," Harris reminded her, an edge to her voice that told me she was a sergeant back in her unit. "None of us have any rank other than cadet while we're here."

I revised my opinion of Harris. She had a take-charge attitude and wasn't afraid to tell other people off, even if she'd just met them. Not so generic after all. Pineda took it silently, seeming a little embarrassed.

"Marisa Vasquez." Nothing there, nothing I could make out past her buzzed hair and interface jacks. She was as much of a cipher as Harris had been before her rebuke of Pineda.

I wondered if they were *trying* to avoid revealing anything about themselves because they didn't want to get picked for a leadership position. That might have made sense before, in Boot and Armor school, but this was a school *about* leadership and I didn't think any of us was going to get away with flying under the radar here.

"Makenzie Krause."

She had a face that could stop a battlesuit in its tracks, and that was impressive in a day when even chawners on the dole in the Underground could get the standard genetic cleanup kit for their children to make sure they were at least average when it came to health and attractiveness. From the colonies then, and not the nice, core colonies like Eden here in the 82 Eridani system. She was from the Periphery, way out where health care was only for those who could afford it and everything that couldn't be produced on a cheap fabricator had to be imported.

The last one in the squad was about my height, close to my build, with the sort of mélange of racial characteristics usually found in the megacities where various ethnic groups had merged, pulled asunder, and merged again over the last two hundred years. He had high cheekbones and the generic light tan skin tone that was practically uniform in Trans Angeles and a hint of suspicion in his eyes that was also uniform in the Underground in my city or any other.

"Hector Fuentes," he said like it was a combination of a curse and an insult. "I've heard of you, Alvarez," he added. "You

13

were on Brigantia. Some guys in my unit were there, said it was a real shit show."

"It was," I agreed. "But a lot of people were there."

"Not a lot of them personally took down the deflector shield."

That got me a lot of stares and I hissed out a sigh.

"We're all here because we got noticed," I said, trying to deflect the matter. "But right now, we have to choose a squad leader and have someone to nominate to the rest of the platoon for Platoon Leader and Platoon Sergeant." I jumped ahead of the train before someone could recommend me. "I nominate Harris for squad leader." I cocked my head to the side. "Anyone object?"

"Yeah, I fucking object," Harris said, but then she rolled her eyes. "But yeah, whatever. I'll do it."

"What about the rest?" Chang demanded. "Who're we gonna tell them for PL and PSG?"

"You volunteering for platoon sergeant?" I asked her.

She scowled but in a thoughtful way, as if she was considering how much work it would be versus how much more control she'd have over her own fate.

"Yeah, fine."

"Hey!" I spoke up, waving a hand for attention from the other squads. Way too many eyes were staring at me, but I supposed I'd have to get used to that if I was going to be an officer. "We got a nominee for platoon sergeant. Cadet Chang here." I waved at the blond woman. "Anyone else want it?"

Silence answered me, along with a dance troupe of shaking heads.

"What about Platoon Leader?" someone asked. I couldn't make out who with all the people clustered together, but it set off a buzz of conversation, until Hector's voice cut through the confusion.

"This guy is Cameron Alvarez," he said and I turned on him, eyes bugging out, ready to tell him to shut up. "He's the one who was all alone on Brigantia with a bunch of civilians and managed to take down the Tahni deflector shields. I think we should make him platoon leader."

"Yeah, that's good with us."

"Better him than me."

And one accession after another and I was just opening my mouth to object when the door slammed open and Reznick blew through it like a thunderstorm.

"At ease!"

"Time's up!" she said, even though I knew for fucking certain we still had ten minutes left. "Somebody better be reporting to me in ten seconds or your asses are grass and I'm a fucking brushfire."

Shit.

I stepped forward and came to attention.

"Cadet Alvarez reports, Gunnery Sergeant Reznick!"

How do I get myself into these things?

15

[2]

"...and you should be aware that your Commonwealth Military Class Three retirement plan will *not* transfer to any of the Class Four civilian plans if you should separate from the military at the end of the war before you've put in a full ten years since your initial enlistment..."

The captain giving the lecture was in love with graphs and charts and the fancy holographic display he was presenting them on, and in love with the sound of his own voice. If they'd kept the temperature cold enough in the classroom, I might have even been able to appear as if I were paying attention, but the combination of the mid-day summer heat of Tartarus, the forty OCS cadets and all the hot air from Captain Economics kept forcing my head back and my eyes closed. I just *knew* that Gunny Reznick would catch me at the exact instant I nodded off.

I had my issue tablet out, not that I planned on taking a single note on it, and I touched a control with my stylus, opening a message box. I couldn't send anything from here— that would have to wait until I had free time. But I could write it now and save it for later and Mother of God I needed something to keep me awake.

Dear Vicky,

I'm sorry I haven't written lately, but we don't get much free time. I'm currently writing this while I'm supposed to be taking notes on a lecture about investment strategies for my post-military life. Silly me, I thought I was here to learn about being an officer and leading Marines in combat. Instead, the first two weeks of this sixteen-week course have been occupied with three days on how to properly wear a dress uniform, two days on how to write an Article-15, three days on how to conduct a formation on a parade ground and now two days of this shit.

Sorry, I don't mean to sound like I wrote you just to whine. It's been frustrating though, particularly since these morons went and made me the cadet platoon leader. I thought it was going to be bad leading troops in combat, but being in charge of a bunch of know-it-all wannabe officers is so much worse. Every single one of them thinks they could be doing my job better and they sure as hell don't hesitate to tell me so, and to tell me what mistakes they think I've made. When you put that together with how often the training NCO tells me I'm fucking up, you'd think I couldn't take a shit without someone around to help me wipe my ass.

Anyway, I hope things are going okay there. I've heard you guys are in an operational hold for a while. The rumor is there's going to be some kind of shift in strategy, and I keep seeing propaganda pieces talking about the "Heroes of Silvanus," the Marines who got trapped behind enemy lines on the colony when it was occupied by the Tahni. The powers-that-be wouldn't say a word in public about the people on the occupied worlds at all this last year and change, and suddenly they're talking all about it. That tells me something is about to change.

I looked up, sure I appeared to be totally engrossed in the

lecture as well as keeping track of what my platoon was doing, in case one of the combat-seasoned NCOs suddenly went nuts and urinated in the middle of the classroom.

"...and as you can see in this chart," the Financial Services officer droned on, indicating something red and green and shaped like a pie split into pieces, "much of the investment the military provides for your retirement account is in the way of long-term government bonds, so it really is in your best interest to...."

The people in my platoon are all older, most at least a couple years older than me, with more time in the service. Even the corporals have more time in the Corps than I do. Not a one of them has more combat experience, though. I'm not sure if I'd count that as a plus, given the nightmares. Are you still having them? I stopped taking the medication because it made me feel sluggish in the morning. I'd rather just deal with the dreams. At least here, I don't have to worry about waking you up, just Freddy, the guy in the bunk beneath me, and he's a heavy sleeper. He's from Lagos, all the way over in Africa, which would have seemed a hell of a long way away back when I was in Trans Angeles, but hell, it's all on the same planet.

It's probably hot in Lagos, but at least Earth has cooler spots. I had almost forgotten how much I hated Inferno. If I live through this war and get out of the service, I am never, ever coming back to this planet. It's the armpit of the galaxy, and it's a sweaty, hairy armpit where the hair is all tangled into knots and smells like the galaxy hasn't take a shower in a week.

Sorry, I may be getting a bit whiney again. I just really hate this place. Fourteen more weeks. Then I get to see you again. I don't know what we're going to do when that happens. According to the regs, we can't have a relationship if I'm the platoon leader and you're even in the same company as me, because I might have to take command of the company. But I

*know you love your squad and you love being their leader and I
can't ask you to change that for me. Maybe I can get Captain
Covington to put me into another company.*

*Shit, I don't want to think about that right now. That seems
far away and as my mom used to say, "sufficient to the day is the
evil thereof." Or in this case, the boredom thereof. Right now, I
just wanted to see how everyone was doing. Tell Scotty it's so
boring here, I even miss his stupid jokes and those history lessons
he used to teach us when we were eating lunch during live fire
exercises. Seriously though, I miss him and the guys from my
squad and I'd appreciate if you could tell them I was thinking
about them.*

*And about you. I think about you a lot. I miss you. I feel
selfish for worrying about us with everything going on, with the
war, with Lt. Ackley dying. But I can't help it. I love you, and I
hope me making the decision to go to OCS doesn't wind up
ruining the best thing that ever happened to me.*

*Write me back. I need something to keep me sane in this
place.*

See you in four months.

Cam.

My eyes flickered upward at a hint of movement, an instinct
that probably went back to apes in the trees catching the motion
of a leopard, but rather than a jungle cat, I found myself being
stalked by Gunny Reznick. I reacted with speed my anthropoid
ancestors would have been proud of and tapped the screen with
my stylus, hiding the message and bringing back up the note-
taking page.

"Cadet platoon leader Alvarez," Reznick snapped, "are you
paying attention to this lecture?"

"Yes, Gunnery Sergeant!" I barked with much more enthusiasm than I'd ever felt about anything, including sex.

"I'm not sure I believe you, Cadet Alvarez." She leaned

down into me, her nose just a few centimeters from mine, her eyes so close that her face was nearly out of focus. "You strike me as one of those know-it-alls who comes through here thinking they don't *need* to listen, that they should just be kicked up to an officer's rank because they're hot shit on a stick. Is that what you are, Alvarez?"

The instructor had stopped talking and was watching the show with a scowl of annoyance, like he had a certain amount of information he was required to get through and this bullshit was just making his day longer. The students seemed less impatient and more fascinated, just as bored with the class as I had been and ready to be entertained.

"No, Gunnery Sergeant!" I assured her, though what I wanted to ask was how many classes they'd actually had and how many know-it-alls she'd managed to encounter in that stretch.

"Is that so?" She cocked her head to the side, squinting like she'd figured out she was too close to actually see me and wanted to get a better look. "Then why don't you tell me what Captain Gilliam was teaching the class?"

I sighed and tried very hard not to roll my eyes.

"He was explaining to us that military retirement is based on investment in government bonds," I said, droning in an almost unconscious imitation of the captain's tone. "And that because of the long-term nature of the investment, it's in our best interest not to cash out if we retire at the minimum ten years, but to get a loan secured against the retirement account and use it to invest in short term stocks."

She frowned, drawing back a step, then motioned at the tablet.

"Is that in your notes?"

"No, Gunnery Sergeant," I admitted. "I just have a good memory." And I'd read ahead in the documentation they'd put in the class syllabus because what the hell else was there to do with my time here?

"You're the cadet platoon leader," she scolded, sounding angrier that she didn't really have anything to be angry about. "The others look to you as an example. Always take notes! Your memory might fail you!"

"Yes, Gunnery Sergeant!"

I didn't even have to turn my head to see a half a dozen barely-smothered laughs, though whether it was at my predicament or Reznick's declaration that I was some sort of role model, I wasn't sure.

Fourteen more weeks.

———

"You know, they say simulators are indistinguishable from real combat nowadays," Freddy Kodjoe mused, sitting half in and half out of the pod next to mine in the training bay. "But I think that's bullshit. Even with the interface jacks...." He pulled one of the cables out of the pod and plugged it into his implant socket. "...I can still tell the difference. What about you, Cam? What do you think?"

"I think," I told him, settling into the armor simulator, "that I'm glad I'm not the platoon leader for the very first simulator run. Everyone here has some kind of combat experience and they're all used to being in charge. This is going to be all kinds of fucked until people get used to working together."

"You got that right, streetboy." I leaned out of the pod and looked back at Fuentes. He was eyeing me again.

"Streetboy" was a term from the Trans-Angeles Underground, a very specific word referring to people like me, the homeless but also those who refused to join one of the gangs. It wasn't something the average chawner would say, and not something I would have called myself. It was meant as an insult and there was only one group that used it.

"Who did you run with?" I asked him. I don't know if I intended to make the question as harsh and clipped off as it came out.

"Kibera 1087s." His smile wasn't at all friendly and I suddenly understood why he'd been so curious about me when we'd met.

"I should thank you, then," I told him. "If you assholes hadn't sent a totally incompetent gun thug to guard your shipment of Kick a few years back, and if he hadn't gotten himself killed by a train chasing me, I wouldn't have wound up in the Marines." I shrugged. "Which, despite the obvious drawbacks of almost getting killed and watching some good friends die, has still managed to be a net positive."

He laughed.

"Yeah, I heard about that. It made you a little famous back home. I think they still have a price on your head, so if I were you, I might avoid coming home to Trans Angeles when the war's over."

"Trans Angeles was never home," I assured him. "And if I never see it again, I won't be crying any tears."

"All right, cadets, cut the chatter!"

The training officer was a slender woman named Perry, her mouth twisted into a perpetual frown and like everyone else I'd met at OCS, she didn't seem too happy to see us. She was a captain, and it seemed odd to me that I hadn't seen any trainer above that rank since I'd arrived apart from the battalion commander, and he was a major. For an institution the Marines had deemed necessary to the war effort, no one seemed to be putting much importance to it.

"Everyone knows why you're here unless you're a complete idiot," she said, already endearing herself to all of us with her personable nature. "This is your first simulator session, the first of many, and from these sessions, you will learn how to lead a platoon in combat. You may think you already know all there is to know about combat, but I am here to tell you that you are *not* ready to take men and women into combat. You may be hot shit in a Vigilante battlesuit, but being able to lead your platoon, keep yourself alive *and* concentrate on accomplishing a big-picture mission is something you have not experienced."

Well, actually... But I said nothing.

There were other skeptical looks beside mine, and I thought I knew people enough to discern that some were based on just the sort of ignorance she was warning against, while others were more from the same place as mine, having actually done what she said we weren't ready for. Still, I got it. This wasn't a job you wanted people going into overconfident. I was just happy to be getting to a part of the training that actually had some practical connection to reality.

"For this first simulated mission, your platoon leader will be Cadet Tomasi."

Tomasi nodded to the rest of us, standing up from his simulator pod. I didn't know the man. He was in a different squad and I'd barely even had time to talk to my own people much less the rest of the platoon. But he gave off an air of competence, so I had hopes he'd do okay.

"All right, cadets, get into your pods and get jacked in." She raised a finger. "And remember, treat this as if it were for real, because if you don't, it will be as close as any of you ever come to leading a platoon."

I pulled the simulator shut, the halves of it closing around me and encasing me in utter blackness for just a moment before the system flickered to life. I was on a barren, rock-strewn plain, the sandstone a blood red under a setting star, the sky a deep amber. We were already down, which seemed to be simplifying the scenario a bit. The platoon was stretched out ahead of me, their battlesuits shifting from foot to foot like toddlers who needed to pee. The interface jacks that lent my reflexes and balance to an actual Vigilante did the opposite in this case, allowing me to feel the ponderous gait of the simulated version of the battlesuit.

"Training Platoon Three," Captain Perry's voice crackled in my headphones as if she was speaking to us from orbit rather than the same room only a few meters away. "Your mission is a movement to contact, across this plain due south for five kilometers, through a canyon and into the next valley over. The enemy will be there in at least platoon level force running patrols in that area and they'll need to be cleared out to allow our troops to penetrate the enemy defenses without being detected."

I frowned. That was some bullshit. I wanted to ask her who the hell had come up with that mission and whether they'd ever once dropped into combat, but I clenched my jaws tight and let Tomasi do his job.

"Okay, Third Platoon," he said, projecting his voice like someone trying to fake being a natural leader, "I want first squad to take point, standard squad wedge formations, second and third abreast, fourth in the rear. Acting Platoon Sergeant Nagano will travel between third and fourth squad and I'll be between first and second. Any questions?"

There were none and surely not from me. I was in fourth squad, dead last, which felt a lot like watching the whole thing instead of participating but, like I'd told Freddy, I could live with that this time.

"Let's move out."

It almost felt strange being in a Vigilante again, even a simulated one. I hadn't had the opportunity in weeks, which was as long as I'd gone without being inside a suit since Armor school. The thought made me laugh softly inside the suit. I was making wearing the suit sound like sex, though the truth was I'd had a lot more of the suit than I'd had time alone with Vicky.

We bounded across the plain with long strides that ate up four meters a piece, nothing stirring on the plain but the odd lizard. Tomasi critiqued our spacing every couple of minutes, seeming to be obsessed with leading, or being seen to lead, and I mostly tuned him out, paying attention to the suit's tactical display, watching the sensors. Nothing showed up, not a hint on thermal, radar, or lidar, and that pissed me off as much as the simplistic, unrealistic operations order. What mission had we ever gone on that we didn't catch sight of the enemy after running through open space for kilometers?

The canyon was generic, like any of a dozen I'd seen on worlds throughout our colonies and the Tahni worlds, dug by some ancient, notional river, but wider and smoother than any I'd traversed in real life. I supposed that was convenient to the scenario, since they didn't want us to spend hours walking through holograms of empty sandstone. We were making good time and I think Tomasi had become so wrapped up in the movement that he forgot about the contact.

They hit us near the end of the canyon, and I was just far enough back to have a ringside seat. Artificial lightning seared away the dusk shadows, the incandescent flares of the proton beams streaking downward from the top of the canyon walls. First squad took the brunt of it, the destruction veiled behind thermal blooms of energy and clouds of angry, black smoke, and the comms were jammed with reports and contradictions, orders and countermanded orders...and then, the IFF transponders began to wink out.

Tomasi's went first, and the rest of us were trapped behind, useless as the front two squads engaged an enemy we couldn't even see behind walls of blinding energy and waves of heat the simulator did its best to duplicate with its internal heaters.

"Nagano!" I snapped, trying to get her to take charge. "Tomasi is down! What are your orders?"

The right thing to do would have been to tell us all to jump. We needed to get out of the canyon and into open space, to break out of the terrain funnel and get room to maneuver. But if I did it on my own, or got just Freddy to follow me, it wouldn't accomplish anything and would only succeed in making me look like a huge Blue Falcon—military slang for buddy fucker. And if this had been real combat, I might have done it anyway and dealt with the consequences later, but this "realistic" training had other purposes not at all connected with combat. So, I stayed where I was and watched for targets and waited for orders. And tried to get Nagano or *someone* to pull their head out of their ass.

"Nagano!" I yelled again. "Tomasi's down, take command! We need to either charge through or break contact!"

But my words were lost in the yells, shouts, and screams of a couple dozen others and so were Nagano's, if she was saying anything. Next in the chain of command was First squad leader, Hasper, but she was tangled up in front, and if her armor wasn't deadlined yet, it was about one good hit away from it. Which left the Second squad leader, Gutierrez. I toggled a private channel to the man, hoping he'd accept it and wasn't already overwhelmed by all the cross-chatter.

"Goot!" I said, using the nickname I remembered from our brief conversations. "Tomasi's down, Nagano's doing fuck-all and Hasper is caught up in the brunt of the attack. You need to take charge of the platoon and get us out of this trap right fucking now!"

"I don't know," Goot said, a hesitant whine unraveling ragged edges off his voice. "I'm fourth in the chain of command, Cam...I don't want to make Nagano look bad."

Oh, sweet Jesus and Mother Mary...

I switched to Bethany Chang's frequency. She was Fourth squad leader for the mission, the very last in the chain, but fuck it, at least she was a link.

"Chang," I snapped. "Everyone's fucked. Take charge and get us out of here or the whole platoon is toast."

"Yeah," she muttered, obviously not happy about the idea. "Maybe I should, at that." When she spoke again, it was on the platoon net and she used the command override the leadership came equipped with to drown out the other confused voices, something Tomasi should have thought to do, but hadn't. "Fourth platoon! Hit your jump-jets and advance out the end of this canyon! We have to break through the ambush!" Everyone, go! Now!"

I didn't know who was in charge of Fourth squad or who was acting as her platoon sergeant and there was no time to find out. The tethers had been slipped and it was time to move.

"Follow me, Fourth squad!" I said and jumped, hoping someone would follow me,

A flood of data washed over me with such speed and vehemence I couldn't sort it all into a coherent picture on a conscious level. I just *knew*, the way you know where your hands and feet are, or where the door is in a room you've lived in for years. I knew the Opposing Force, the OpFor, was arrayed in an inverted V across the front of the canyon entrance, dug in behind hasty fighting positions stacked with rock and sandstone, something we trained with but I had never actually seen fighting the Tahni.

I targeted the two closest and fired off a pair of fire-and-forget missiles, the pod jolting me with the simulated shudder of the weapons rocketing out of my shoulder launcher, one after another. I didn't wait to judge their effectiveness because things were even worse than I'd thought. Most of First squad was dead, right alongside Tomasi, and the enemy's reserve was taking to the air, arcing over the elements in contact to try to take us in the rear.

We could bypass the ones who'd dug in, but the reserve squad was going to take us head-on and I made the decision to deal with them first.

"Freddy, stay on my shoulder."

They were the last words I said before I was in the fight, before conscious thought slipped away, stepping back and letting something instinctive and unthinking take over. The suit was an extension of me, the maneuvers a dance I'd learned so long ago that it was a part of my identity. It came as a surprise when my plasma gun fired, as if someone else's finger had been on the trigger, as if the roiling ball of super-ionized gas had come from the accusatory finger of an angry god rather than by any intention of my own.

Whether it was Zeus or me pulling the trigger, the results were the same. A simulated Tahni High Guard battlesuit took the blast in the left shoulder and lost its arm in a splash of starfire, leaving only blackened, charred metal behind. The enemy suit had been in mid-jump and it tumbled out of the air, the jets still operational but the mind behind them gone into deep shock, or at least so the simulation's AI shepherd had decided. I didn't follow its descent, moving to the next target.

I had two missiles left and I used them now, deciding they probably wouldn't let me take them home after the war. I was less than three hundred meters from the enemy now, barely enough space for the warheads to arm before they slammed into the Tahni High Guard troopers. Again, I couldn't wait to do a Battle Damage Assessment, could only afford the time to run a quick scan of my surroundings, find the next one in line.

I was vaguely aware of my own movement, the way a boxer in the ring isn't consciously moving his feet, just letting years and years of training guide his footwork, letting it lead him to the right spot. I was down, then up, then down again, bouncing left and right in a zigzag pattern over the ancient, dry riverbed, and Freddy kept at my shoulder as I'd directed, moving with a natural flow I admired. He knew his business and it was clear why he'd been sent here. Enemy targets were dropping off the scope and some of them were his, enough that I allowed myself the space of a half-second to feel impressed.

The next half-second I gave to checking my own status and finding, to my shock, that not only had I not been hit yet, but that my whole squad was intact. That was enough back-patting, though. The attack of the reserve squad had been disrupted, but there was still most of a platoon dug in behind us, still engaging the rest of our people.

"Turn back and hit 'em from behind," I instructed.

Somewhere, Chang was shouting orders and I should have been listening, but I figured she had her hands full with the rest of the platoon and I should try to do my best to help out without distracting her. Fourth squad followed my lead and our approach didn't go unnoticed. The High Guard troops backed out of their fighting positions and turned to face us.

Their missiles were gone, as were ours, spent in the first, mad minute of fighting, and it was down to our energy weapons, as it usually was in real combat. I didn't have to remind my people to randomize their movement, to cut their jets and bounce off in a new direction, to stutter-step in the face of gouts of proton lightning. Every one of us was a natural in a Vigilante or we wouldn't have been sent here, wouldn't have been given this opportunity. We were all the best fighters and this simulation's computerized OpFor didn't stand a chance against us.

But computers, as they so often do in these sorts of situations, tend to cheat. The enemy platoon was toast, as good as gone. My squad was blasting it from the rear, almost at point-blank, while Chang led the charge from the canyon. But this was the computer's show and it wasn't about to be upstaged.

"I'm picking up multiple contacts inbound from behind us!"

The voice was unfamiliar and I didn't have time to check the IFF transponders to see who it was. The truth of the message was evident in my own sensor display, the thermal and radar hits popping up like Christmas tree lights, closing in from the plateau atop the canyon walls. They were heavy, slow-moving aerospacecraft, the Tahni equivalent of a drop-ship, each laden down with the burden of two platoons of enemy battlesuits, and I counted at least five of the ships burning in on superheated air sucked through their intakes and heated in reactors before being expelled at hypersonic speeds.

And if the ships hadn't fired on us already, it was only because we were too mixed with their own forces. There was no question of standing and fighting, no hope of reinforcement, and if Chang hadn't made the call, I would have.

"Scatter!" she said, the word explosive, a gunshot. "Everyone scatter by twos and meet back at Rally Point Alpha! Go!"

I echoed the command and then Freddy and I were gone, jetting forward in short, frantic hops across the high desert terrain in what was likely a forlorn hope, and for just the briefest of moments, I forgot this was a simulation and felt the hind-brain panic of flight, the wolves at the heels of one of my hunter-gatherer ancestors.

"Index, index, index. End simulation."

The world around me faded into darkness and the pod hissed open automatically, letting in the painful light of the training center and a sea of scowling, disapproving faces.

"All right, cadets!" I had almost forgotten about Captain Perry, but there she was again, along with Lt. Manzer, Sgt. Reznick, and a couple of other trainers I didn't recognize.

"Everyone out of the pods and double-time to the briefing room for the AAR!"

"You heard the Captain!" Reznick bellowed. "Go! Go! Go! If you're not all there and standing at attention by your seats in thirty seconds, I will take you outside and smoke you till you collapse from the heat and the medics drag your asses to sick call!"

Reznick, I thought as I yanked free the interface cables from my implanted sockets and let them spool back into the pod's housings, was a joke. I wondered if she thought her Boot-Camp schtick was getting to us, if she realized we'd all been yelled at before. If she even considered how much more stressful it was to see your friends die around you than to have some idiot who'd never seen combat try to make you panic by yelling at you.

"Come on, Freddy," I said to my bunkmate. I could see a muscle twitching on his cheek and I thought maybe he was having the exact thought about our training NCO. "I think the circus is about to start."

[3]

"Can anyone tell me what they think went wrong with this exercise?"

Perry was very self-consciously trying to sound in command. Which, I suppose, was necessary for a training officer, but it was so deliberate, so obvious it made me want to laugh in her face. I wanted to raise my hand, wanted to answer, but I didn't think she'd like what I had to say.

Behind her, the whole cluster fuck was unfolding on a screen stretched across the back wall of the conference room, playing out in two-D because the Marines were too cheap to spring for a holotank. The Vigilantes looked like toys in some giant sandbox, or perhaps, more accurately, like pieces in a giant Virtual Reality computer game, each labeled with the wearer's name, squad and leadership position, if any.

It wasn't a pretty picture. The lead elements of our platoon had been royally sodomized by the enemy troops, and the long seconds between the start of the ambush and Chang taking charge had been enough to give our platoon five KIAs and three suits too damaged to continue fighting. Three more of us had notionally died in the counterattack and God alone knew whether anyone would have survived the flight away from the incoming drop-ships.

Tomasi raised his hand.

Oh, jeez, this should be good.

"Yes, Cadet Tomasi?"

He stood and came to attention, as we'd been instructed, projecting his voice as if he were on the parade field. It sounded ridiculous and I wondered how stupid we all looked to anyone who wasn't part of the OCS class.

"Ma'am, I accept full responsibility for the failure of this mission, ma'am. I should have taken control of the situation."

"It *was* your responsibility, Cadet Tomasi," Perry agreed. "But your suit was badly damaged in the initial attack and your communications were out even before you took a critical hit and were ruled KIA. Which means acting Platoon Sergeant Nagano should have stepped up and taken control of the unit." Her face hardened and she speared Nagano with a glare. "Sit down, Tomasi."

Tomasi managed to make sitting in his folding chair look as stiff and uncomfortable as any drill and ceremony move we'd practiced on the parade field.

"Cadet Nagano," Perry said, and Nagano stood and braced to attention.

"Ma'am, yes, ma'am?" Nagano tried to bark the words but they came out as more of a squeak.

"Why don't *you* tell us what you think went wrong with the operation?"

"Ma'am, I neglected to engage command override on the communications net and my orders were drowned out by everyone else, ma'am." Which was, at least, concise and accurate and showed some self-awareness. I wondered if she'd figured that out herself while we were still in the simulators or if someone else had told her on the way into the conference room.

"Yes, you did neglect to do that, Nagano," Perry agreed. "And do you know what would happen if you did that in real combat? You'd all be dead. That's why you're here, because none of you are ready for this job. I hope to God you're prepared by the time you leave here."

Perry was on a stage at the front of the conference room, a meter above the main floor where we sat, and she paced across the five-meter stretch of platform, hands clasped at the small of her back, eyes fixed on the floor ahead of her.

"Anyone else?" she asked. "Anyone know what the last problem is, what might have been the worst failing of the training mission?"

Chang's hand went up and she rose, coming to attention, not waiting for Perry to call on her.

"Ma'am," she said, her voice much steadier and more confident than the others had been, "once our platoon leadership had been compromised, the chain of command fell apart. No one wanted to be the one to take charge and make a decision." She paused, then seemed to remember the proper etiquette of addressing the officer and added a final, "ma'am."

"Very good, Cadet Chang," Perry acknowledged. "And yet you did, taking command of the platoon out of your turn, not waiting for the others ahead of you to do so. Why was that?"

"Ma'am," she said, and her eyes flickered toward me, "Cadet Alvarez suggested we didn't have time to wait for the others to realize the leadership structure was compromised, and recommended I take control of the platoon, ma'am."

Fuck. Thank you all to hell, Chang.

I tried to keep my face neutral, stifling the surge of irritation roiling around in my gut.

"Sit down, Chang." Perry's voice was flat as she stepped across the stage and singled me out with a piercing glare. "Cadet Alvarez."

I stood and came to attention, perhaps not as eager and energetic as the others had been.

"Ma'am, yes, ma'am!" Just as loud, though.

"Tell me, Cadet Alvarez," she went on, "what exactly gave you the idea that you had the authority to put Cadet Chang in command of the platoon?"

"Ma'am," I said, my words harsh and clipped off, not because I was trying to sound angry but more because it was the only way to hide my disgust, "the platoon was in immediate danger of becoming combat ineffective. No one was stepping forward to take command. I knew the First squad leader was too busy fighting for his own life up front to be able to control the rest of the platoon and I am not as familiar with Second and Third squad's personnel as I am with my own. Ma'am."

"In other words, Cadet Alvarez," Perry said, a growling undertone in her voice, "you decided that you knew better who should be running the platoon than the chain of command, did you not?"

I wasn't sure what she wanted, but I was fairly certain that whatever I said was going to land me in deep shit, so I figured I might as well be honest.

"Ma'am, I believed we didn't have the time to waste waiting for someone to step up, ma'am."

"And you didn't think that the chain of command is there for a reason, Cadet Alvarez?" Her eyebrow shot up, as if in disbelief. "You didn't consider the chaos and destruction that could result from ignoring it?"

"Ma'am, I did consider it, ma'am. Marines were dying in the simulation, and I have always been taught since Armor School to treat simulations the same way I would treat actual combat, ma'am."

I'd probably said too much, I knew that already. I should have just admitted to being wrong no matter how I actually felt about it and let her have her way. That was the lesson I should have learned in Boot Camp and Armor School. But dammit, this was supposed to be different. We were supposed to be learning how to be leaders, how to make these sorts of decisions.

"These exercises are meant to teach you, Cadet," Perry told me, strained patience grating like metal on metal in her tone. "They are lessons you're supposed to learn, each about a different subject, and this subject was the chain of command. If you can't accept the nature of our learning process, I'm sure we'll be happy to send you back to your unit until you've matured enough to learn how to obey instructions. Is that what you want?"

"Ma'am, no ma'am!" I barked, giving in to the inevitable. I was about to sit back down, but one last rebellious spark lit up behind my eyes. "Ma'am, may I ask a question, ma'am?"

Perry didn't *want* to let me, but she didn't have any good reason not to and she answered through gritted teeth.

"What is it, Cadet Alvarez?"

"Should the platoon have had the point man or maybe a buddy team up front a couple hundred meters to scout the end of the canyon, ma'am?"

"What does Marine doctrine state?" she asked by way of a reply. She was phrasing it that way on purpose, trying to make it sound like an attempt to make sure I knew doctrine, but I had the sense she was asking because she had no idea.

"According to what I was taught in Armor school, ma'am, it's generally advised, but it's also command discretion in a situation where avoiding detection is vital. I was just wondering what you think we should have done, ma'am?"

I sat down, feeling Gunny Reznick's glare from the other side of the room. *She* knew what I was doing, even if Perry didn't. Perry had tried to make me look like a reckless know-it-all, a Blue Falcon out to undermine the other cadets. I was returning the favor by putting her on the spot, and if she really knew as little as I suspected about combat...

"It wasn't important in this exercise," she said, a note of huff in her voice, her lips pursing in a narrowly-aborted pout. "This is about leadership."

I said nothing, but the look in her eyes said everything.

———

"This is, I believe," Freddy told me, not looking up from polishing his boots, "the most worthless, useless training I have ever had."

I nodded, not bothering to comment. Rage burned in my chest and I took it out on the uppers of my combat boots. Maybe if I wore a hole in the damned things, they'd give up on the stupid-ass tradition of making us shine them every single day. As stupid as it was, though, it had nothing on the simulator training we'd been doing.

"Man, you said it," Fuentes piped up from the bunk across from us, though I don't believe Freddy had meant to include him in the conversation.

Fuentes was sprawled out on the floor, legs hanging out in the middle of the aisle between the bunks in a way that was sure to get him dropped for pushups if Gunny Reznick popped in for a check...which would, of course, get *me* in trouble.

"I thought that first simulator run was lame, first-week-of-Armor-school shit, but the last couple were even worse." He sputtered something between a laugh and a grunt of disgust. "Fuck, man, how many deserts we gonna run through with nothing in them? Shit, you seen a lot of combat, *Jefe*, how much has been running through the fucking desert?"

Jefe was what he'd started calling me ever since I'd been

made cadet platoon leader, and I was fairly certain he didn't mean it in an affectionate way.

"I think maybe once," I admitted. I laughed without humor. "I never thought I'd get to the point where I'd been on so many different worlds, I couldn't even remember them all."

"Long way from the streets back home, huh, *Jefe?*" Fuentes cackled. "Not some outsider scrambling around trying to beg a place to sleep, anymore."

"I don't think about that much anymore, Fuentes." I shook my head, not willing to take the bait. "That was someone else's life, and I didn't miss it the second I left it behind." I eyed him with a curious tilt of my head. "What about you? You miss being one of the old gang, throwing your weight around in the 'hood, and getting all the women you wanted?"

"Shit no, man! I wasn't no fucking shot-caller! I was the kid they sent to do the shit no one else wanted to do. I spent a shit-load of time in juvenile confinement, just waiting for the day I did something bad enough they'd finally throw me into the Freezer."

The Freezer was what the gangbangers called punitive hibernation. Some of them had even come back from it, returning right back to the gang, stepping in as if nothing had changed because nothing ever did in the Underground.

"What'd you get pegged for?" I asked him, honestly curious. "You don't strike me as a guy who would have volunteered in a fit of patriotism."

His eyes narrowed.

"Man, if I *was* still in the gang, I'd think you was an under-cover cop. Why you talk so fancy for a streetboy?"

"My mom thought learning was important." I let my eyes drop from him back to the boot top I'd been working on, buffing out one last scrape. "And the library was always open if I wanted a place to sit somewhere comfortable and plug into a ViR education program."

"What happened to your mom?" Freddy asked.

I glanced up sharply but forced my eyes back to the boot. It wasn't a question you'd ask someone if you were from the Underground, but I knew he wasn't. He was a surface dweller and bad things didn't happen to people he knew.

"We lived in Tijuana," I said, and that *should* have been enough explanation if he'd known anything about the place.

"People still live there?" Fuentes asked, dead serious. I wasn't shocked. Most people in Trans Angeles, even in the Underground, had never heard of it.

"It's in old Mexico," I continued. "The country doesn't exist anymore, and most of the cities are in ruins, but people still live in parts of them." I spat on my boot top and polished it away. "And if you think the gangs in the Underground were rough, you should try living with the cartels in Tijuana. Mom wanted me to learn because she wanted me to be able to survive, and Tijuana is a hard place to survive. Mom took a bullet standing right next to me on our front steps, a stray shot from two guys trying to kill each other over money."

Freddy gasped. I don't know if I'd ever heard a man gasp before. His right hand moved a centimeter toward me and stopped, as if he'd felt an urge to put a comforting hand on my shoulder but reconsidered.

"And you know, that was the final straw for Dad. He put me and my brother in a gas-powered car someone had fabricated off old specs and tried to take us to Trans Angeles because he heard they'd take anyone who came. Lots of people try to make that trip, though, and the reason most never get there is the bandits in the desert. They got us, too. I hid in the trunk until they left, until they'd killed my father and older brother and took every-thing we had, which wasn't much. Then I started walking across the desert and would have died if a maintenance tech hadn't stumbled across me."

"*Jesus Christo*," Fuentes murmured, crossing himself. I chuckled. For some reason, the Catholic reflex struck me as funny coming from him. "I'm sorry, man, I didn't know."

"No reason you should have."

I put the polishing cloth down, judging the boot with a critical eye. It was as good as I could get it. Whether Gunny Reznick agreed, I couldn't be sure.

"You're right about the simulator missions, though," I told Freddy. "They're worse than useless, they're fucking dangerous. They're going to send a bunch of new platoon leaders out there thinking they know how to command, and when everything goes to shit, like it always does, maybe their platoon sergeant will have it together enough to pull their asses out of the fire but maybe they won't. Hell, I could come up with a better set of simulation parameters just from...."

I realized I'd left my mouth hanging open and I closed it before something flew in.

"What?" Fuentes asked, shaking his head.

I stuffed my polishing gear and my boots in my locker and jumped to my feet. My fatigue blouse was hanging on the aluminum frame of the bunk and I grabbed it and my cap and started toward the door.

"I'll be right back," I told them.

Lt. Manzer's office was in the same building as our barracks, but it had to be accessed from the exterior, mostly, I suppose, so they didn't have to worry about cadets sneaking in there at night. I departed our blessed island of air conditioning and ventured out into the blast furnace of a Tartarus summer, sweat beading on my forehead and the small of my back almost immediately. I kept my eye out for officers or, worse, training NCOs, but it was mid-afternoon on one of our rare days off and they were all off doing whatever training NCOs had to do to keep sane.

Manzer's door was closed and I hesitated for just a moment before I knocked on it, wondering how much trouble I was going to get in for not going through Reznick first before talking to him.

"Come in." Manzer didn't quite have the impatient snap of command like Covington. His invitation was almost friendly.

I pulled the door open and stepped into a position of attention, saluting before I'd had so much as a chance to take a glance at the interior of the office.

"Close the door behind you," Manzer said, his tone plaintive and nearly whining, but his return salute crisp and textbook sharp.

"Yes, sir." I got the door with one hand and pulled off my cover—my cap. The Marines call it a "cover," like my head was some sort of preserves jar and my brains would go bad if I left the top off.

It was blissfully cool in Manzer's tiny office, probably due to the small space the system had to work on. The room was plain white and unadorned, the only decoration on the walls a certificate of commissioning from the Commonwealth Service Academy back on Earth. The desk was metal and must have been older than Tartarus base. It looked as if the Marines had salvaged it from some ancient American military base after the Sino-Russian War and brought it to Inferno out of some misplaced sense of nostalgia.

"Cadet Alvarez," Manzer said, "I don't recall Gunnery Sgt. Reznick informing me of any scheduled appointment to speak with you."

"No, sir," I admitted. "I do not know where Gunnery Sgt. Reznick is, sir. But I had something important I wanted to ask you, sir, something you would have to okay."

Manzer leaned back in his chair, which, from the incessant squeaking, had to have been just as old as the desk. He rested his chin on his chest and regarded me with skepticism in his eyes.

"All right," he said, finally. "Tell me." He sighed. "And at ease."

"Sir," I said, hands clasping behind my back, "I wondered if I might program a few scenarios into the simulator pods that the platoon could run on our own time."

"Why?" He shook his head. "What would you want to do that for?"

"Sir, I'm concerned that the scenarios we're running in training are too simplistic and dumbed-down to realistically reflect combat."

"Major Brena," Manzer told me, mouth twisting in a scowl, "and the commandants for the other OCS training battalions have made the decision that the simulations should be as simple as possible to keep the trainees from being distracted or confused." He seemed pissed off, but I wasn't sure if it was with me.

"Do any of the battalion commanders have actual combat experience, sir?"

"No." Now the bitterness was plain to see and I knew it wasn't my suggestion or my questions that had upset him. "Not a one of them."

"Sir, I've never been an officer," I said, approaching the subject like I would unexploded enemy ordnance, checking out every side before I took a step closer. "But I had to lead a platoon in combat once. I had to because the platoon leader sacrificed herself to save us, and the platoon sergeant was badly injured. I wound up almost getting killed myself and I got to tell you, sir, I didn't know at the time how the hell I would have handled that mission, how I would have been able to do anything to get us all out of it alive. I still don't."

I sagged just slightly, a feeling like walking back out into the heat from the air conditioning.

"Coming here wasn't my idea. My company commander sent me and I didn't want to go. I didn't want to be a platoon leader. I'm good in a Vigilante. Better than anyone I've ever run into, if I'm being honest, sir. I wanted to stay with my squad, with my friends, to do what I could to keep them alive. But Captain Covington had a different idea for me. He thought the kind of talent I had could be used to lead others, to teach them to see what I see and think like I think. I have my doubts, but I owe my platoon leader, Lt. Ackley, a debt I can't pay any other way."

"And it has to start right here. If I just do what I have to do in order to graduate OCS, get my butterbar and wash my hands of the place, I won't be paying her back for the lessons she taught me. I have to try to make sure I try to help everyone I can who leaves here as an officer to know what they're going to face."

Manzer stared at me for so long, I was convinced he was debating whether to simply throw me out on my ear, or actually call the MPs and have me hauled away. But when he moved, it was slow, measured, and deliberate.

"This can only be on your free time," he said.

I blinked, certain I'd misunderstood, but he kept on.

"And you can't touch the scenarios reserved for training. This will have to be a self-contained module you can insert and take out completely. And I have to be there when you use it. Don't involve Gunny Reznick, just come get me yourself."

I nodded, wondering if he was concerned that Reznick might report the violation to higher authority, or concerned that she wouldn't and not wanting her to get in trouble.

"Yes, sir," I said, realizing the nod might be taken as disrespectful.

"I'll give you an extra hour after lights-out each night to construct the scenarios. I'll come get you. Don't tell anyone about this until I've had the chance to review what you've done."

"Yes, sir," I said, sucking in a deep breath as if I'd been holding it the whole time. "Thank you, sir."

"Don't thank me yet, Alvarez." He rubbed a hand over his face. "I get the feeling I'm making a huge mistake."

[4]

"Contact right!" Fuentes yelled.

Tahni High Guard battlesuits swarmed from the underground bunker like rats deserting a demolished building, some taking flight and arcing across the 1200 meters between us, other sprinting headlong, straight into our front lines.

"Launch missiles by rank!" I snapped, operating my own suit from instinct, not thinking about what I was doing, only what I wanted the others to do. "Staggered fire, maintain the volley until you're dry! Keep your formation, don't fucking panic!"

The words might have been wasted. These men and women were all experienced and well-trained. But it helped me to say it and I thought it helped them to hear it, helped us all to organize our thoughts in the face of chaos.

I'd been here before, but the familiarity did nothing to ease the fear and tension. Even the knowledge it was a simulation was offset by the nervousness of leading my platoon in combat for the first time, of knowing they'd be watching me as closely as they watched the enemy.

Things were different this time and not just because I knew

what was coming. The first time I'd gone through this battle, I'd let my conscious mind drift, let my instincts and training take charge and tried *not* to think, not to absorb the bigger picture at all. It had been a comfort of sorts, not letting myself realize what was happening. This time, I had to keep the formation at the front of my brain, watch every meter of the Tahni advance, looking for weaknesses, for gaps, in our lines and theirs. I had to figure out where to throw troops to block them from getting behind us or cutting us off from the next platoon over, which was just as much a product of logic gates and computer simulation as the enemy.

"Fourth squad," I transmitted, firing my plasma gun and not remembering I'd aimed or even conscious of whether I'd hit anything, "hit the jets, hop over First and lay down suppressive fire! First, move up to support them and fill the gaps! Second and Third, close in on the flanks! The company is advancing at the tip of our formation so move!"

Shuttles were exploding, proton beams crashing, missiles were arcing back and forth between our lines and theirs. Mortar rounds were launching automatically from my backpack to lay down countermeasures for the incoming fire but it was all just a buzz of background noise. It slid past my mind, past the only thing that mattered, where my platoon was and what we had to do in order to accomplish the mission.

"First platoon," a female voice said in my ear, what could have been a human but was actually the computer masquerading as one, "pull back and prepare for incoming air support."

And things went from there just like they had the first time, with our shuttles coming in and cutting down the enemy ranks, then the company command group taking down the deflector dishes with the Boomer fire support suits. And then, quite unlike last time, there were no Tahni civilian females swarming us and being slaughtered in a fit of rage. It was just a voice.

"Index, index, index."

The projections around me went dark and I unplugged from the deck and pushed my pod open. Lt. Manzer was waiting there for me, arms crossed over his chest, eyes downcast, staring at the floor without seeing it.

"And that was an actual place?" he asked me.

I climbed out of the simulator, laughs and curses and muttering coming from the rest of the platoon. The simulation had been a kick in the teeth after the milk runs we'd been sent on so far, and I thought it had produced the effect I'd been looking for. Some of them hadn't wanted to give up their free time to come back to the pods, but I'd promised them something different, something that wouldn't bore them.

"Confluence," I told him. "I was there. I nearly died. My point man, the best Vigilante operator in the platoon besides me, was killed by a civilian female with an IED."

"I can't believe *anyone* survived that," Manzer said, shaking his head. "How could they?"

"This wasn't even the worst. People died, a lot of people, but it wasn't the worst."

"Goddamn," he hissed the word like a prayer. "Other cadets have to get a chance at this. This needs to be SOP, not just something our platoon does on its free time."

"What the *fuck* is going on in here?" The voice was as familiar as it was unwelcome.

Gunny Reznick stormed through the door from the training bay's outer hallway, hair on fire and ready to tear someone a new asshole until she spotted Manzer and stopped in her tracks.

"Lieutenant?" Disbelief and confusion had replaced her anger. "Sir, might I have a word in private?"

Manzer blew out a breath and eyed me sidelong.

"Alvarez, police up the platoon and get back to the barracks."

"Do you want me to yank the program module, sir?" I asked him, motioning toward the control station at the front of the room.

"No. I'll take care of it. I want to show it to Major Brena."

"Yes, sir," I said and started to turn before I stopped and added, "Good luck, sir."

I got the feeling he was going to need it.

———

"Out of your racks, maggots! Move your asses, now!"

It wasn't the first time I'd been woken up from a sound sleep well before reveille by a bellowing Gunnery Sergeant, though I held out hope that, after OCS, it might not happen again. I didn't even bother bitching and moaning because no one wanted to hear me complain and I certainly didn't want to hear it from them. I just rolled out of my bunk, my bare feet slapping the cold floor, then turned and made my bunk by rote, not even needing the light. It took ten seconds and then I was slipping into my PT shoes and running up to Gunny Reznick, bracing to attention.

"Yes, Gunnery Sergeant!" I said, as loud as I could manage on three hours of sleep.

"Alvarez," she growled, more venom in her tone and her eyes than usual, "get these maggots in their fatigues and into formation in ten minutes or I will haul your ass into the Goddamned yard naked and have you do pushups with your fucking dick!"

"Yes, Gunnery Sergeant!"

I didn't make the obvious jokes about being *able* to do pushups with my dick, which would have been very Marine-like of me, but wasn't really my style. And probably would have had me doing pushups, not with my dick and likely not naked, but pushups just the same.

"Get into your fatigues!" I bellowed, then had to repeat it for the females on the intercom before I ran to grab my own.

"What the hell is going on, anyway?" Freddy asked, rubbing sleep from his eyes with one hand and fastening his blouse with the other. "There wasn't any training scheduled this morning, was there? Do you think they're going to drop us in the jungle or something? Make us all find our way back on foot?"

I rolled my eyes. He'd been going on about that since we got here.

"This isn't Force Recon OCS, Freddy. They've barely let us get into a real suit outside the armory, they aren't going to drop us in the fucking jungle."

"I hope it's not just another boring lecture by some colonel about military decorum," Fuentes murmured, fastening the straps on his boots. "If I have to sit through one more of those useless wastes of time...."

"We ain't gonna find out sitting in here bitching," Beth Chang said, bounding down the stairs just past Fuentes' bunk.

"I'm heading outside," I told Chang. "I'll take everyone who's ready and wait up at the front of the formation and you get everyone out of here, okay?"

"Yeah, I gotcha Cam, get on out there."

"Fourth platoon!" I yelled, bringing my shout up from my diaphragm instead of my throat, pitching my voice to carry. "Everyone who's good to go, follow me outside and form up! If you're not squared away yet, *get* that way! Acting Platoon Sergeant Chang is going to be shoving you out the door, ready or not, in five minutes! You got me?"

"Ooh-rah!"

It was raining outside because of course it was. It was one of those twice-daily rains Tartarus got that made the northern continent of Inferno just barely habitable in the summer, and if it had been mid-afternoon, I might not have even complained. Anything was better than the too-close 82 Eridani glare beating down on us in the middle of a summer afternoon here. But in the zero-dark-thirty blackness, when you can barely see shit anyway by the streetlights that always seemed too dim and too far away, the driving rain added one more filter of invisibility and all I could hope for was that Reznick wouldn't be able to tell how ate-up we were.

I found what I thought was the right place to stand to form up the platoon and the Marines who'd followed me out began to line up by squad, leaving gaps for the ones still inside to fill. I started counting automatically, knowing by heart just how many men and women were in our platoon. While I did, I noticed peripherally the broad-shouldered form of Gunny Reznick prowling around, draped in a rain jacket, which, of course, she hadn't cautioned us to wear. She was speaking to someone else, a figure I didn't recognize even after weeks of practicing trying to tell one NCO and training officer from another at night and from a distance. This one was standing tall and ramrod-straight in defiance of the elements, not bending to the rain, not so much as tilting his head forward to keep the tip of his hood down far enough to keep the water out of his face.

I couldn't make out much of the face and what I did see wasn't familiar. What *was* familiar were the two other Marines striding purposefully down the street, boots kicking up sprays of water as if they resented God for sending the rain. One was the Top, the training First Sergeant, a loose-jowled, dead-eyed fucker named Palermo and you did *not* want to get that asshole's attention.

The other was Major Brena.

Shit. What the hell is the Major doing out here this time of the morning?

We'd gotten pulled out of the barracks early before, but I had never, not once, seen Brena's worthless, lazy ass out of doors before 0800.

"They're all out here, Cam," Chang told me and I blinked, not even realizing she was there between the rain and the revelation that Brena was present. I wiped a hand over my eyes and tossed excess water off my fingers.

"Thanks." I counted twice myself just to make sure, then braced to attention. "Platoon! Attention!"

I about-faced and waited, knowing it could be a while but also knowing Reznick would have dinged me if I'd waited till the last minute. But Reznick didn't post up in front of me. Brena did. If the storm hadn't featured any thunder and lightning before, it surely had some now. Brena's face was twisted in what could have been anger or perhaps resentment, his eyes narrowed against the rain, and he didn't even bother have us go to parade rest.

Prick.

"Fourth platoon, you're out here because your training officer, Lt. Manzer has been relieved and you will have a new trainer. Lt. Steiner! Front and center!"

Oh. Oh, shit.

I was suddenly in free-fall, or at least that was how it felt to my stomach, like the world had dropped away. Manzer was a good officer.

The tall man, whom I now assumed was Lt. Steiner, seemed to be perpetually at attention, so I couldn't tell much difference when he posted in front of Brena. They exchanged salutes, droplets of water flying as their hands sliced through the air. Once Brena had left the formation, Steiner executed an about-face and favored us with a glare, and I knew immediately that Brena had found his spirit animal.

"Cadets!" His voice was a whipcrack. "Up until now, you've had it easy. That ends this morning. From this point on, you will work harder than you ever have in your life. You will run twice as far, do twice as much PT, and you will do it without complaint and without fail, or you will be dropped from this course. Standards have slacked off, which is why my predecessor has been replaced. You will no longer be able to cruise along, marking time until you graduate."

What a load of shit.

It was all I could do not to say it aloud. Who the fuck *was* this asshole to say shit like that about a fellow officer? What kind of unprofessional bullshit *was* this? My head felt hot enough that I was surprised the rain didn't turn to steam where it touched me.

"I have also heard," Steiner went on, his eyes on me this time, boring into me like drilling lasers, "that your former trainer was unwise enough to allow nonstandard scenarios to be loaded into the training simulators. This practice will cease immediately, as will any use of the simulator pods outside established, scheduled training sessions. Your training will come straight from the book and *only* from the book. Do I make myself clear, cadets?"

"Yes, sir." The reply was lukewarm and anger flared behind that mask of iron.

"I know it's raining, but I can't believe you didn't hear me!" he bellowed. "I said, do I make myself *clear*, cadets?"

"Sir, yes, sir!" Louder this time, if no more enthusiastic. It seemed to be enough to satisfy the shitstain though.

"Gunnery Sgt. Reznick, front and center!"

The Gunny took over while Steiner stalked off to speak with Brena.

"All right, you maggots," Reznick said, shoulders hunched up against the rain, "when I dismiss you, I want you to change into your PT uniforms and clean up the fucking floor because I know you sloppy morons are going to get water and mud all over it. But before you do that, you're going to need to get your heads together, gather those few working brain cells you have left and pick a new set of cadet leaders. Alvarez has had his chance to fuck things up and he's done it so well, we're sending him back into the ranks to figure out just where he went wrong."

I didn't look at her eyes. I wasn't going to give her the satisfaction.

"Dismissed!"

I clamped down on an urge to yell for the platoon to get inside. Instead, I simply walked inside, not saying a word.

"Cam!" Freddy was running to catch up with me and he grabbed my arm just as I was passing through the door. "Hey Cam! What are we going to do now?"

I stared at him like I would have if he'd asked me what color Thursday was or any other nonsensical question.

"What the hell do you mean?" I demanded. "Do about what?"

"About them getting rid of Manzer," Fuentes said. I hadn't even noticed him walking up behind Freddy. "This ain't right, man."

"What do you guys want me to say? There's nothing we can do now except try to graduate from this shit show." I stripped off my shirt, ignoring the puddle of muddy water on the floor.

Someone should clean that up. But not me. I wasn't in charge anymore.

Thank God.

5

I should have known that wouldn't be the end of it.

We were sitting in a class covering how to tell a legal order from an illegal one when Gunny Reznick pushed the rear doors open with a metallic clunk of the locking mechanism and stomped down the aisles between the platoons and stopped right beside me.

"Get up, Alvarez," she snapped. "You're coming with me."

"Yes, Gunnery Sergeant." The words were quiet, numb. I'd given up on the forced enthusiasm around the same time I'd given up on the genuine version.

I said nothing as I followed her out of the classroom, out of the building and into the searing heat of the streets of the training base. A half a kilometer away, a Force Recon OCS class was getting smoked in a sand pit, dropped for pushups, turned over for flutter kicks, popped to their feet for squats, and then back to pushups. It could go on for an hour, I knew. I'd been there. We'd done plenty of pushups, plenty of marching, plenty of running, and endless classes on every piece of minutiae some officious asshole had considered vital, but I could count the number of times we'd done live fire training on one hand and still have four fingers left.

We stopped at a set of offices I didn't recognize except that it was in the middle of brass country, where the senior officers squatted in air-conditioned comfort and shuffled data from one system to another. By the time we stopped in front of a door marked with Major Brena's name, I knew why I was here. I took a deep breath and let it out slowly, preparing myself while Reznick knocked.

Brena grunted something through the door and Reznick stuck her head inside.

"He's here."

"Send him in."

Reznick gestured and I might have let my lip curl in a sneer as I passed her. She was a fucking gunnery sergeant and it was beginning to piss me off how important she thought she was. She wasn't worth the sweat on Gunnery Sgt. Scott Hayes' boxer shorts.

Brena was sitting at his desk, looking at me expectantly and I at least afforded him the military courtesy of coming to attention and saluting.

"Cadet Alvarez reports, sir."

He took forever to return the salute, and I wasn't a bit surprised. He was that sort of officer. I distracted myself by taking stock of his office. It was thoroughly decorated with what military officers call an "I love me" wall covered with his graduation certificates and commendations. None of them had come in combat, I noted.

"Sit down, Alvarez," he told me after he'd finally tossed back a sloppy wave of his hand.

I sat and didn't try to stay stiff and attentive. He didn't deserve it.

"You think you're special, don't you, Alvarez?" His piggish

little eyes stared at me with resentment he wasn't even trying to hide. "You think because you got a few medals that the rules don't apply to you? That you can do whatever you want?"

I thought about staying silent, reflected that it would probably be the smartest thing to do, then didn't.

"I didn't break any rules, sir. I asked for and received permission for everything I did."

There was no point in pretending I didn't know what he was talking about, and I wouldn't have tried even if there had been.

"Lt. Manzer did *not* have the authority to allow you to change *my* combat scenarios!" Brena shouted, slamming a palm down on his desk. "That bullshit you programmed into the simulators would never have been approved by me or the curriculum committee! No one would ever face that sort of opposition in a real battle." His tone was scornful, as if he was speaking to a wayward teenager who'd played too many ViR games. "The briefings we've been given by our Intelligence officers say there's no way we've taken that many casualties."

"Every one of the programs I created," I said, keeping my voice low and calm by a force of will, "is a battle I fought in. Each one is a scenario I've played out over and over again in simulators, live-fire exercises and force-on-force field training missions. And in my nightmares. My team leader was killed in the first of them. We lost half a company at Brigantia. And at the last one, the one where they gave me a silver star, we lost my platoon leader. Her name was Joyce Ackley and she was the finest officer I've ever met." *Present company included, you fucking circus clown.* "To answer your question, Major, no, I don't think I'm special, but I do think she was. She saw something in me and took a chance when others wouldn't have, and I've been trying to pay her back ever since. I felt like the best way I could do that was to give the other candidates here a chance to see what real combat is like."

It was a waste of time. I already knew it. Scotty told me once that there are two types of majors. One is what he called the perennial staff officer, the one who knows they're not going to be promoted, or if they are, it's years away, and until then they're stuck in one staff position after another. A few are bitter with their lot in life, but most are fairly cool about it. Brena was one of those other type of majors who had his eye on Lt. Colonel and knew it was so close he could taste it. He was sitting in a Lt. Colonel's position so he had to expect the notification any day. That by itself didn't necessarily make him an asshole, but if an officer had any assholish tendencies, this was the situation that would bring them to the forefront.

"You are an insubordinate piece of gutter trash from the Underground," he growled at me, leaning across his desk and jabbing at me with his finger, just begging to get it broken for him. "I don't know who's been filling your head with the idea you can come in here, into *my* command and tell me what's real and what isn't, but that's not going to be my problem from now on."

He pulled a tablet out of a drawer and tapped at it with a stylus until he reached the page he was looking for and then he held it in front of me. I didn't bother to try to read it, but I caught a fleeting glimpse of my name and rank before he set it back down on the desk in front of him.

"You are here at the pleasure of the Marine Corps and at *my* discretion, Sergeant." Not cadet, I noted. He'd said sergeant. "And I am recommending," he went on, tapping the stylus against a control, "that you be dropped from this course effective immediately." His sneer of satisfaction really needed a fist through it, but as much as I hated to return to my unit a failure, staying in the brig for a few months first didn't really appeal to me, either. "It will be reviewed by the brigade commander's office, but that's mostly a formality. You should go pack your shit, Sergeant. You'll be on the next ship back to the front."

———

The barracks floor was comfortably cool under me and I had lost track of how long I'd sat there, staring at my open footlocker, before the others started to file in from training.

"What's going on?" Freddy asked, dropping his tablet and stylus on his bunk, following it with his sweat-soaked cover. "What did Gunnery Sgt. Reznick want?"

"Yeah, man," Fuentes said, snickering, "they kick you out or something?"

"Yeah." He'd been joking. I wasn't.

Fuentes' face froze somewhere between a sarcastic, teasing smile and a look of utter disbelief.

"No shit?" Bethany Chang asked, stopping her tracks and staring at me. "What the hell happened?"

"Reznick took me to Brena's office," I explained, amazed at how dispassionate I sounded for all that my gut was still roiling. I pulled open my duffle bag and stuffed my running shoes into the bottom of it, still unable to work up the energy to put any real effort into packing. "He told me I was insubordinate and disrupting their training and he was recommending to the brigade commander that I be dismissed from the course."

"That is such *bullshit!*" Fuentes raged, and I was a bit surprised at the passion behind the words. "Jesus, dude, you are the *only* motherfucker in this place who cared if we learned a damned thing or not." He slammed his fist into the wall and if it hurt, he didn't seem to register it. "Goddammit!"

"What's going on?"

It was Tomasi, the new cadet platoon leader. I'd gotten to

know him a little bit since our first simulator run. He wasn't the smartest guy I'd ever met, but he wasn't a dick, either, and if I'd thought otherwise when he'd been in charge of our movement to contact a few weeks ago, well, he'd been just as nervous as the rest of us. He'd hurried over as soon as he came in, sensing something was out of place in his newly acquired platoon.

"That stupid motherfucker Brena is kicking Cam out of the program," Chang said, nearly as vehement as Fuentes, "because he programmed those alternate training programs into the simulator for us."

"Oh, dude, that sucks," Tomasi said, his long, horsey face suddenly stricken. "Those were the best training I've ever had!"

"Yeah, that was some awesome shit, man." Vin Lee Trang agreed. I didn't know him beyond his name, but he was in Third squad and he'd been there for the off-hours training. "It was even more intense than the real combat I seen."

"Thanks, guys," I said. I tried to smile but I thought it came out more of a grimace. "You just keep on working, keep your noses clean and go be some first-rate officers, okay? Maybe I'll get lucky and have one of you for my platoon leader."

"Umm...," Tomasi dithered, "we gotta get ready for lunch. We only have ten minutes before we have to be out in formation." He brightened a bit. "You coming with us, Cam?"

"I don't really have much of an appetite right now," I said. "Besides, I still have to pack. If I'm not here when you get back, well...." I shrugged. "I've got you guys' 'link addresses and I'll make sure to keep in touch."

It was a nice thought, but probably as much of a fantasy as me becoming an officer. Once I left here, I'd likely never see any of these people again.

"Officer on deck!"

I sprang to my feet out of habit, coming to attention microseconds before I remembered it was probably that stick-up-his-ass Steiner. Oh well, we respected the rank even if we couldn't respect the person.

But it wasn't Steiner, and it wasn't even Brena. The woman who walked through the door to the platoon bay was older than either of them. It was harder to tell in the military than it had been in the Underground, and harder there than Tijuana, because the availability of advanced medical care decreased with each step down that ladder, but after a while, I'd learned how to spot them. The docs might be able to stop the aging process, might be able to make someone a hundred years old look like they were thirty, but there's a difference to the way an older person carries themselves, a certain care to their stride, a weight that I thought had to come from knowing how easy it was to get killed and having lived long enough to try to avoid that at all costs.

There was something in the face, too, something I couldn't quite define. Not exactly a weathering, not physical anyway. More a set to the eyes and the jaw, the sort of jaded cynicism someone might develop when they'd seen the worst humanity had to offer for longer than the human consciousness was built to last.

This woman was old. Not as old as Top or the Skipper, who were both pushing two hundred, but somewhere north of a century. And the golden eagles on her shoulders proved she hadn't wasted that time. She was a full bird colonel in the Marines, with a chest-full of fruit salad, campaign ribbons, commendations and medals for valor that had to date back to the First War with the Tahni.

"I'm looking for a Cadet Alvarez," she said, her voice clear and almost lyrical, like she'd once been a trained singer.

"Ma'am!" I sounded off, the bombastic energy I thought I'd lost somehow back in my bellowing reply. "This cadet is Cadet Alvarez, ma'am!"

"Cut that ooh-rah shit out, Marine," she said, sounding more amused than impatient, a mischievous twinkle in her grey eyes. "I'm Colonel Bell, commander of the 33rd Training Brigade. I'd like to talk to you." She turned a baleful glare on the others. "Alone. Get everyone out of this barracks and get to the mess hall."

"Ma'am, yes, ma'am!" Tomasi said, reddening as the last part came out in a squeak. "Platoon! Everyone out now! Drop what you're doing and form up outside! Double-time!"

It took less than a minute for the whole platoon to rush out the doors, some of them pulling on boots or fastening their fatigue blouses as they went, and I thought it must have been some kind of record.

"At ease, Alvarez," Bell told me. "Actually, as you were."

I nodded my thanks, though I didn't actually go back to as I was, because I had been sitting cross-legged on the floor. But the command gave me leave to speak, which I wouldn't have had standing at ease.

"You're probably wondering why I'm here, Cadet Alvarez," she said.

"And why you're still calling me 'cadet' instead of 'sergeant,' ma'am," I agreed. "I thought I'd been dismissed from the program."

"Major Brena doesn't have the authority to dismiss OCS candidates," she told me. "He can only make recommendations to *me*, and I make the final decision."

Bell moved over beside my bunk and leaned against the frame, her stance casual, as if we were of equal rank and she was shooting the shit.

"Sit down," she invited, waving at Freddy's bunk.

I hesitated, more from not wanting to mess up Freddy's perfectly-made bed than fear of accidentally disrespecting her, but I sat down anyway. I could always fix it for him before I left.

"Something else Major Brena didn't have the authority to do was to have Lt. Manzer relieved. That should have run across my desk *before* the fact rather than being presented to me as a *fait accompli* after Josip had already found a replacement." She grinned. "Just in case you're wondering, I did *not* drop everything and rush down here simply because Brena sent your name across my desk. I'd had my adjutant looking into this ever since Manzer had been relieved, and seeing the report recommending your dismissal, put together with Manzer's testimony gave me all the information I needed."

"To do what, ma'am?" I asked, treading carefully. This was a full colonel, probably close to being promoted to general, and I was an E-5 and close to being thrown in the brig.

"To have the man relieved, Cadet Alvarez." She cocked an eyebrow at me. "Believe it or not, it was *not* the intent of the Marine Corps to turn OCS into a punishment intended to flunk most of you out and discourage enrollment. This is a work in progress and there's a lot of pushback, but we will get it working eventually." She snorted a humorless laugh. "Probably about the time the war ends. But the Corps *needs* officers, and I think, from your record, you know why."

"Yes, ma'am," I confirmed, a grim frown settling on my face at the memories.

"And we need them trained well. Which is why I am ordering your scenarios programmed into the simulators on a permanent basis. Along with a few more we've collected from students in other companies. And I'm also reinstating Lt. Manzer as your platoon trainer. My adjutant, Major Breslov, will take over the battalion temporarily, until a permanent replacement can be found."

I realized I was staring at her, open-mouthed, and I shook myself like a dog shedding water and smiled.

"Thank you, ma'am."

"Don't thank me, Alvarez," she warned. "I'm not doing this because I like you. I'm doing this because you have experience that's valuable to the Corps and to the Drop Troopers. If you want to thank me, help others learn from it. And pass this fucking course so we can plug you and the rest of these cadets here into platoons and keep fighting the damned war."

I jumped to my feet and came to attention, feeling as if God Himself had breathed life into me.

"Ooh-rah, ma'am!"

6

"Hi, Cam." Vicky gave a little wave at the camera and I waved back at the recorded message even though she couldn't see, my breath catching in my chest at the sight of her.

It hadn't been that long, just four months, yet I thought there was something different about her. Maybe it was the two-D flat screen, or maybe it was the lighting in the barracks room where she'd recorded the video, but there was something harder about the lines of her face, something sharper in her cheekbones, some darker glint to her eyes.

"I hope you're doing okay. I know you have to be close to graduation by now." She smiled and the harshness I'd perceived melted away. "I guess that means you didn't fuck up too badly and you're actually going to be an officer, which seems like it should be scary as shit, but I've seen some of the Academy kids they're kicking out lately and OCS grads can't be any worse."

She sobered, the smile fading.

"I hope this doesn't get censored. I mean, I don't know why it would." She shrugged. "The enemy already knows and no one has told us it's a secret. But we've been on an operational hold since just a couple weeks after you left. The scuttlebutt is that the whole kinetic strike strategy is being shelved. I guess that must mean it either worked or someone decided it was a bust. I don't know if we'll ever be told which is the truth. But I've heard it has something to do with a colony world called Canaan."

"Canaan," I mumbled. "Where the hell is that?"

"I don't know where the hell it is, either," she said as if she heard me. "Some Periphery colony that happens to be a Transition line hub. I guess the Tahni occupied it over a year ago, a few months after Demeter. Well, the word is, we took it back." She grinned. "Fucking citizen's militia of some kind working with intelligence spooks set something up and some guys I know from the 3rd of 598th Drop Troopers came in for the clean-up. They said it was a beautiful operation. The spooks knocked out the ground defense lasers and tied up the Tahni forces while the Fleet jumped insystem and launched an attack. The Marines barely had to do anything, just take out a few hold-outs. I kind of envied them the milk run."

She seemed to lean in toward the video pickup as if she was sharing a confidence with me that she didn't want anyone else to hear.

"I think the Fleet brass needed this, like a kick in the ass telling them it was time to start trying to take back the occupied colonies. I talked about it with the Skipper and he says it's what they call a 'tipping point.' He thinks that's what's going on, that we got the Tahni to withdraw their fleet back to protect their core systems and now we're going to dig out the troops they left behind on our worlds. I don't know how long we have before it kicks off...so, I'm doing this now."

"Doing what?" I whispered, knowing she was about to tell me and suspecting I might not want to hear it.

"I asked the Skipper to put me in for OCS."

There it was, the other shoe dropping. It was a gut-punch. It meant she would be in a different platoon, likely a different company unless ours had another opening at platoon leader I hadn't heard about. But I was, I decided, happy for her. She deserved it, and she'd be good at it.

"I leave for Inferno in three weeks," she went on, a hint of regret in her eyes, in the fall of her voice. "I don't know if you'll be back before I go. I hope so. I'd like to get the chance to see you again before I go. If I don't...." The breath went out of her. "I love you, Cam. And I know we'll find each other once this is over."

She reached out a hand to touch a control on her 'link and the image froze as the recording ended. I touched my fingers to the screen to meet hers and answered under my breath.

"I love you, too."

I put the tablet down on the drum-tight bedding of my bunk, pulled out the ear bud that had kept the audio private, and began fastening the brass buttons of my dress blues.

"Why we gotta wear this shit for the graduation ceremony anyway?" Fuentes whined, tugging at the collar of his uniform. "Brass buttons and medals...this is like from a hundred years ago. And it's gonna be hot as shit out there in these damn jackets."

"It's tradition, Hector," Freddy told him. "The Marines are all about tradition, man."

"Yeah, and the fucking tradition makes us spend a month's pay on these stupid fucking money suits we're never gonna wear again." Fuentes wandered off toward the head, probably looking for a mirror, and Freddy turned back to me.

"Was that your girlfriend?" he asked, nodding toward the tablet. "The one you keep talking about?"

"Yeah." I didn't really want to say anything else, but I knew Freddy by now, and I knew he wasn't going to give up until I'd had some long, heartfelt conversation because that was what they did in his family, and we were all his family now. "She's leaving for OCS. Probably be gone before I get back."

"Oh, man, I am so sorry," he said, putting a supporting hand on my shoulder. "That's rough."

"That's how it goes," I said, shrugging, trying to act more blasé and accepting about the whole thing than I really felt. "We were lucky to get the time we had. You hear much from your girlfriend back home, Freddy?" I asked, hoping to change the subject. "I see you recording messages to her all the time, but I don't know that I've ever seen you watching one she sent back the whole time we've been here."

"She doesn't like to do video messages," he said. "She just does text."

"Just admit it, Freddy," Horan said, nudging Freddy in the shoulder. "She ain't real. You're in love with a computer simulation you met on one of them lonely hearts sites or something!"

"Yeah, you're just jealous, X," Freddy pushed him back, but they were both laughing. "Just because you haven't found a girl willing to put up with your smelly, hairy ass..."

"Officer on deck!"

We came to attention, but Lt. Manzer waved it off quickly. He was all smiles and I knew why. I'd asked around and the graduation rate for the average OCS class was just over sixty percent. Our company was commissioning ninety percent of the cadets, and the only reason it wasn't more was that we'd had a couple drop out. And our platoon had stayed intact for all sixteen weeks, not a single failure, not a single drop-out. Together with the Brigade Commander being in his cheering section, Manzer was looking at the fast-track to captain.

"Are all of you ready to have those gold bars pinned on?" he asked.

"Ooh-rah!" The reply was deafening, echoing off the walls

of the barracks and Manzer seemed to lean back and let it wash over him.

"Get ready, people," he said, hooking a thumb back at the barracks door. "I want you all formed up in twenty minutes and looking sharp out there! What's the best platoon in OCS?"

"Fourth platoon!"

"You're damned straight it is!"

He was still smiling when he came up beside me and leaned against the railing of the bunks.

"Cam," he said softly. "I know you guys are supposed to have a week of out-processing, but we got a request for expedited transport. Apparently, your unit's about to move bases soon and they want you back before it happens. After the ceremony, you need to get your shit packed up quick. You're hopping a transport heading for Hachiman in twenty hours."

"Yes, sir," I said, nodding. "Guess I won't make the party at the O-club after."

"Sorry about that," he said. He chuckled. "I owe you a drink."

"Me, sir?" I blinked. "For what?"

"If you hadn't come to me and asked for that extra training," he confided, "I wouldn't have gotten in deep shit with Major Brena, but I also would have been serving under him here for another two years. You met the man. You tell me, do you think he would have recommended me for the Officers Advanced Course and a promotion?"

"Probably not, sir," I admitted.

"As things stand," he said, "Major Blake has me to thank for his position as Brena's replacement, and a colonel who's about to be a general knows my name."

"It's not all me, sir," I insisted, a little embarrassed by the attention. "Things went right for you because you did the right thing."

"So did you, *Lieutenant* Alvarez." He offered me a hand and I shook it. "And you weren't afraid of the consequences. Whoever gets you for a platoon leader could do a lot worse." He nodded toward the door. "I have to go get ready for the ceremony. Make sure your shit's on straight. You're an Honor Graduate, after all."

————

"Thanks again for coming with me to the shuttle," I said, shouldering my duffle as the bus came to a jolting, squeaking halt. The bag was heavy but nothing felt as heavy as the subdued, gold bars on my shoulders.

Holy shit, I'm a fucking officer now. Who the hell thought this was a good idea?

Insects drawn to the interior lights flitted about us, tormenting the line of bleary-eyed Marines waiting to get off the vehicle.

"You had to miss the party, man," Fuentes said, rubbing a hand reflexively against the back of his shaven head as a mosquito tried to gain purchase on it. "Couldn't let you slip away at zero-dark-thirty with no one to say goodbye."

"I wish you could stay longer, my friend," Freddy told me, and I thought he'd been about to say more but the line began moving as the troops in front grabbed their luggage and headed down the steps to the pavement below.

It was still early morning and 82 Eridani was hours from rising above the horizon, but it was still cloyingly humid and I thought again how happy I would be to leave this planet and never set foot on it again.

"Do you two know what units you're getting yet?" I asked.

"I got my orders right after the commissioning ceremony," Fuentes said. "I head out for Canaan in a week. 3rd of the 598th

is settling in there for the rest of the war and Fourth platoon, Alpha Company needs a new LT."

"Congrats, Hector," I told him. "I know you'll do great."

And the lucky bastard probably wouldn't see any combat for a while. I wish I could have said the same. It was probably heresy for a Marine to think, but I'd seen more combat than I ever wanted to and I would have been just as happy never to hear a shot fired in anger again.

"I'm going back to my old unit," Freddy said, brightening. "Not the same platoon, but the same company. They're good troops."

The others from the bus milled around at the tram station, some squinting into the distance, looking for the open wagons that would take us out to our shuttles on the tarmac. Some of them, I imagined, would be going on my plane, heading up to the same transport, their destination Hachiman. There was a whole battalion of Drop-Troops there and another of Force Recon, as well as a few squadrons of Attack Command missile cutters. And they were about to move out.

Where would we be going? Vicky thought we'd be pushing in on the occupied colonies, which probably meant we'd be withdrawing from the Tahni frontier, heading back into Commonwealth space. It was funny, the war had turned and we were taking the offensive...by moving backwards.

"You have to promise me you will stay in contact," Freddy said, jabbing a finger into my shoulder for emphasis. "I mean it, Alvarez. You have our 'link addresses and I had better hear back from you."

"All right, I promise." I raised my hands in surrender. "It's...," I trailed off, shaking my head. "It's not something I'm used to. But I'll do my best."

"Hey, man," Fuentes said, "I know you said you don't want to go back to T-A again, but in case you ever do, I know some

guys. I could make some calls, see if I can get them to cool things
down for you."

"Don't put yourself in a hole for me, Hector," I told him.
"You can ask, but don't call in any markers. If you wind up going
back there after the war, you might need them for yourself."

"You know, man," he mused, looking up at the stars in the
early morning sky, "I think you might have the right idea on
that. T-A is home, but there's so much else out here. Not *this*
fucking place." He snorted at the idea. "But I seen a bunch of
other worlds and I don't know if I want to particularly live on
any of them, but I wouldn't mind finding a job that would keep
me travelling around them. It's too big a universe to be living in
a hole under the ground, trying to claw my way to the top of the
garbage heap to be the head rat."

"Not a bad thought." I heard a commotion and glanced over
to see people pointing at the tram approaching from the landing
field. "Here's my ride, guys. You should get back on the bus
before you get stuck here for another half an hour, getting eaten
alive by mosquitos."

I hadn't expected the hug from Freddy, but I suppose I
should have. He struck me as a hugger.

"Be careful."

"You too."

Fuentes settled for bumping forearms, and then the tram
pulled up, settling in with a squeal of brakes and a rasp of plastic
tires against the pavement. It was operated by a fairly basic automated driving program and built low to the ground, with bare,
plastic seats lacking any sort of safety restraints, designed to
simply slow down and let the passengers pile off at their destination. I grabbed a seat and let my duffle bag ride beside me, then
barely had time to wave a last goodbye to my friends before the
tram rolled off again, continuing its cycle around the perimeter
of the landing field.

I'd woken up at 0200 local time and I wouldn't have minded the opportunity to close my eyes and grab a catnap on the drive to the shuttle, but the tram didn't announce stops and I'd have to keep my eyes open or else ride the damned thing the whole way around the edge of the field again. I tried to keep myself awake by swatting at mosquitos.

"You here for OCS?"

It took me a second to realize the question had been for me. I twisted around, cradling an arm over my duffle bag and met the eyes of the man beside me. He was generic in utility fatigues and a brimmed cap, the dim glow of the streetlights barely penetrating the shadows to give me a glimpse of a square jaw and a nose that had been broken a couple times too many. I eyed his rank and saw that he was an E5, a buck sergeant.

I suppose I was too new to being an officer to be take offense at the lack of a "sir" at the end of his question, though maybe I should have said something. As I'd had to tell myself several times, you respected the rank, not the officer wearing it.

But I was too tired to be outraged.

"Yeah," I said, not adding "sergeant" just to let him know I hadn't missed his casual disrespect.

"You think it's a good idea?" he asked, and I could tell by the edge of skepticism in his voice that he didn't. "I mean, I figure they can teach you how to lead Marines in combat in four months, sure...but isn't there more to being an officer than just knowing how to run a platoon in combat?"

"Like what?" I wondered, curious in spite of myself.

He tilted his head and a single blue eye emerged from the shadow long enough to meet mine.

"Like, they send 'em to the Academy for a reason. They teach 'em history and science and shit. I figure they don't do that just because it's always been that way, it's gotta be important for something. Like, it's gotta give them perspective, you know? On people, on what's been tried before and failed. Maybe that's just the little bit of extra edge you need when you have to make decisions you don't want to have to make, right?"

"You might be right," I admitted. "But there's more than one way to learn perspective. And there's more than one perspective to have, you know?" I thought about Tijuana, about the death and chaos, about the Underground and the gangs and the cops.

"You were what?" he asked me. "A corporal?"

"E5," I told him. "Same as you."

"And you really think you're ready for this?"

"Probably not," I admitted. "But this whole war has been one thing after another I wasn't ready for." I saw the shuttle up ahead, knew it was mine from the tail number. I grabbed the strap of my duffle bag and was up and stepping off as soon as the tram slowed down. I threw an ironic salute at the mouthy E-5 as he passed on into the darkness and muttered the rest of the thought aloud, not caring he wouldn't hear it.

"Why should this be any different?"

[7]

I was never so glad to be cold in my whole life.

Hachiman was a little too far away from its star to be called temperate. In fact, only the equator was ice-free year-round, and the only land at the equator was a few, small islands. I'd only seen them from the air, but even from a thousand meters up, I could tell they weren't suitable for a military base. The Fleet had constructed the base on the southern edge of the largest continent and there were still glaciers only a few dozen kilometers north of it. Even the summers never got warm enough to venture outside without a field jacket, and the winters were four long, miserable months of sub-freezing temperatures and endless blizzards.

And I hadn't realized how much I'd missed it until I stepped off the ramp of the shuttle and didn't begin sweating immediately. I'd neglected to check the local calendar on the flight from Inferno, but by the fact that the wind coming in from the north didn't blister my uncovered face, and the fresh sprouts of flowering plants pushing out of the mud toward the late morning sunshine, I deduced we were in late spring.

After the brisk rush of spring chill, the next thing that hit me was the noise. The spaceport at Hachiman was always active, Marine dropships or Fleet missile cutters or cargo shuttles coming and going at all hours. This was orders of magnitude different, an unending roll of thunder from cargo ships landing and taking off, served by a ceaseless swarm of freight trucks that seemed to be disassembling the base right in front of my eyes.

Enthralled by the sight, I barely noticed the other passengers crowding down the boarding ramp around me, and didn't even glance downward at the passenger bus pulling up to the base of the ramp until someone smacked me on the arm and told me to move my ass.

"Oh, sorry, Lieutenant," the Corporal corrected himself, finally catching sight of my rank. "I meant to say, move your ass, *sir*."

I didn't recognize any of the other people on the bus. There was no reason I should have, but the whole flight back, I'd felt as if I were coming home, and it was unsettling to be in the midst of strangers while the whole place was torn down around my ears.

The shuttle had landed near the far side of the port and it was a good three-kilometer drive just to get to the edge of the landing field, then four more to get us to the center of the base. Mud sprayed from the tires as the vehicle came to a sudden halt outside the admin center, a square, ugly, functional building for the ugly function of personnel allocation, and it was as close to a state religion as the Commonwealth military had. Anyone who reported to any base, even their own, had to stop at the admin center to make obeisance to the Gods of data processing, and newly-minted lieutenants were no exception.

At least there wasn't much of a line. I didn't actually have to report to a human clerk—even the military wasn't *that* inefficient. I just had to input my biometrics to one of a dozen consoles in the personnel office and then wait for the system to reward with me with a ping, a green flash of confirmation, and a message to my 'link confirming my unit and who I should report to. Of course, there was always the possibility that the God of data would judge me a sinner, give me the dreaded red light, and be forced into another chamber of outer darkness while I waited for some ill-tempered Fleet functionary to come sort me out. Those were the sort of nightmares that could wake a Marine up from a deep sleep screaming in fear.

I breathed a sigh of relief at the green flash of approval and turned back toward the door, and nearly ran chest-first into the Skipper.

There was nothing physically intimidating about Captain Phillip Covington. He was lean and rangy, with a hawkish face and a coiled-spring stance, but so were a thousand other Marine officers. What marked him as different were his eyes, and not just the gun-metal-grey color, but the depth of experience stored up behind them. He was a man who was on a first-name basis with Death.

I stiffened and nearly saluted him before I realized we were indoors and it wouldn't be appropriate.

"Sir!" I exclaimed, then adjusted my volume downward at the further realization I was no longer in OCS and didn't have to scream the word every time. "I was just about to go report in..."

"I got the notice you were arriving on the last shuttle," Covington said. "I figured I'd catch you here." He shook my hand. "Congratulations, Lt. Alvarez."

"Thank you, sir. I'm glad to be back." I blew out a sigh, showing more exasperation than I'd intended. "*Very* glad."

He chuckled, a harsh, knowing sound.

"This iteration of OCS may be new," he said, "but the idea certainly isn't, and it's never been a particularly pleasant experience. Although most candidates don't wind up nearly getting their platoon trainer cashiered and themselves dropped from the course."

Ice crystallized in my veins and the words caught in my throat. I'd been about to ask him how he'd heard, but it was a stupid question. Covington had been in the Marines since the Pirate Wars, over twenty-five years ago, and had connections everywhere. Of course he'd be following a Marine he'd recommended for OCS, and of course someone would tell him what had happened.

"Do you think I did the right thing, sir?" I was finally able to get out.

"The *right* thing?" He shrugged. "Almost certainly. The *smart* thing? Oh, definitely not. Your job was to get your ass through OCS and get back here as the platoon leader I still need for Third Platoon." An edge of anger had crept into his voice and I tried not to cringe. Making the Skipper mad was usually a horrible mistake, and most people didn't make it twice. But the anger faded and he cocked an eyebrow. "But I suppose, knowing your history, I shouldn't have expected anything different. And as usual, despite fucking everything up with your damned good intentions, you still got the job done."

I felt a sudden suspicion take hold and I couldn't keep myself from blurting the question out.

"Did you call Colonel Bell, sir? Did you know I was in trouble?"

"Knowing you're in trouble, Alvarez, is about as difficult as figuring out the sun is going to rise in the east." He nodded toward the door. "Come on, I brought a car to pick you up. We've got a shitload of work to do and the whole battalion is shipping out of here in less than seventy-two hours."

The groundcar was the basic, boxy, utilitarian military vehicle, but after months of riding packed busses and the back of cargo trucks in the sweltering heat, it was a taste of Heaven. I let myself sink into the plastic upholstery and blew out a breath as the driver pulled away from the curb and into the muddy streets. This was real. I was back.

"Tell me something, Alvarez," Covington said, and I sat up straight, paying attention. The Skipper was a fair man, but if you weren't on your toes with him every second, you'd regret it. "I know OCS has a fair amount of worthless bullshit, but did you actually learn anything?"

"You mean something they were *trying* to teach me, sir?" I asked. "Or at all?"

That brought a full-throated laugh, something I hadn't heard much from the Skipper.

"Let's start with what they were trying to teach you."

"Well, believe it or not, sir," I said, almost feeling embarrassed to say it, "but the classes on finances and investment actually did seem useful. Not useful enough to spend *two days* on it, but honestly, I didn't know shit about money or investing it until now."

He grunted, obviously amused.

"Not what I expected, but I suppose. Now, what did you learn that they weren't actually trying to drive through your skull with a sledgehammer?"

"That's easy, sir. I learned that being good at working a Vigilante isn't enough. There's a lot of Marines who can run a suit just as good as me, but they still get tunnel vision when they're trying to see the big picture."

"What about you? Do you see the big picture?"

"I can in a simulator, sir." I spread my hands. "I guess we're going to find out if that translates to real life." I hesitated. "Sir, I got a message from Vic...." I closed my mouth, opened it again. "From Sgt. Sandoval. She said she was leaving for OCS herself. Has her transport left yet?"

"Not yet," he said. "It's the same one you just came in on.

She leaves in your shuttle in...." He checked the wrist display connected to his 'link. "...four hours." He smiled thinly. "Don't worry, son, I'll get you back in time to say goodbye."

"Yes, sir. Thank you, sir."

The town had grown since I'd been gone, which was ironic since now they were ripping it apart again. Not all of it, of course. The admin buildings and the Fleet base would stay, because the Fleet always needed waystations for their Attack Command ships and carriers where they could pick up supplies and fresh crew. But the Marines were pulling out and I didn't know if we'd be back. Fleet Corps of Engineers troops were everywhere, stripping down all the gear we didn't want to leave behind and loading it onto the backs of cargo trucks for the short drive out to the spaceport, where the trucks would wait in lines, sometimes for hours, sometimes for days, for a cargo shuttle to come free.

The farther out into the Marine section of the base we got, the more stripped and naked it felt, until all that was left were a few bare, buildfoam domes, barracks buildings and storage huts and a couple of armories where we kept the Vigilantes. Those were being hauled out, too, some walked out by the troopers assigned to them, some on maintenance racks, carried by load-lifters, one exoskeleton in the arms of another. Which made no sense, but this was the military and things didn't usually need to make sense.

The driver, a corporal I didn't recognize, dropped us off in front of a line of barracks and stuck around long enough for me to grab my bags from the cargo compartment before he tore away, gone on some other errand.

"Alvarez," Covington said, raising a finger. "Leaders meeting in two hours in the Company area. Don't be late."

"Roger that, sir."

I slung the duffle over my shoulder and ran through the

centimeters-thick mud, ignoring the insistent suction trying to drag the boots off my feet, heading for her barracks room. I hoped she hadn't changed with someone else since I'd left, or I was going to bust in on the wrong Marine. I should have been introducing myself to my platoon, should have been checking in with Scotty, my platoon sergeant, should have been packing the shit I'd left behind in my barracks room, but I didn't even consider it.

I had to see her before she left.

There were other members of her platoon wandering through the halls of the barracks, some carrying duffle bags, taking their belongings out to one of the cargo trucks, others cleaning and scouring and doing all the shit that was irrelevant because we were vacating the premises anyway. God forbid we leave a bare buildfoam floor dirty for the next poor assholes who moved in here after us, because the first thing their NCOs would make them do is to clean those same fucking floors over again.

Her door was closed, and I wondered if I should have called and told her I was coming from the spaceport, but I'd kept thinking, what if she didn't *want* to see me before she left? What if she wanted to break things off clean and keep her head clear? Why was I so damned scared?

I knocked on the door.

"Just a minute." It was her voice. I hadn't heard it in person in months and I nearly collapsed at the realization she was on the other side of a few centimeters of plastic. I knocked again. "Damn it, I said just a minute, I'm packing here!"

Vicky Sandoval yanked the door open and I nearly fell inside. Her eyes went wide and she froze in place, a curse half-formed on her lips.

"Oh, my God!" she whispered, then grabbed me by the lapels of my jacket and pulled me into a kiss.

Her lips were chapped by the wind, and her mouth tasted of coffee and this morning's breakfast and I just didn't give a shit. I pulled back against her and squeezed her against me, drinking her in like the first taste of water for a man who'd been dying of thirst. One of us closed the door. I wasn't sure who and didn't care, but I heard it close.

I didn't remember taking my clothes off and wasn't sure if she had undressed me or it had been the other way around, and the next hour was a blur of warmth that vanquished the chill spring air of Hachiman. When I could think again, we were tangled up together on the bare mattress of the bed and she was crying. I think I was, too.

"I didn't think you'd make it back in time," Vicky said, sobbing, burying her face in my shoulder like I'd just arrived and we hadn't spent an hour in bed together. "I thought I was going to leave and I'd never see you again. That if one of us didn't die, we'd lose touch and that would be it and I'd spend the rest of my life wondering what had happened to you."

"I would never let that happen," I said, sniffing. My face was wet, and the tears could have come from either of us. "I made a promise, didn't I? Have you ever known me to break one?"

I ran my fingers down her cheek, brushing away moisture, moving a stray hair out of her face.

"I have to get ready," she moaned, sounding miserable. "I have to leave for the port in an hour!"

"I know," I told her. "The Skipper told me. He met me at the admin building and drove me here."

"He *knows* about us?" she asked, sitting bolt upright in bed, the blood draining from her face. "Oh, shit!"

"That ship has sailed, honey," I assured her, laughing softly. "In another hour, you're going to be gone, and if I see you afterward, we won't be breaking regulations anymore, will we?"

"He knows and he didn't care?" There was wonder and disbelief in her voice.

"He doesn't care now that it doesn't make any difference," I corrected her. "And maybe he knew before but only cared that we kept it quiet. Who knows, between Top and the Skipper? I doubt there's much you could get past either of them. But right now, I'd throw myself in front of a missile for him, because he got me back to you in time."

I grabbed her hands in mine.

"We've said all the words we need to say," I declared. "I just wanted to get here before you left so you could go to OCS without worrying about us. We're good. I *will* be here for you when you get back, no matter how long it takes. That's a promise. And I always keep my promises."

Vicky pulled me into a hug and I reveled in the warm softness of her, could have held here there forever.

"I have to go get a shower," she said, the words plaintive. "Do you want to go with me to the spaceport?"

"I wish I could. I have a company leaders meeting." I shrugged. "And maybe it's better to say goodbye like this, anyway." I grinned, tracing a line down her bare back with my fingertips. "Anything else would seem...anticlimactic."

"Shit, *someone* has a pretty high opinion of themselves." She yanked at my chest hair and I winced. "Is that something that comes with the gold bar?"

"It's standard-issue," I agreed. "When you get back, you'll hardly be able to fit your head into your suit's helmet."

I was laughing, but the smile didn't go any deeper than my eyes. She was leaving. I'd just got back and she was leaving. I'd known it would be this way, if I was lucky enough to see her at all, tried to prepare myself for it, but it hadn't helped at all.

"Go," she told me, pushing against my chest as if she could read what I was feeling. And maybe she could. "Get your clothes on and get to your meeting. If the Skipper knows about us, then this is just as much a test as any you took at OCS. You can't be late, not even for me."

You don't spend three years in the Marines without being able to get dressed in a hurry, and it was less than a minute before we were both standing at the door, me with my duffle slung across my shoulder. She kissed me one last time, and then shoved me out the door.

I think I said "I love you" before it closed, but I might have just thought it.

"The target," Captain Covington said, "is Demeter."

The hologram shifted behind him, the view rushing past a dozen other labelled star systems in an image that was an amalgamation of stock footage from Scout Service probes and computer simulations and zooming in on a star much like the sun, though just a touch brighter. It was labelled "Delta Pavonis" and it was a bit under twenty light-years from Earth, according to the readout. I don't know if I'd ever heard the name of the star before, but everyone knew its only habitable planet. The view shifted again, closer now, as the star grew so large it dominated the screen and then faded off to the side to make room for the planets orbiting it. There were six of them, a lifeless, charred rock close in, and its frozen twin at the outer edge, a pair of ice giants and a gas giant a bit smaller than Saturn.

And then there was Demeter.

"The colony was settled about forty years ago," the Skipper went on, pacing across the front of the double line of folding chairs, "after a century of terraforming."

He paused to jab a finger toward one of the other platoon leaders, one of the many new faces in the company since I'd left.

I'd introduced myself before the briefing had begun, but I couldn't for the life of me remember...

"Yes, Lt. Cano?"

Cano was a short, round-faced man a little younger than me, fresh out of the Academy if I'd had to guess. He wasn't exactly pudgy but he had the look of someone who could turn that way quickly when he went out into the civilian world.

"Sorry, sir," he apologized. "Terraformed it?"

"I was being approximate," Covington admitted, the barest hint of a tug at the corner of his eye showing he was irritated at being interrupted for something irrelevant to the mission. "It was already habitable, but the ecosphere was basic, not much more than algae and bacteria. The Commonwealth decided to use the world as a test case for introducing a full, Earth-based ecosystem from the ground up."

"That's where they introduced all those extinct animals," Kovacs, the First Platoon leader chimed in. "They cloned them from tissue samples, right? Like saber-tooth cats and mastodons and shit."

"Yes, Lt. Kovacs," Covington replied, his words so dry a man could have died of dehydration just hearing them. "They cloned mastodons and shit. Researchers from several Earthside universities maintained watch stations sprinkled around what they called Revenant Forest, a huge track of woodland a few dozen kilometers outside the capital city of Amity. They were underground, connected by tunnels, designed to monitor all the Earth species, but especially the revenants. Apparently, the local militia and some Intelligence spooks have been using them as hidey-holes so they can pop out and sabotage the Tahni."

"We're gonna count on a civilian militia to back us up, Skipper?" Cano asked, sounding dubious about the proposition. I wasn't Cano's biggest fan so far, but I had to admit I shared the concern.

"They're not backing us up, Lieutenant, they're doing the heavy lifting. Here's the situation, at least so far as Fleet Intelligence is relaying it to us, for what that's worth. Things are bad on Demeter for everyone, but they're almost worse for the Tahni than they are for our people. The Imperium has withdrawn most of their ships from the occupied systems to defend their core colonies from the sort of strikes the Attack Command and us have been making, which means the Tahni troops they left behind aren't getting resupplied and have no hope in sight of relief. They've basically been abandoned and they *know* it."

The thin smile that spread across his face was not at all sympathetic to the plight of the Tahni, and I mirrored it.

"The Tahni aren't human, and I think we've fought them enough to know how motivated they can be, but something like this has to fuck with even the most motivated troops out there. They're coming apart at the seams and the militias are taking advantage of it. It's all coming to a head in less than two weeks, and we're gonna have a ringside seat. Some Intelligence spooks, a special operations unit I understand, though they decline to be more specific than that, is going to lead the militia in a strike against the fusion reactor to cut off power to the planetary defense laser outside Amity. With most of their fleet withdrawn from the system, that laser and a few orbital platforms are the only space defenses they have. They don't even have deflector dishes built, because they were counting on us not being willing to bombard a city while they were using the colonists as human shields."

A distant rumble of jets shook the walls of the buildfoam dome we'd used for two years as the company conference room and offices, starting low and chest-deep and climbing in pitch as the shuttle ascended. And took my heart with it. I wanted to look up, but I kept my eyes on Covington, and I thought I saw recognition in his face of what was happening.

"Their regular infantry's going to be tied up with the militia," Covington went on. "From the intelligence passed along to us, their heavy infantry Shock Troopers have had their numbers badly attenuated by sabotage and ambushes and shouldn't be a factor. What they *do* have is a full battalion of High Guard battlesuits, and if we can't suppress and destroy them, the militia is going to get slaughtered. So, we're going to take a major risk and insert our dropships right at the No Later Than time and not wait to confirm they took down the reactor. And if we're wrong, they'll slice us right out of the air." He shrugged. "If we're right and they take care of business, it'll be a straightforward armor-on-armor fight. Don't expect any air support, though, because we still have civilians in the area and we're trying to minimize collateral damage." His eyes flickered back and forth between his platoon leaders, all five of us, First through Fourth and the Special Weapons platoon. "Any questions?"

"Do we have intelligence about where they're keeping the civilians remaining in the city?" I asked him. It was a stretch, but apparently, we had assets on the ground, so I figured it was worth a shot.

I'd seen Covington angry, and it was a fearful sight. But seeing his face turn despairing and melancholic was somehow so much more terrifying.

"There are none, other than the militia. They freed as many as they could and took them into the woods, into the tunnels and other hiding places. The rest...." He closed his eyes for just a moment. "The rest starved to death. Thousands of them, minimum. Others were executed in retaliation for the resistance strikes."

It shouldn't have hit me as hard as it did. I *knew* what the Tahni could do to a civilian population. I'd seen it first-hand.

But letting them starve to death...I knew what real hunger was, and there just didn't seem to be any worse way to go.

Covington touched a control on his wrist display and the hologram disappeared.

"You'll get a detailed op order on board the transport, along with scenarios for simulator training. Right now, I need you to go tell your people what we're heading into and make sure everyone has their shit wrapped tight. We've been sitting on our asses too long and I'm ready to go visit some vengeance on the Imperium. Who's with me?"

From another commander, the words could have been cheesy, melodramatic, easy to dismiss as motivational bullshit. But from the Skipper, they were enough to send a surge of enthusiasm and rage up from my gut, and there could be only one response, the one we call gave in an abrupt and ear-pounding shout.

"Ooh-rah!"

"Holy shit," Gunnery Sgt. Scott Hayes murmured, eyes widening as I turned the corner into the platoon area, the central oval between the barracks. Then he shook himself, seeming to remember where he was. "Officer on deck!" he barked, coming to attention.

Most of the platoon was gathered, waiting for me. I'd sent the message on the way over from the company meeting and I'd regretted on a personal level that I wouldn't be able to surprise Scotty the way I had Vicky, but the sight of me had still rocked him back on his heels.

He saluted, a grin breaking through his stern platoon-sergeant-serious expression despite his best efforts.

"Welcome back, sir," he said, after I'd returned the gesture.

"Are you here to take charge of your Marines?"

"I sure as hell am, Sergeant. At ease."

Forty-one sets of eyes stared at me, and I realized with a twisting turn of my stomach that most of them were strangers. I shouldn't have been surprised. Life didn't sit still just because I was away for training, and the wartime military promoted fast. Men and women had been shipped to NCO school, given their own squads in other companies, other platoons, wherever the need had arisen. Some of the fire team leaders were familiar to me, but I'd known them as privates.

It's better this way. It wouldn't be easy stepping back into the old platoon and expecting them to treat me like an officer when I used to be just another one of the guys.

"I'm Lt. Alvarez," I said, struggling to sound confident, the way I remembered Lt. Ackley sounding. "I'm your new platoon leader and I got here just in time. We leave on an operation in sixty-eight hours, and we're barely going to have ten days transit time to train in the simulators shipboard."

I was talking on autopilot, matching faces and name-tapes to the files I'd been sent by Covington en route. Joanna Carson, Francis Houghton, Ernst Kreis and Christian Majid. Those were my squad leaders and I knew their faces, how they'd scored in NCO school, their service record, and not a damn thing else about them.

"We're heading into combat," I warned them, "to take back one of the colonies the enemy has held for too long. You'll get a full op order on board the transport, but I want the squad leaders in my barracks room for a short briefing at 1800, right before we head to dinner." I held up a finger. "When you come to that meeting, I want a full report of our readiness and what still needs to get done before we ship out. We clear?"

"Yes, sir!" Their answers were enthusiastic if not well-choreographed, and I could live with that.

"Dismissed," I said, nodding to them. "Go get to work."

They hurried off, trying to look busy. I knew because I'd been one of them not so long ago. Scotty waited until they were gone before he turned back to me, shaking his head in disbelief.

"Wow, look at you, *sir*," he said, grinning. "Goddamn, I remember the day you walked in the door as a PFC and now I gotta salute you!"

"Jesus, Scotty." I let out a long, hissing breath. "I'm glad you're still here. It's hard enough taking charge of a bunch of strangers three days before we ship out, without having to break in a new platoon sergeant!"

"You mean without your platoon sergeant having to break in a new butterbar," he corrected me, arching an eyebrow.

"Hey now," I warned him, less than half serious, "don't try that all-second-lieutenants-are-dumbasses thing with *me*. I was an NCO just a few months ago so I'm not some fucking greenhorn Academy grad."

"And thank God for it, sir," he assured me.

It was so weird Scotty calling me sir. For as long as I'd known him, over two years now, he'd been my superior, first my squad leader and then my platoon sergeant. But then, of all the things that had changed for me since I'd joined the Marines, Scotty was the one thing that had not. He was an open-faced farmboy from Hermes, his hair as blond as the flax in his family's fields, still with the same "aw-shucks" accent as he'd had the day that I'd first met him.

And yet it hadn't seemed to be a problem for him as a platoon sergeant. Most gunnery sergeants I knew came across as complete hardasses, whether it was honest or them putting on a show for the troops, but Scotty never changed who he was and still made it work.

"What do they know about me?" I asked him, nodding toward the direction the squad leaders had gone.

"If you mean what did *I* tell them," Scotty replied, shrugging, "then just that you're the best I've ever seen in a Vigilante and you were the best squad leader I had before you got it into your head that you wanted to be an officer. What they've heard from the grapevine, well, I don't know for sure, but everyone knows about Brigantia and the infiltration mission on Ambergris. Hell, you got the Silver Star. They don't hand those things out like good-conduct medals, you know?"

"I suppose it helps if your LT has a bit of awe and mystery connected with him," I mused. "Of course, that means I can't slip up and act like an idiot in front of them."

Scotty squinted; his expression dubious.

"Not sure you can go that long without looking like an idiot, sir."

We both laughed, because it was either that or yell at him for being overly familiar with his new platoon leader, and I was neither enough of a hardass or a dumbass to yell at my platoon sergeant.

"Did you get back in time to talk to Vicky?" he wondered, sounding like he'd been reluctant to bring it up first.

"I did." I very purposefully did *not* sigh. "She's going to make a great officer."

"Wish she was coming along with us on this one," he said. "We haven't had a combat mission in three months. If I didn't know better, I'd say the Skipper told them to hold off until *you* got back!"

"Well, of course he did, Scotty," I told him, deadpan. "What would you guys do without me?" More laughter, and suddenly it felt as if I'd never left. "Come on, let's go to my office while I still have one and you can tell me all about the platoon."

"Yes, sir." He took a step to lead me toward the office, but paused and offered a hand. I shook it. "It's good to have you back, Cam."

[9]

"Drop! Drop! Drop!"

It was a familiar feeling, the world falling out from beneath me, utter darkness giving way to the flashes of light I couldn't separate into lightning strikes, missile warheads, proton cannons and the inevitable explosions of inbound ships. The city was a distant glow near the horizon, a couple dozen kilometers away, while our target was much closer, squatting in the shadows of night.

Demeter might have been a beautiful world, full of natural wonder and antique architecture, a paradise of long-extinct animals living in harmony with their new ecology, but I'd never know it. I was falling into a world where the sun had set and everything alight beneath me was glowing with thermal energy and had to be destroyed.

I wasn't sure if I should have been happy or disappointed that they didn't drop our platoon with the rest of the company into Amity City. We'd received intelligence when we transitioned into the system that an enemy High Guard platoon was holed up at one of the tourist resorts outside the city, dug into fixed positions and just waiting for the Marines to come get them. Contrary to earlier reports, they had apparently gathered together the last of the human prisoners and were holding them in the resort facility as human shields to prevent us from simply bombarding the resort from orbit or calling in an air strike.

The Skipper hadn't been sure if he bought the new intelligence, but it wasn't something we could ignore, so he'd sent Third in to check it out. In a way, it was exactly what we needed, a platoon-level live-fire training exercise. The only difference being the live-fire was two-way and we could get killed. But the isolation, the separation from the rest of the company, felt strange and unsettling at a time when I was already unsettled enough about my first combat operation as an officer.

Deal with it, Alvarez. Watch the big picture.

The resort was huge, a giant building built from whole logs thirty meters tall, stripped and polished, with the base filled in with bleached white limestone. The roof was sloped and shingled with green-tinted slate tiles, and each room had its own window of hand-blown glass. Captain Covington had told me it was built on the pattern of national park lodges on Earth, particularly Old Faithful, and I had no idea what the hell that meant, but it was pretty and probably way too expensive for me to afford a night's stay, much less the ticket for a voyage to Demeter, if the Fleet hadn't given me a ride free of charge.

First squad had taken point out of the dropship, Sgt. Joanna Carson's squad, with a promising young corporal named Delp on point. Scotty had said the kid reminded him of Henckel and that was high praise coming from anyone who'd served with Henckel. Carson, Scotty hadn't been so sure of, which was why I was positioning myself just behind her squad in the drop.

The white glow of jump-jets was a giant target on the cool, dark night, but there was nothing to be done about it. I didn't believe the enemy would take potshots at us while we were in the air, not if they wanted to force us to come to them and dig them out, take as many of us with them as they could. That was the Tahni way. They didn't surrender. It wasn't in their nature, wasn't part of their cultural psychology. Instructors at OCS had compared them to the Imperial Japanese Army from World War Two with a good dash of Egypt under the Pharaohs thrown in for good measure. I'd had to take their word for it since most of what I knew about military history I'd learned from the Marines.

But I knew if they wanted to draw us in and get us too close to use missiles, they'd wait until we were on the ground to attack. I'd talked about that with the Skipper, about how to approach without springing any traps they might have set up.

"It's your call, Cam," he'd told me. "You're the leader on the ground. But given what I know of the Tahni, I'd think they expect you to form up at a distance and advance carefully in formation."

Since the Skipper was almost always right, I had First squad drop right through the fucking roof.

"Firing!" Carson announced when all eight of them were still fifty meters up.

Missiles streaked away from the launchers on the shoulders of their Vigilante battlesuits and hammered into that beautiful, deep-green slate roof, ceiling tiles, and wooden cross-beams disappeared in a row of fireballs, one beside another all along the west wing of the giant hotel.

It had been a risk. If the Tahni had been keeping their hostages on the top floor, I could have been responsible for the deaths of dozens of innocent civilians. I'd been worried about that, too, but the Skipper had been grimly pragmatic.

"If they're still in Tahni hands at this point," he'd said, "it's a choice between maybe being killed by us or definitely being

97

killed by the enemy...or starving to death. Do what you have to do."

Do what you have to do. How was that going to play in my nightmares? The playlist was already long and varied, the faces haunting me a mixture of Marines and civilians, people I'd loathed and those I'd cared about. *What's a few more?*

Delp dropped into the billowing smoke of the burning roof, the weight of his Vigilante smashing the weakened building material beneath him, the fire nothing compared to the punishment the suit was constructed to take. This was where it got really tricky. First was going to drop into a suite of hotel rooms and smash their way down from the top, while Second and Third came in through the front and Fourth hit the rear freight entrance. Someone was going to hit the ambush. I could have better command and control from the outside, with Second and Third, but I needed to know what First was hitting and I needed to see it with my own eyes.

Carson went in between fire teams, and I dropped through the biggest of the four smoking, shattered holes in the gabled roof just behind the last of them. Once again, I was swallowed up, awash in flames for a moment before I dived into smoke so thick my sensors were nearly useless.

The power was out. That much was clear by the fires still burning. If there'd still been power to the resort, fire suppression would have switched on automatically. The place must have run on underground cables from the fusion reactor and when it had gone down, so had this place.

I was in a hotel suite, or what had once been a hotel suite. Now it was a pile of kindling, what hadn't been destroyed by the missiles had been trampled underfoot by the Vigilante suits that had come through before me. Even the hardwood floor was burning, splintered, revealing a layer of concrete beneath it, and what remained crunched under the soles of my battlesuit, sending me lurching from side to side.

"Top floor, negative contact!" Carson was saying, her voice strident with the adrenaline of her first real fight as squad leader. Lots of firsts today. My first drop as an officer, the first step in a new phase of the war. "Moving to the next level."

I'd barely had time to talk to each of the squad leaders for more than a few minutes during the voyage from Hachiman. The rest of the flight had been packed with maintenance checks, simulator runs, meetings and mandatory sleep. Some Fleet types had laughed at me when I mentioned mandatory sleep, but it was necessary. If command didn't make it mandatory, way too many officers and NCOs would have been up every single hour of the voyage trying to cram two months' worth of work into ten days.

In our brief one-on-one, Joanna Carson had struck me as someone floundering with her newfound responsibilities. Scotty wouldn't come right out and say she wasn't ready to be a squad leader and it wouldn't have mattered if he had, because we just didn't have enough qualified NCOs to go around. The good ones were being promoted to platoon sergeant or sent to OCS and for the rest, we'd just have to make do.

Carson wasn't going to be sent to OCS. She was barely twenty years old and it was obvious she hadn't put enough time in at team leader before she'd been kicked up in rank and position.

The doorway of the suite hadn't been large enough to let a Vigilante battlesuit through it, but it was now, and I picked my way through it, careful not to stumble into any of the holes blown in the floor.

"Scotty, sitrep," I snapped, stepping through a haze of smoke and onto the interior balcony of the hotel's upper floor, open at the center through to the ground floor courtyard.

The central opening began narrow and widened as it descended, mirroring the hotel's exterior appearance, and through the tiny gap at the top jutted a cluster of wooden support columns six meters across, the remains of the trunks of massive redwoods. I caught a glimpse of one of the Vigilantes on thermal disappearing into one of the hotel suites on the next floor down, but nothing below them. The lobby below was barren, deserted.

"Second and Third squads are in position at the front, three hundred meters out. Fourth is circling around to the back now, be in place in two mikes. No sight of the enemy so far, sir. No sign of anything." A pause. "It's kind of looking like a dry hole. I wonder if the intel is bad."

"Keep your eyes open for demo charges," I warned him. "The Tahni might have a lookout on the trigger."

One of the crazier things about the Tahni religion was that it didn't allow autonomous weapons of any kind. No robots, no drones, and more important to our immediate concerns, no mines unless they were manually detonated. I think the exact words of the translation they'd given our OCS class from a fragment of their Tahni scriptures, or whatever they called them were: "no thinking being may die except by the hand of another." The idea was that the Tahni were made in their god's image, and only they had the right to take life.

Which was damned convenient, since Commonwealth law also forbade the use of autonomous weapons for our side, a legacy of the sad and bloody days after the Sino-Russian War when tens of thousands of refugees had died at the cybernetic hands of automated sentry guns lining the borders of the irradiated zones. But it made some of our troops complacent. Just because the Tahni were restricted by their weird beliefs didn't mean they couldn't be damned clever about how they applied them. And one of those clever ways was laying down demo charges as a trap, but leaving a lookout with his finger on the trigger.

"Negative contact on this floor," Carson said. "Heading to the next."

She wouldn't find anything on that floor, either. I don't know how I knew, but I felt it. These guys were holding up on the ground floor, dug in like ticks to make it harder to dig them out.

"Carson, bypass and head down to the lobby." I ran the blueprint I'd seen of the place through my head. "There's a storage room off to the right of the service desk on the north side. Prep it with missiles and go."

"Sir," she dithered, "we could be leaving enemy troops behind us...."

"Do it, Sergeant."

She relayed the orders and I let my attention drift away from the edge of the balcony, checking the IFF on the troops outside. Fourth squad had made it to the rear entrance of the hotel, skirting the low hills the back end of the place was cut into and circling to the freight entrance. My hunch was any trap would be laid there, at the freight entrance, another reason I wanted First squad on the ground floor, so they could back up Fourth if they needed it.

The question was, where did I need to be?

Not up here on the top floor, that was for sure. I waited until First was dropping off the balcony below me, their jump-jets kicking up sprays of dust and curling billows of smoke, then I vaulted kicked through the solid oak railing and jumped. I remembered a day when the stomach-in-my-throat feeling of falling would have immobilized me with terror, but that fear was one of the first things you lost in the Drop Troopers, right after any aversion you might have had to swearing and any taste for good food.

I didn't need a long burst of jets, just a couple of kicks and then a lean forward and one last goose to get me down to the fourth floor. I banged the top of my helmet casing on the ceiling as I landed and I was thankful the rest of the platoon couldn't see it. It wasn't painful, but it was a rookie mistake, and I made it simply because I was so busy trying to keep track of everyone on the HUD map.

"We're ready to go in, boss," Scotty told me.

I scuffled to a halt on the heart-of-pine floor, feeling it crunch under the weight of the suit. Wood flooring was as alien to me as it was to the Tahni, something only the richest of the rich could afford on Earth, with decades upon decades of conservation laws in the wake of the Sino-Russian War and the havoc the nuclear fallout had wreaked on the globe. Here, it was a mild extravagance, and yet I still felt as if I were pissing on a DaVinci painting.

"You're about to hear some explosions from inside," I told Scotty. "Hit from the front and back simultaneously the second you do."

Which was a risk. If there was a trap, the missiles might or might not distract the Tahni long enough to keep them from springing it.

"And watch for civilian hostages," I added, and felt like an idiot saying it. Of course, he knew to look for the civilians, but I was in command and had to make sure I reminded everyone of the obvious because if someone forgot, it would be on me.

I jumped off the fourth-floor balcony just as First squad launched their missiles and everything slipped into slow motion inside my head. It was what the combat psychology experts called "tachypsychia," and it was an illusion. Everything was going full speed, but my conscious mind was running a fraction of a second behind reality, instinct and habit controlling my actions and giving me the illusion that I'd thought everything through while I was watching time unfold at half speed.

The missiles streaked away from the launchers of the lead fire team, arrayed in a wedge formation even in mid-air, converging on the double-doors of the storage room behind the check-in desk. I tensed up, anticipating the blast, but the blast that came was one I had *not* anticipated. The roof trees blew. I didn't know it at the time, had to piece it together afterward, but the best I could tell, the Tahni had planted charges at the base of the support columns and when a few kilograms of Hyper-Explosives touched off, it turned tons of redwood into thousands upon thousands of pieces of shrapnel.

The wood itself couldn't penetrate our armor, but the concussion slammed into my Vigilante like the hammer of some ancient god and I was suddenly tumbling out of the air, my jets cutting out from my lack of concentration, the floor a black and shrouded mystery concealed by a roiling cloud of smoke.

I tried to cry out, tried to shout a warning, tried to give an order, but the world rushed up and punched me in the face and everything went numb.

It felt as if a baseball bat the size of a building had smashed into my whole body at once, and stars floated across my vision. I couldn't see through the flares of light, couldn't hear past the roaring in my ears, couldn't move past a dull blanket of pain. I tasted blood and tried to spit it out but I couldn't make my body do what I wanted and it went down my throat. I choked and tried to spit again and a wave of fire seemed to surge out of my chest and take the glob of blood with it.

Adrenaline. Not my own, it had been loaned to me by the suit's medical systems. Loaned because you always had to pay something like that back, eventually, in a few hours when I collapsed from exhaustion. If I made it those few hours, I'd gladly accept the price.

Stars cleared, replaced by flashes of yellow and red from my suit's displays telling me exactly how bad a shape I was in and what parts would work if I managed to get out of all this rubble and up on my feet. It seemed that the roof had caved in once all those beautiful redwood logs stopped supporting it, and now half of it was on top of me.

Okay, not quite half, just a pile a meter deep with me at the bottom.

"Report!" I tried to shout the word but it came out a croak and I grabbed at the water nipple beside my face and took a long draw off the bladder. It was blissfully cool. "Report! Third Platoon, report, damn it!"

Nothing. It could be my comm antennae had been damaged or it could be they were just too busy. Or dead. I thrashed with my arms and almost screamed at the pain in my shoulders and back but kept it up. It wasn't my own muscles lifting the weight, I just had to pretend to move to get the sensors to read how serious I was about getting the hell out from under this rubble. So, if I had broken ribs or torn ligaments and couldn't lift a quarter-liter beer can to my lips, it wouldn't matter so long as the damn suit sensors figured out that I *wanted* to.

Rubble shifted and fell away and flickering firelight showed past the blackness of the pile of debris in my helmet screen. It wasn't a visor, it was the end result of a software simulation based on tiny external cameras, thermal filters, sonic and lidar sensors and whatever else they'd crammed into the armor that I'd forgotten, but when you piled rock and wood and brick on top of it, it wasn't going to see a damned thing. I had to get out.

I bent my legs and pushed with my feet, rolled onto one side and heard a shriek of stone scraping against stone, the clatter of wooden beams meters long. How much could this suit lift? Had they ever experimented with it, buried the stuff under cement blocks and then tried to have it dig itself out? That hadn't been in the training. Maybe they thought no one would ever be stupid enough to get a building dropped on their heads.

Well, that was their mistake. Nothing is ever fool-proof because fools are so damned ingenious.

I felt as if I should be grunting with the effort, but the servo-motors were doing all the work. The Vigilante burst free of the burial cairn the Tahni had laid atop it and suddenly, I could see again. The hotel had been run down, neglected. It would have needed renovating after the war. The Tahni had saved them the trouble. Half of the building had collapsed outward, and that twist of fate was the only thing that had saved us all from dying under hundreds of tons of rubble, enough to crush even the hard shell of a battlesuit.

The other half had collapsed backward toward the freight entrance, undermined by the missile strikes and maybe more Tahni demo charges, which left tiny islands of stability inside all the destruction like little jokes God was playing on us. A spiral staircase went up to nowhere, the floors it had serviced vanished in billowing clouds of smoke and dust, and the only reason I could see through the blackness was through the helmet optics turning ink black to a milky twilight. A data terminal with shelves filled with complementary tablets for use by the hotel guests still stood, its battery blinking two-year-old tourist information, the display glowing neon in the haze.

I didn't care about the fate of the furniture, but the motion of hulking, oversized battlesuits picking their way out of the rubble unclenched a fist that had been squeezing my chest so tight I couldn't breathe. Some of them were alive. I couldn't even tell who. Either their IFF transponders were fragged or my receiver wasn't working...and neither was my suit's communications link. I switched to my external PA speakers and shouted into the pickup.

"First squad!" My amplified voice sent quivers of sonic vibration through the clouds of dust. "Sound off! Respond via public address speakers!"

Nothing for a moment. Maybe they couldn't hear me. Maybe they were still stunned. Or maybe they were just trying to figure out who was supposed to talk first, which was the most likely scenario.

"Carson!" Her voice was choked, rasping, her throat sounding dry from fear. "Squad leader!" My sonic sensors picked her out of the cluster of Vigilantes, homing in on a battered suit covered in dust and marred by gouges, burns and scraped metal.

"Gingold. Alpha team leader." The young corporal's words almost tripped over Carson's and I knew I'd been right; they'd been waiting on her to get her shit together.

"Delp. Alpha team." He didn't sound too rattled, which either meant he was a steely-eyed point man who knew no fear, or he was a teenager too young and stupid and inexperienced to know he should be afraid, that death was hanging over his shoulder, just waiting.

"Fujiyama. Alpha team."

"Rogan. Alpha team."

"Bradford. Bravo team leader."

Closer to me now, near the center of the lobby. Bravo team had been in the trailing group on the way down from the top floors.

"Benitez. Bravo team."

"Mariota. Bravo team."

"Woodside. Bravo team."

"Haskell is down." That was Bradford, the Bravo team leader, the voice coming from the far left, towards where the collapse had begun. "She's not moving." He was standing unsteadily on a displaced slab of concrete beside a three-meter-tall pile of debris, and beneath it I could just make out the leg of a Vigilante.

"Shit."

I'd shut off the PA mic, not wanting them to hear my frustration. She *might* be alive under that mess, but her suit wouldn't be getting out without heavy equipment, and it sure as hell wouldn't be fighting. Worse, we couldn't leave it behind, not with the possibility she was still breathing inside. I switched the mic back on.

"Carson, take Woodside and Rogan and wait here with Haskell. The rest of you, get behind me and form up. We won't be able to communicate so just follow my lead and shoot the bad guys. And don't shoot *me*."

What would Scotty be doing? He had to have seen the collapse and was too smart to just charge into that. He would have tried to call us, and when he couldn't get through, he would have called Fourth squad and told them to hold in place, assuming they hadn't been caught in the collapse of the building.

We were alone in here for the moment. Except for the Tahni. They were in here somewhere. Downstairs. The basement. It had to be. It was the only place safe from the explosion and the collapse, or as safe as possible inside the building...

"Oh, damn."

I hit the jump-jets and soared upward, out over the truncated walls, hoping the others would follow me. The Tahni weren't inside the hotel at all. We hadn't detected them coming down, but they'd had plenty of time to dig spider holes and disguise their thermal signatures. They'd suckered us. Our comms weren't out from the explosion, they were out because laser line-of-sight was fucked by the haze and smoke and the Tahni were jamming microwave.

They'd suckered *me*.

Twenty meters up, clearing the top of the hotel, it was all stretched out before me. Fourth squad had pulled back from the rear entrance when the charges had blown, nearly to the edge of the woods, and out of those woods was coming a light-show of thermal energy, a platoon of High Guard battlesuits jetting from their hidey holes, probably dug into the side of the hill. Fourth squad wouldn't see them in time, and wouldn't be able to warn each other if they did.

I fired off every missile in my battery, all four exiting the launch tube with a dull thump of cold-gas pushing them clear before their solid-rocket boosters ignited. There'd been no time to pick out multiple targets, so I'd sent all four into the lead suit. I would have followed them in, but my jets had reached the limit of their power and were starting to overheat and I had to come down.

The Tahni troopers were less than half a klick out and the missiles took barely two seconds to reach the first of them. The thermal glow of his reactor and jets turned into a supernova of flaring white as the missiles struck one after another, ripping him to burning shreds in a very satisfying paroxysm of overkill. Besides venting my frustration, it also had the effect of disrupting their advance, sending the tight formation scattering. More of the weapons were streaking in from behind me and I whispered a prayer of thanks that at least some of them had been listening.

Fourth squad was turning now, a ragged line of troops arrayed ahead of me, barely noticing my Vigilante touching down behind them. The Tahni were too close for missiles, at least for Fourth's missiles, and they cut loose with an unorganized and nearly un-aimed barrage of plasma blasts, half of them just splattering harmlessly into the dirt. I hit the jets again, hopping over their position, no way to talk to them and not enough time even if I could have.

The Tahni were down now, jets cooling, the platoon splitting in two, half of them loping around the northern edge of the wrecked hotel, trying to get to the two squads up front. The other half were circling back around, trying to force Fourth squad toward the thick forest where they wouldn't be able to maneuver.

I came down in the middle of the group circling back south, blasting one of them with my plasma gun before I'd even touched dirt. Metal flared, sublimating into burning gas, and the High Guard battlesuit stumbled forward, its balance gone, and plowed face-first into the dirt. The gun took seconds to recycle, far too long when I was this close, but I'd bought myself spare time by coming down in a spot where the Tahni fields of fire would intersect their own troops. Not *much* time, because soldiers are more willing to risk friendly fire in combat than most people would expect when it's their neck on the line, but a beat, a breath.

I swung my left fist in a backhand blow across the shoulder of the nearest of them as he tried to rush past me, the impact vibrating through the armor of the Vigilante like the head of a drum. It was slightly more dramatic for him. The blow took the power feed for his electron beamer right at one of the junctions and it blew with a shower of sparks, pulling his teeth. He tried to turn, his foot pads digging into the rich, black dirt and sending it showering as he grabbed at balance, but I was already moving. I stamped down on his left knee joint and the suit's leg bent the wrong way, which wouldn't kill him and might not even have injured him, depending on how tall he was and how far his biological legs extended down into the metal version, but it put him out of the fight and that was enough for now.

A green light flickered at the edge of my vision, letting me know the plasma gun's capacitors were charged and I fired again without realizing I'd picked out a target. Another High Guard suit went down in the false dawn of an artificial sun, but I'd lost the time I'd gained and they knew I was here. The lightning bolt of an electron beam sought me out and I backpedaled four meters in two steps and hit the jets again. The beam tracked upward and he would have hit me if a pair of incandescent plasmoids hadn't converged on the chest plastron of his suit.

I didn't know who I had to thank for saving my life, but that was three down that I'd seen, and another two dropped at the periphery of my vision. The pincer attack had failed and Fourth squad could handle what was left. I had to get back to the front of the hotel, where the rest of the Tahni platoon would be coming at Scotty.

My suit warned me the turbines were close to overheating but I stomped on the jets anyway, needing to get ahead of them, needing this all not to have been my fault. Fire and smoke and wreckage passed beneath me, accompanied by a soundtrack of warning buzzers letting me know just how banged up my suit was and how close it was to heating up, shutting down, exploding, or all other sorts of nasty possibilities. I ignored it, just needing to get through the next couple of minutes.

Just a couple minutes, I prayed, though whether to God or the suit, I wasn't sure. Whichever was listening.

And as it turned out, Scotty was the one who'd been listening. I had a ringside seat, cruising in about twenty meters up, watching the two squads of Tahni High Guard troopers stomp their way right into the path of flight after flight of missiles. T82s, they were called, standard for the battlesuit and I'd never thought about them except for the occasional regret that they needed too great a distance to arm. But they were versatile and simple and hellaciously destructive when they hit.

I couldn't count them all and I doubt the Tahni could either, but by the time the last of them had detonated, the High Guard assault was shattered and burning, and the few who'd survived long enough to try to make it out of the kill zone went down to a well-timed fusillade of plasma.

"Scotty!" I yelled into the audio pickup, hoping the smoke had thinned out enough for laser line-of-sight to work. "Get a squad to the rear! Fourth is still mopping up!"

"Holy shit, boss, you're alive!" Scotty blurted before he

acknowledged my order. "Right, on it, sir. Second, get back there and support Fourth!"

Eight Vigilante suits rocketed into the air, heading back the way I'd come. I stumbled to a halt and my suit's left hip servo gave out, taking me down to one knee.

"Shit." Red flashed in my Heads-Up Display, telling me the obvious. I pushed the suit up with its left hand and locked the hip, letting me at least stay on my feet. "We have one down inside. Haskell got buried when the demo charges blew; not sure if she's alive. Any casualties out here?"

"Meehan took some damage when the building collapsed outward, but he's fine. Suit is immobile until we get it to a repair rack, though." On the comm display, I saw him switch to the general net. "Kreis, set up a perimeter with Third squad and keep a thermal scan going, try to find those civilians, if they even exist."

"I think I know where they are," I told him. "Follow me."

It would probably have been easier for him to lead me as slow as I was moving, but it was the principle of the thing. I used the jump-jets as a crutch, spurring the suit along with a half-second burst every other step, sending clouds of dust and smoke rising behind us. The hotel was more of a piece of the landscape now than it had been before. If blending in with nature had been the aim of the design, well, mission accomplished now. It was part of the hill, like a landslide at its base, and all that was left a man-made cave.

"Carson!" I said over the external speakers as we rounded the front of the building. "It's Alvarez! We're coming in!"

"Sir!" Carson said, sifting through the debris-strewn floor toward us, her voice static-filled on her speakers. "Haskell is alive! She moved!"

"Stay with her," I ordered. "Send Woodside and Rogan with me and the Gunny."

The missiles First squad had launched had taken out the storage room and more. They'd blown open the entranceway to the basement and it yawned below us through a three-meter gap in the flooring, inky blackness clouded with ash and dust. I'd often questioned the wisdom of having a spotlight built into the chest of the Vigilante, wondering what possible use it could be in combat. I found out shining it down the hole. The basement was intact apart from a pile of debris beneath the hole where the stairs had been. Past the splinters of polished hardwood, past the crumbled remains of demolished brick was bare floor.

I tracked the circle of light from side to side, over deactivated cleaning robots, pallets full of supplies and others picked clean...and then to a series of chicken-wire cages. I thought they were for more supplies, but then something flickered through the edge of the light and I shifted it over. My breath caught in my throat and when it returned, it brought a stream of bile I barely kept down.

Inside the cages were skeletons. Living skeletons, their skin sallow and covered in sores, their hair patchy and falling out, their ragged clothes hanging off their starved bodies. Men and women, teenagers, but no younger children, no babies, because they couldn't have made it this long with so little food. There were at least a couple dozen of them in three cages, some standing and staring up at me with wide, white eyes, not even trying to shield themselves from the light, while others were laid out on the floor, unmoving. I wondered if they'd died before we arrived or if the concussion of the blast had been too much for them.

"Jesus Christ," Scotty murmured.

I turned back to the two privates we'd brought with us.

"Woodside," I said, barely able to get the words out. "Get clear of the jamming and call for Search and Rescue. Now. Tell them it can't wait,"

"Yes, sir." Her voice was shaky, wavering, but she backed out of the wreckage of the storeroom and kicked in her jets, flying clear of the ruin of the hotel.

"Listen to me," I said to the hostages. "I'm Lt. Alvarez, Commonwealth Fleet Marine Corps and we are here to help you. We've called for medical aid and they'll be here soon. Just wait here."

They said nothing. Where else would they go?

"Rogan, stay here," I instructed him. "Don't go down there, the floor is too unstable. Just keep it secure for the rescue team."

I left them there and limped outside, needing to take charge of the platoon. Scotty stayed in step with me and I wondered why he didn't just move out ahead of me to make sure everyone was okay.

"Cam," he said, and I saw that it was on our private net. "This was a royal fuck-up, you know that, right?"

"I got suckered," I agreed. "They knew we had to try and they knew just how to nail us."

"Not that." He blew out a breath and I thought he was barely controlling an anger he knew he couldn't and shouldn't let show. "We had to do that. No matter how we handled it, they were going to spring that trap. I'm talking about you going in there with First squad. You cut yourself off from the rest of the platoon, left us all hanging out there. You're not a fucking squad leader anymore. You can't be doing that shit." I nearly stopped, but I was walking slow enough as it was. It took me a second to find my voice.

"You told me you didn't think Carson was ready," I reminded him. "She would've...."

"Would have walked into a trap?" he interrupted. "Tell me, sir, what would have gone down differently if you'd been outside and Carson had gone in alone? Would anyone have died who didn't? Or would you have been outside where you could control the situation better?" I wanted to argue, but I couldn't. He was exactly right.

"I'm sorry, Scotty," I told him. "I'll do better next time, I promise."

"I know you will, sir. Everyone makes mistakes." His tone softened. "This ain't your first. But you always learn from them, which is why you haven't let me down yet."

"I know it's policy to always send an OCS grad back to a different platoon than they served in before," I told him, "but I'm glad they sent me back to this one. It would sting pretty bad to get my ass chewed like that by a stranger."

"Always happy to help, sir." I couldn't see his grin, but I could hear it. "That's why God made platoon sergeants."

[11]

It felt very odd to be walking on what had just hours before been a battlefield without my suit on. The armor insulated me from reality, from the ugliness of it, but now I was naked to the casual brutality of it, seeing through my own eyes, unfiltered by the impersonal display of my helmet screen.

In the harsh light of the morning, Amity was the smoking, shattered remnants of a nightmare, the ruins of the downtown area jagged talons raising up from the charred pavement. Tahni High Guard battlesuits stood like memorials to the battle, frozen in death. I shivered and pulled my field jacket hood up over my ears, walking only meters past one of the blackened and burnt armor suits as I headed for the temporary command center. It was a grand name for a tent stretched over steel anchors driven into the pavement of the city's central square.

Force Recon Marines were guarding the perimeter of the square, against what I wasn't sure. The Tahni were dead. They hadn't run, hadn't surrendered, they'd just fought to the last and died in place. And I suppose I understood. They'd been here without resupply or reinforcement for a year. They'd known no help was coming and they'd known the choice would be between an uncertain future as a prisoner of war or the comforting certainty of death. I couldn't say I would have done anything differently than they had.

I smelled smoke and blood in the air. The city was depressing, a mutilated corpse dumped by the side of the road. The whole planet felt dead and I wondered if we had arrived too late to do anything more than finish off the last of the enemy and bury the bodies.

The tent flap was hanging closed and I ducked through it, grateful for a barrier from a world I didn't want to see anymore. Inside was the comforting familiarity of a military field station, communications and sensor gear, holographic displays, and a swarm of clerks and technicians, performing whatever arcane tasks they were assigned. A single Force Recon Marine stood guard near the entrance, his Gauss rifle cradled in his arms, the visor of his helmet thrown back, revealing a face etched with exhaustion and boredom.

"Captain Covington?" I asked him.

"You got me, sir," he said. "They just told me to stand here and don't let any civilians through."

I snorted and brushed past him, scanning back and forth as I zigzagged through the interior of the tent, squeezing between quantum computer cores and holographic projectors, until I finally found a cluster of officers gathered around a tactical display, a holographic terrain table showing the area around the city along with avatars representing our deployed units.

A colonel was finishing a briefing and I held back, not wanting to act like I was crashing their party, barely catching the end of his summary.

"...don't think we're going to need more than a few companies of Fleet Engineers and a medical support unit, and maybe a couple platoons of Force Recon as guards."

"Guards against what, sir?" The one who'd asked was a

captain, and from the lack of interface sockets in his temples, likely Recon himself. "I'd heard there weren't any Tahni left."

"There aren't. But this occupation was...." The colonel hesitated. "Well, to call it rough would be an insult to those who survived. And many of the locals who made it through are going to have trouble adjusting. I'm not saying they're crazy or violent, but the possibility exists that some might tend that way. I don't believe it would be wise to neglect the security of the Engineers and Medical Service technicians. If nothing else, there are the wild animals to think of, at least until we can get the sonic barriers repaired."

He paused and surveyed the officers gathered around the table.

"If there are no other questions, I'll leave you to your duties. We haven't been assigned a new permanent base yet, so we're going to take at least ten to fourteen days here to repair and refit. I'll need a rotation from you all to send troops through guard duty and to help with constructing temporary shelters for the civilians. Get those to my 'link within twelve hours."

The meeting broke up and I caught Captain Covington's eye before he headed back to whatever else he'd been doing.

"Lt. Alvarez," he said, nodding. "Glad you caught me before I headed out."

"I ran into Top over at the spaceport, sir," I told him. "They've set up repair racks there. She said you wanted to see me."

"I won't keep you long," he assured me, seeming almost solicitous, which worried me. "I heard you found the hostages. I saw them after Search and Rescue turned them over to the Medical Service units."

"It was...unimaginable, sir," I confessed. "I hope to God I never see anything like it again."

"Tell me how it went." I knew he wasn't still talking about

the hostages, and I didn't bother to pretend I didn't know what he meant.

I glanced around me to make sure no one would overhear, but all the rest of the officers who'd been gathered at the terrain table had scattered.

"Sir, I feel like I may have reached the level of my incompetence."

I expected him to agree, or possibly to get upset and tell me to get over it and stop feeling sorry for myself. I didn't expect him to laugh.

"And I suppose you believe you're the first brand new platoon leader who's ever said that to me."

"Probably not," I admitted. "But sir, I felt so at home as a squad leader...I don't know if I ever felt I was out of my depth or didn't know what I was doing. After last night...." I shook my head. "You must have audited the report. I made the wrong call on just about everything."

Covington leaned back against the terrain table and regarded me with crossed arms.

"Tell me," he prompted. "Lay it out for me."

"I should have gone in the rear with Fourth squad," I told him without hesitation. I'd thought about this quite a bit the last few hours. "Going in with First through the roof was removing myself from the command equation and limiting my ability to respond to a changing battlespace."

"Changing battlespace?" Covington repeated, snorting amusement. "Someone's been playing buzzword bingo at OCS. You mean the fucking building blowing up."

"I should have expected they'd rigged the building," I insisted. "Hell, sir, I *did* expect them to rig the building, and I still went in through the roof. I was thinking like a door-kicker, not a platoon leader."

"It was a mistake," he agreed, his tone casual. "One I believe

I might have made a time or two myself back when I was a platoon leader. The first time around. But it wasn't fatal, not for any of your Marines. You accomplished the mission, freed most of the hostages alive and killed the enemy. And if the hotel needs to be rebuilt, well, we don't work for the Demeter Tourism Administration. We're Marines. Our job is to kill the enemy and break shit."

"It was only blind luck it wasn't fatal, sir."

"Was it?" The question was sharp, the crack of a whip, and it startled me into coming to attention. "Tell me something, Cameron, if you hadn't ordered First squad to skip the intervening floors and go straight to the lobby, what do you suppose would have happened when the supports blew?"

"Some of them would have been caught in the collapse, sir."

"And likely gotten themselves killed. So yes, perhaps you should have stayed with Fourth squad and retained more control over the platoon, but you went where your instincts told you to go." He closed his eyes for a moment and let out a slow breath, as if forcing himself to calm down. "Your problem isn't the decisions you made, Cameron. Your problem is, you're still thinking bottom-up. You didn't trust Carson to make the calls she would need to make if she'd gone inside alone, so you went with her. But if you didn't trust her, why put her squad inside at all?"

"Because Delp is our best running point, sir," I said, not quite understanding.

"And that's exactly what I'm talking about. That's squad leader thinking. Bottom-up thinking. You are an officer now and you need to be thinking top-down. If you need to be outside, you send a *leader* you trust inside, even if their troops aren't the very best in your platoon. Because, in the end, a good leader will save more lives than a good gunfighter. You get what I mean?"

"Yes, sir," I said, "I think I do, now."

'Good." He clapped me on the arm and I blinked, not used to him being quite so comradely before. "Because it only gets harder from here, son. This...." He waved a hand around him. "...was a cakewalk. The enemy was barely holding on by their fingernails. You probably heard the colonel. We have ten days here." He rolled his eyes. "Theoretically. You know how that goes; it could be anywhere from twenty-four hours to a solid month. But while we're here, I want to take advantage of the terrain and the lack of an enemy threat and do some field training. Simulators are fine if that's all you have, but they're no substitute for actually operating your suit."

"Ooh-rah, sir."

Shit. I winced at the fake enthusiasm, something else I'd learned at OCS. Covington laughed again.

"Get your suits running," he told me, then give your people a twenty-four-hour rest. And you," he emphasized the word, pointing at me, "turn off your 'link and get a solid eight hours sleep. That's an order, by the way. Grab a sleeping pill from the medics if you need it. Then get me a training schedule for the rest of the week by no later 1200 local tomorrow."

"Yes, sir." I turned to go but hesitated. "Sir, the way the Tahni treated those people...." I squeezed my eyes shut against an unbidden image of the living skeletons, starved so nearly to death. "Is that what we're going to be seeing from now on?"

"I don't know," he admitted. "Supposedly, things here were about as bad as it gets. Guerilla warfare, assassination, atrocities on both sides, retaliation, infighting between factions of the human resistance and the Tahni command...." He shook his head as if to clear it of the ugliness. "I'm hoping it's the worst we'll see, but you know the old saying. Hope in one hand...."

"...and shit in the other," I finished for him. "And see which one fills up first. Yes, sir."

"It's a war. Despite anything you might see in the movies,

it's never clean and rarely noble. And if it's ever heroic, it's not because men and women are determined to be heroes, it's because they care about their brothers and sisters more than they care about themselves. You know that as well as anyone. It's always been true, and it's twice as bad when you're fighting an enemy who isn't even human."

He motioned at the door.

"Go get some rest."

I walked out of the tent and pointed myself back toward the spaceport. The Fleet engineers and the Marine techs had dropped most of the gear from their cargo shuttles there and left it to make another run up to orbit, and until we got the trucks from the civilians or load-lifters from the *Iwo* or the other ships, any and all repairs were going to be done at the spaceport.

It was a long walk and I suppose I could have waited for a vehicle, but I was zoning out and by the time I blinked and realized where I was, I'd already gone a good three kilometers and I was passing the perimeter fence the Tahni had set up on the outskirts of town. Most of it was torn to shreds, ripped apart either by the civilian militia or the other Drop-Trooper companies hitting the city.

The primary star was higher now and it was warming up, the mist burning away, and as it withdrew, an image clarified off to the side of the road, as strange and spectral as if I had stumbled onto a ghostly apparition. A group of civilians were gathered by the side of the road, digging into the sodden ground with hand tools. I stopped in mid-step and stared at them, wondering what the hell they were digging holes for, before I noticed the body bags.

They were digging graves. It seemed even stranger once I understood that. Why would they be burying their dead on their own? Why wouldn't they let us do that for them with machinery? Then I noticed the Gauss rifles stacked off to the side, barrels supporting each other with the butts planted into the ground, very professional, the way a Marine squad would have done it.

I looked closer at the civilians. Their clothes were mended and patched over and over, but they weren't ragged or torn. They were lean and hard, but not painfully skinny or starving. Their hair was cut short and a few were still wearing bits and pieces of what I recognized as Tahni armor. Their faces were hard, one or two marred by long-healed scars.

This was the resistance, the civilian militia. The ones who'd done the dirty work. Which was why they were burying their own dead.

One of them, a dark-haired young woman close to my age, who would have been beautiful if it hadn't been for the case-hardened set to her face, stared back at me with eyes so dark they were nearly black, burning with a lingering rage like the smoldering ruins of yesterday's fire.

"You a Marine?" she asked me.

"I'm Lt. Alvarez. Cam."

"Sophia," she returned. I didn't know why she'd decided to talk to me, but I felt compelled to fill the awkward silence.

"Are those your friends?" I asked, gesturing to the bodies. "People you fought beside?"

"No," she said. "Those are people who the Tahni let starve to death. They tossed them into a ditch over that way." She pointed north along the fence line. "We just found them."

"They're all dead now, you know. The Tahni, I mean. They're gone." I didn't say it because I didn't want to piss her off, but I was implying they didn't need to keep the rifles handy.

"I know." The corner of her mouth twitched, like she wanted to smile but had forgotten how. "I killed sixty-seven of them in the last fourteen months."

"Was that enough?" I wondered. "I mean, do you think you got even?"

Her eyes flickered toward the bodies and she shook her head.

"Not even close."

[12]

"What the hell was the name of this planet again?" Joanna Carson wanted to know.

I frowned, wondering if I should be the one to tell her to keep her chatter off the general platoon net or if I should leave it to Scotty. My eyes flickered to the left, not seeing her or anything in the view from the external cameras except the bare metal of the drop rack. A shudder ran through the aerospace-craft and I wondered if we were hitting more turbulence or actually taking fire this time. I could have accessed the drop-ship's tactical feed, but I was too busy trying to run through the op order in my head.

"Vistula," Scotty's voice came over the line, sounding annoyed. "Like you've been told at about three briefings now."

"I know," Carson admitted. "I just never heard of the place."

For that, I couldn't blame her. I hadn't known it even existed until about a week ago, and even the Skipper didn't seem convinced it had any strategic importance.

"The only reason we're taking this planet," he'd confided to the platoon leaders gathered around an overturned spool of superconductive cable outside the headquarters tent, "is that there are human colonists still alive on it. It's a wildcat colony, established by an independent mining cooperative that came out here without authorization and started digging for iridium on one of the moons of the interior-system gas giant. It wasn't habitable, but the larger moon is, and parts of it have a pretty temperate climate, so they made their home there and started breeding cattle and growing luxury crops."

He'd sniffed in disdain, casting a baleful glare at the holographic projection of the single—well, not *city*, more like a town, barely as big as the tiny section of Tijuana where I was born—hovering over the portable field display on top of the metal spool.

"The Tahni only bothered to take it because it was the last system on the way to Silvanus and the iridium mines were handy for their fabricators to manufacture weapons and drive components for their fleet. Why they're trying to hold onto it, God only knows. The spooks believe it's a sort of religious imperative with them not to give up a living world once they've taken it, but I think they're just guessing. They're aliens, and what we would think of as foolishly stubborn, they might consider perfectly reasonable. We could and probably *should* just bypass it, but it wouldn't look good for the politicians if they left a bunch of colonists, even outlaw colonists, in Tahni hands."

"There can't be that many Tahni troops on Vistula though, can there?" Lt. Cano had asked, worry pinching folds beside his eyes. "Not by this point, right? I mean, it's just a resupply base...."

"There likely won't be any starships, but I'm sure they'll still have plenty of cargo shuttles. And they've been there long enough to rig up weapons for them. As for ground troops...." Covington's eyebrow had arched in the "you-should-know-better" expression that all of us were so familiar with. "The Tahni have never been reticent about leaving their soldiers to die in meaningless rear-guard actions, and I doubt they'll start here. There's sure to be at least a battalion of conventional soldiers to run the resupply base and the fabrication facility, maybe as much as a full brigade. They're sure to have Shock Troopers, but as for High Guard suits...." He'd shrugged. "None of the Scout Service drones have reported any, but they're taking snapshots from a few hundred thousand kilometers away before Transitioning out again, so the odds are, they wouldn't see them even if there was a whole battalion of them. As always, hope for the best, prepare for the worst. We ship out in forty hours and Transition time will be about five days subjective. We'll use as much of that for simulator time as we can." He'd nodded back to where we'd established the temporary barracks, in what had been the Tahni troop quarters and, before that, some government building for storing heavy machinery. There'd been a lot of dried blood inside that building and hosing it off had taken the better part of a day, but no one had minded the extra work. "Go tell your people. Give them the rest of today off, then we start loading our gear first thing in the morning."

The other platoon leaders had been upbeat and talkative on the way back to the barracks, like we were planning a vacation outing instead of a battle, and I'd had to remind myself that the drop on Demeter had been the first combat experience Cano and Kovacs had ever had, and only the second for Burke and Patel. All four were Academy grads, which made them about my age and yet, somehow, so much younger.

"Hey," Burke had piped up when we were nearly to the barrack building, "I heard the locals re-opened one of the bars in town and have it stocked with home-made moonshine. We got tonight off. Anyone want to check it out?"

"Oh, shit yeah," Cano had enthused. "I haven't had anything to drink in like two months. Maybe I could find one of the local girls who wants a roll in the sack. Been even longer since I got laid."

Dark, vengeful eyes and the smell of newly-turned earth had teased at my memory.

"I'd be pretty fucking careful about messing with any of the locals. They've been living on the edge of a knife for over a year and they're not going to be too receptive to some jackhead Marine coming in here with clean clothes and a full belly, expecting gratitude."

I had been, I'd realized a couple seconds too late, using my NCO voice. When they'd warned us about that in OCS, using our NCO voice instead of our officer voice, they'd mostly been worried about presenting ourselves in our new identity to our troops, but I discovered that it was just as important when dealing with my peers.

"Yeah, okay, man," Cano had said, his voice suddenly subdued. The others had seemed reluctant to meet my eyes, and when they'd gone out to that bar later in the evening, I had not been invited along.

Lesson learned.

Scotty wasn't going to say it, so I did.

"Keep the channel clear, Carson." I hesitated. They should at least get the explanation I got. "The moon is important for the same reason this mission is more dangerous than you think. There are humans down there, being held prisoner by the Tahni. That means we can't just pound the base from orbit, then walk in with a broom and sweep up the pieces. We have to slog our way in from the outside and do our best not to kill the hostages, which gives the enemy the chance to kill as many of us as possible. And we're jumping into that shit in about five minutes, so button up your shit and get your head in the game."

"Yes, sir," Carson said, her voice subdued.

I cursed in the privacy of my helmet. That was my NCO voice again.

Another shudder wrenched the dropship, more violent this time and I gave in to curiosity, tapping into the external video feed. Once upon a time, I'd had to run a backdoor program and sneak into the feed without authorization, using a trick I'd learned from the company armorer. Now, as an officer, I just had to touch a control.

I really shouldn't have bothered. It was black as coal outside, except when lightning crashed through the clouds and the lifting body shape of another dropship was silhouetted from kilometers away. That was spitting distance for spacecraft flying down through the atmosphere, but the target was small and so was the drop zone. If we didn't pack the flight path, we had the choice of dropping the troops over too big an area and having them take longer to reach the target, or sending the ships in a few at a time and not concentrating our force on the enemy.

"What do you see out there?" Scotty asked me on a private channel. The corner of my mouth turned up at how well he could read me.

"Two things," I told him. "And Jack just left town."

"Going in blind with no orbital prep. I like it, I love it, I want more of it."

I grunted an unwilling laugh at his use of the age-old response of a Boot Camp recruit to the announcement that it was time for more physical training.

"One minute to drop," the crew chief's voice echoed inside my helmet.

Scotty would be telling the platoon, giving them last-second warnings and assurance. I found myself missing the days when there'd been someone to do that for me. I didn't even get a pep talk from the Skipper, not with a dropship only capable of carrying a single platoon. All I had was my own doubts swirling around inside my brain, which was exactly as depressing as it sounds.

I didn't remember hearing the crew chief announce it was time to drop, barely realized I was echoing the command, and had no clue I'd yanked the drop lever until I was falling into the night, still unable to see a damned thing. The clouds were low and thick and full of moisture, ideal for killing thermal and lidar, and all the radar could tell me was there was a shitload of other Vigilantes in the air, all heading for the same place.

Thanks, I never would have figured that out on my own.

At least the mapping software was still working, using dead-reckoning rather than any reliance on sensors. The one useful thing the Scout Service had been able to tell us about this place was that the minute our ships had appeared from Transition Space, the Tahni troops had begun chivvying the human settlers out of the single, boxy housing unit where they'd been keeping them and distributing them into hardened bunkers scattered around the fabrication plant. And each of those bunkers housed a heavy, rapid-fire coil gun that could knock a dropship out of the air, much less turn a Vigilante battlesuit into so much shrapnel.

Other companies were assigned to taking down the spaceport and the cargo-handling facilities, each of which had its own bunkers and its own human hostages. Delta had been given the plumb prize, the fabrication plant right at the center of town, twenty kilometers downriver from the spaceport. Estimates were that between twelve to twenty thousand human settlers had lived in Vistula proper before the war, and the Intelligence analysts who'd been parsing the data from the Scout Service drones had told us they estimated half of them were still alive.

Now, all we had to do was kill the Tahni who were using them as shields without killing the humans.

The platoon was spread out over nearly half a kilometer, the point of the company spear once again, the others coming in along our flanks, surrounding the bunkers, trying to keep them from having a single, massed target. The coil guns were firing. I knew it in my gut, even if I couldn't see them, couldn't detect anything even with the radar. Somewhere in those thoughts we don't want to admit we have, I hoped they were shooting at the dropships or the assault shuttles and not us. I felt guilty about that, but I still hoped.

God had been listening, though, and just to show me what a shitheel He thought I was, he arranged for me to be in the perfect position to see the dropship go down. It had been burning a high-g boost upward, out of the drop dive, having divested itself of its load of Marines, but it hadn't gotten away in time. The coil gun round took out its port turbines in a spray of fire and it went into a spin as the thrust all came from one side of the craft for just a heartbeat before the computers shut the other engine down.

If they'd had another three or four hundred meters, they might have pulled out of it, but the ship was too big and ungainly and unresponsive for that. I couldn't even see the ground yet, but I heard the roar of the explosion, felt the gust of wind from the shockwave jolt me in mid-air, felt the heat from the flare of the blast even a kilometer away. The crew might have ejected. At least I told myself that.

Then the clouds parted and we were looking straight down the magnetic coils of the weapon, yawning like a cavern despite only being about 10mm across and nearly a kilometer away.

"First squad, take out that damned gun!"

Carson, for a change, didn't need to be told twice. Or maybe it was Delp acting without orders, simply out of self-preservation, the way I would have if I could get away with running point. Missiles launched at the same time as the gun fired. It didn't hit me or anyone in front of me, and my soles slammed into the ground with a jolt of reality, like the Skipper slapping me in the back of the head and telling me I wasn't dead and needed to get to work.

The coil gun erupted in plumes of sublimated metal and ten-meter-long sparks of static electricity coming off the shattered superconductor cabling running along the inside of the electromagnets. A cold knife plunged into my guts at the thought of what the blast would do to the human captives inside the bunker, but the coil gun had been mounted on a gimballed turret near the rear of the reinforced concrete dome, and the force of the explosions had blown it backwards. Powdered concrete filled the air with a white haze and chunks of it carpeted the hard-pack dirt around the fabricator plant, but most of the dome was intact.

It was too much, too many details. I was watching IFF transponder signals in my HUD, keeping track of the rest of the company to make sure we weren't drifting into their firing arcs, trying to keep my own position, trying to keep an eye on the sensors and the urgent messages coming in via text alerts. It was only a few seconds, but that was an eternity to be standing still in combat, and I didn't see the Shock Troops pouring out from the hole in the back of the bunker until one of them shot me in the face.

I cried out, half a curse, half an incoherent shout at the pain of the gong-like ringing in my ears from the burst of tantalum darts punching into the armor of my helmet. I had often wondered why they didn't put an actual visor on the front of the helmet, just in case the power went down or the sensors were damaged. Now I knew. If I'd had a transparent visor, no matter what it was made of, no matter how small it was, I would have been dead. Instead, my visual display flickered as a few of the micro-cameras built into the surface of the helmet died under the barrage, but the other sensors remained alive, and so did I.

I jerked the trigger of the plasma gun and the Tahni Shock-trooper disappeared in a star-bright explosion, the top half of his body disappearing, heavy infantry armor that might take an off-center hit from a Gauss gun no match at all for super-ionized hydrogen travelling at tens of thousands of meters per second. The exoskeleton the Shocktroopers used to move around the heavier armor, and what was basically a crew-served KE gun, kept the lower body standing despite the disintegration of every-thing above the hips, like some absurdist art piece in one of the more upscale parks in Trans Angeles.

The plasma shot had blown through the point-blank target and gone on to strike two more of the Tahni heavy infantry behind him, not quite achieving the same dramatic effect on them but still managing to burn through their armor and send them spinning to the dirt and mud. The Shocktroopers were schoolchildren trying to tackle full-grown adults, a good meter shorter than the Vigilante suits, lacking the isotope reactor, the heavy weapons and the massive armor that made us devastating in a fight. They were designed to fight the last war, when the best we'd had was powered armor that was the equivalent of theirs, and now they had High Guard suits to fight us and the Shocktroopers were obsolete and even a tactical liability with their thermal signature and lack of mobility, but the military is the military, no matter the species and when the military has that much gear sitting around, well, hell, they might as well use it.

The plasma gun's capacitors were recharging and I was too close for missiles, even if I would have wasted one on the metal midgets, so I swung with my armored left fist and smashed two of them aside as if they were nothing. And abruptly, there were no more of them in front of me, the balance of the troops who had swarmed out of the damaged bunker charred into cinders by the fire of a platoon's worth of plasma gunfire.

"Carson, check the bunker."

But I could see Delp's IFF transponder already inside, near the hole we'd blown in the back where the coil gun had been mounted, anticipating my order and Carson's relay of it. The kid was good. If I could just make sure he didn't wind up getting killed like Henckel, he might wind up a squad leader himself.

"Clear of enemy in here," Delp reported. "But we got some civilians and they're in pretty bad shape."

I loped around to the other side of the bunker, keeping an eye on the display, watching Second and Third squads carry out the plan and push forward to the fabrication plant with Scotty riding herd on them. Fourth hung back and watched our six, staying in reserve in case Covington called on us for help. The other platoons were dealing with their own bunkers, and I pushed down an instinct to send people to help them, or go myself.

Follow the op order. Fight to the plan.

The hole in the wall of the bunker was big enough, the ceiling high enough that I could fit my armor through if I scrambled over some fallen concrete. I had steeled myself to the civilians inside being injured by the heat of the missile strike, even some being buried by rubble, but that wasn't the problem.

I had also prepared myself for them being starved almost to death, the way the captives had been on Demeter. They were skinny, but not skeleton-thin, not malnutrition-thin. They'd been eating regularly, though clearly not as much as they would have liked. Their clothes were dirty and patched, but they didn't hang off their bodies, and they had jackets and boots, so they hadn't been left exposed to the elements.

They'd been shot.

It was clear what had happened from the divots in the walls, the blood spatter behind them. There'd been twenty, maybe thirty of them pushed against the far wall, their hands bound behind their backs, feet hobbled. The attempted execution had been hasty, performed with a long burst of fire from two or three of the Shocktroopers firing their heavy KE guns, and it had been far from efficient. Ten or twelve of the captives had been killed outright, torn apart, taking the brunt of the bursts of tiny, tantalum darts, but there were at least as many wounded, some of them horribly. I saw white bone and missing fingers and someone holding their insides with their hands before I pulled out and closed my eyes and still couldn't get the image out of my head.

"We need Search and Rescue down here," I called on the general campaign net and heard nothing in reply. We were still being jammed. *Dammit.*

"What should we do, sir?" Delp asked. There was anguish in his voice.

"There's nothing we *can* do right now," I told him. "Search and Rescue will come down here once we've secured the place, so that's the best thing we can do for them." I found Carson on the IFF overlay and turned toward her. "First squad, leapfrog Second and Third and..."

I'd been working it out in my head, keeping the big picture in mind, doing everything I'd been told to do, and everything seemed to be going according to plan. For once. I should have known it wouldn't last.

"We got High Guard!" Scotty called from somewhere ahead of us, closer to the fabrication plant. "Company strength!"

He was still talking but I could see it for myself, the battle-suits bursting through the upper-floor windows of the fabricator plant on jump-jets, shrouded in the launch-trail smoke of their missiles and I wanted to lead, wanted to direct, and there was absolutely no time and the only thing I could say, the only thing I had time to think of, was two words.

"Assault through!"

[13]

I'd just ordered the entire company to attack.

I had, I realized in a horrified flash of insight, been switched over to the company net, ready to report the attack to Covington. It made sense and it was probably the correct call, and I don't know if it made a difference since there wasn't anything else to be done, but I could see the IFF transponders of the whole company surging forward behind my platoon.

We were outrunning the missiles by flying straight into them, a tactic I'd learned from Lt. Ackley. Their warheads, like ours, had a minimum arming distance, and unlike ours, they were manually guided by an ocular inside the helmets, because of that whole business of a Tahni having to personally be responsible for every life they took. Which meant that charging into a swarm of missiles wasn't *actually* insane, it just looked that way.

It certainly *felt* that way, watching firefly swarms of rocket engines heading straight for me, but all I could do was open the throttle for the suit's jets and...

"Fire!"

I'd been giving the order to my own platoon, but the whole

company followed it, a barrage of plasma lighting up the whole front wall of the fabrication plant like a false sunrise for just a fraction of a second. Not all the shots hit home because we were jetting in at maximum thrust, the acceleration pushing us into the bottom of our suits, chins buried in our chests. The enemy was careening headlong into us and the missiles were only a few dozen meters away...but where they didn't hit, they *distracted*, which was the point.

Tahni missiles went corkscrewing out of control, or slammed into the ground with flares of impotent rage and if any of them hit, they didn't hit *my* people.

And then I began to break the rules. There was no way to keep track of my Marines, not in the madness and chaos of the melee, and I concentrated on just surviving the next few seconds. I'd fired my plasma gun and I wasn't a hundred percent certain I'd hit anything with it because there were so many enemy suits and so many of ours firing, but I knew I couldn't fire again for two seconds, and that was eternity.

The High Guard suit coming straight at me could still fire, and did, and a crackling electron beam hit my suit in the lower leg and I screamed. Heat flooded the suit and I was suddenly trapped inside a convection oven, the breath stolen from my lungs, sweat baked away before it could cool me, and searing pain shot up from my right foot. I couldn't stop to figure out how badly I was hurt; however bad it was, it wasn't as bad as dead, which was my destination if I hesitated. I forced my eyes back into focus, swerved at just the last second, then spun and slammed the suit's left fist into the side of the High Guard trooper's helmet.

The concussion nearly sent me tumbling out of control in the air, but it did worse to him. His suit went spinning head over heels, the jets pinwheeling him into the ground and burying his armor half a meter into the mud. I knew what that would do to him because I knew what it would have done to me, and I knew if he wasn't dead from a shattered spine, he certainly wouldn't be rejoining the fight.

All I could concentrate on was a narrow space around me, and another suit popped into it, coming into view as I swung my legs around and decelerated. We fired at the same time and I wasn't sure where his electron beam went but my plasmoid took him directly through the chest. The Tahni soldier inside was incinerated and the blast of super-ionized hydrogen passed right through and spent the balance of its kinetic and thermal energy in the isotope power pack worn like a rucksack behind the suit's shoulders. The reactor died and the battlesuit's jets sputtered out a microsecond later, sending him downward with sickening certainty.

And then it was over, just as quickly as it had begun, and there were no more High Guard suits, just burning hulks on the ground. And a few of ours were burning down there with them. I'd killed two, maybe three, and disappointment at the middling performance warred with disappointment at breaking my own rules and getting involved in the fighting.

I checked the IFF transponders as I descended, before I even checked my own damage, running down through each squad and finding...

Shit.

"Majid!" I called to the Fourth squad leader. Fourth was still back behind the lines of the bunkers, not close enough to have been part of the assault and one of the transponders had gone black. Maybe it was a malfunction. It was possible. I touched the ground and my leg didn't give way, which was a good sign.

"Majid!" I repeated. "Where's Valentine?"

"Sir...." Christian Majid's voice was hoarse, like he'd swallowed cotton, and I wasn't sure if he was going to finish the thought. "One of the missiles, sir. It just...she's gone, sir."

I limped toward him, not willing to accept it, needing to see for myself. It was hard to believe it was the same ground I'd passed over only a couple minutes before. Everything was on fire, buried under layers of white smoke, and the ground was torn to shreds, as if an excavator had begun prep work for some big construction project. The remains of the dropship were burning fiercely, lighting the whole place up like mid-day and throwing eerie shadows from the concrete domes of the bunkers.

The bunkers were cracked and crumbled and pouring smoke, and civilians were shuffling out of a couple of them, barely able to walk with their ankles hobbled by plastic straps. I felt like someone should cut them free, but that was precision work for something three meters tall with one articulated hand and the fingers on that six centimeters wide. I wasn't about to tell one of my troops to get out of their armor yet.

I didn't want to look at Valentine. I'd been letting my eyes wander about the battlefield, willing to take in all the other ugliness, all the death and destruction, but she was one of mine. She would be the first casualty under my command. I didn't want it to be true, and if I could put off know it, put off seeing it, maybe it wouldn't be real. But life didn't work that way, and I should have known. I'd never seen my father's body, or my brother's, never wanted to look at them, but they'd both been just as dead.

So was Private Sera Valentine. The missile had hit her just right, center mass, and there was nothing left of her suit's torso but twisted, burning metal. The arms and legs had blown off and were scattered in the cardinal directions and I was grateful I couldn't see whether her own limbs were still inside.

I tried to say something to Majid but my mouth was dry and I couldn't get the words out.

"Mark the spot," I managed to tell him. "We'll come back and...take care of her."

"Third Platoon, do you read?" It was Covington, and the fact he was able to talk to me meant he was within line of sight. I found his IFF signal and picked him out of the Headquarters Platoon, just now descending from their drop, the coil-gun-toting Boomers strolling in like a police tactical team back in the Underground, always too late to do any good.

"This is Third Platoon." I almost didn't recognize my own voice, so dull and lifeless was its tone. "We have our section of the perimeter secured. One KIA, Private Valentine." I finally noticed the damage report on my own suit. The Tahni electron beam hadn't actually touched flesh, just burned off a few centimeters of the suit's footpad, but I did have second-degree burns from the knee down. I shrugged it off. "No serious WIA. Some minor suit damage. We have multiple civilian dead and badly wounded and need Search and Rescue in here ASAP."

"They're on their way," he assured me. "I need you to move into the fabrication center and root out any conventional infantry the Tahni might have still holed up in there before they get the idea of taking the civilians out before we get to them."

"Too late," I told him, more cold-blooded and matter-of-fact than I'd meant to. "Yes, sir, on it." I switched nets back to the platoon. "Carson, take First squad, head up to the second floor and make entry through the busted-out windows. Grenade launchers only unless you spot more High Guard troopers inside. Scotty, you stay with Second and Third and bust through the front cargo doors. Careful for demo charges. Use plasma guns to take down the doors before you enter."

"Roger that, sir," Scotty acknowledged.

"What about Fourth, LT?" Majid asked me. He still sounded shaken by Valentine's death and I was tempted to have him sit this out, but Fourth had already been held in reserve during the initial assault and still managed to take a casualty.

"Follow First squad through the upper windows," I told him, "and maintain position on the upper floors as overwatch." Which, I thought, sounded better than "stay back in case we need you, because I don't trust that your head's in the game."

I'd already given the order, and I had resigned myself to restating it to get Carson moving, but she surprised me again by taking the initiative and moving her people ahead without having to be told. Delp rocketed upward through the shattered polymer windows of the fabrication plant's upper floor, with the rest of his fire-team close behind. I waited for the Bravo team and Carson to disappear through the lingering clouds of smoke and into the giant windows, gave it a silent count of three, then hit my own jets and followed.

"Second and Third, move in," I called from ten meters up, just before I hit the hole.

Smoke and dust refracted stray shafts of light from what was left of the ceiling lamps, fighting a losing battle with the deep shadows inside the place. The upper floor of the plant was a catwalk surrounding the slapdash, cobbled-together machinery of the industrial fabricators, built from spare parts by the wildcat settlers and expanded as they'd acquired more pieces. It had extended outward and upward and they'd added the catwalk as an afterthought to service the parts that were too high to reach even with maintenance gantries. I landed on the wooden floorboards gingerly, fearing the weight of the Vigilante would send me crashing through, but it was sturdy enough to support me and I took a step toward the edge.

Below, on the factory floor, the machinery was a cold blue on thermal, and my troops were red-hot, moving through it, maintaining their formation as best they could among the obstacles in their way. My gut clenched, expecting the stacks of fabricators to be rigged with explosives like the roof supports back on Demeter, but perhaps I'd given this particular Tahni garrison more credit for fanaticism than they deserved. I tried to put myself in their place, abandoned, left without support or guidance, but not quite as desperate as the troops on Demeter. No civilian resistance to speak of, no sabotage, nothing to make them bitter and enraged.

Yet they'd tried to execute the prisoners anyway, were using them as shields. Maybe the Tahni didn't *need* to be desperate to massacre our civilians. Maybe they knew better than we did just what sort of war this was.

Deep-throated thumps floated upward from the floor, the distinctive sound of grenade launchers, and two seconds later, the kettle-drum rattle of detonation, a rolling echo through the forest of metal. The floor cracked beneath me as I jumped over the railing and fed a burst of power to the jets, turning a leg-breaking, ten-meter fall into a stomp of spiked soles against the concrete. I resisted the urge to ask for a status report, not wanting to be one of *those* platoon leaders, but finding myself with a new-found appreciation of their frustration at being responsible for everything and in control of nothing.

Fabrication machinery loomed over me, from floor to ceiling, simple enough that the settlers had been able to construct it from nothing, but far too complicated for me to understand. I weaved through the maze of the machines, following the hollow bang of grenades and the spiteful crack of Tahni KE guns and lasers replying, until there was no more response.

The Tahni and their human prisoners had been squeezed into a storage room connected to the fabrication plant by a broad cargo door. There'd once been pallet after pallet of manufactured goods lined up along the walls in the room, their square outlines still present as stains on the concrete, but now the cargo crates were packed together into barricades, cover for the Tahni soldiers. A crew-served KE gun had been mounted behind one of the barricades, but its barrels were canted downward now, the Tahni soldiers who had crewed it splashed across the floor by grenade rounds. Their light armor was next to useless against modern military weapons, though I suppose it might offer protection against sidearms or the obsolete slug-shooters they still used out in the colonies.

Makeshift barricades had been bulldozed over by First squad's Vigilantes and more of the enemy troops were buried beneath heavy cargo boxes, their weapons lying on the ground beside them. Laser carbines. I didn't recall ever seeing one on the battlefield before. They were only issued to rear-echelon troops, the Tahni equivalent of clerks and technicians, and they were nearly useless against Drop Troopers, not even really effective against Force Recon personal armor.

They were perfect for unarmored civilians though.

There'd been probably two hundred people jammed against the far wall of the warehouse, tied and hobbled like the others. None of these had escaped. They'd had time to be thorough, to fire burst after burst of their laser carbines into the huddled mass of humanity, hundreds of rounds, maybe thousands, until the cement-block wall behind them was charred and blackened and spattered with blood. Not a single body stirred, not a single moan rose from the corpses piled on the floor. Most had been chopped to pieces.

These weren't like the survivors at Demeter, just the young and strong. There were children, toddlers and the only reason I hadn't descended into madness was that I couldn't see their faces in the sullen darkness of the unlit warehouse. I checked on thermal for body heat, checked the sonic sensors for heartbeats, for breathing and found nothing. They were all dead, every single one.

The bulk of the Tahni were still alive. I'd never seen it

before, but they'd laid down their guns and gone to their knees, a cluster of at least a hundred of them, maybe half again more than that. Some were wounded, but most didn't have dirt on their uniforms. They were surrendering.

Delp stood a few meters from the front rank of them, unmoving, as if staring at them in disbelief, and the rest of the squad hadn't even formed into a combat wedge, just standing and watching. I couldn't see their faces, but decided if I could, they might have been as stunned as I was.

I switched on my shoulder spotlight and shone it across the Tahni. They'd taken off their helmets and their faces were clearly visible, so close to human and yet not quite there. The ridged brows, the flattened noses, the broad, cauliflower ears, those were just the external signs. The real differences were inside, and not the internal organs, which weren't entirely dissimilar to ours, but inside those heads.

Captain Covington had told me once that he'd gotten his college degree in Ancient History, specializing in the Roman Republic. He'd said the way those humans of ancient Rome thought about life, the way they'd approached it, the way they'd believed with every fiber of their beings in gods who controlled every aspect of existence, was more alien to us today than the Tahni could ever be. But staring at them now, I didn't believe him. The Romans would never have expected to be able to surrender after what they'd done.

"Sir...," Joanna Carson choked off, her voice failing her. "Sir, what do we do?"

What *should* I do? What would the Skipper do? What would Lt. Ackley have done?

I looked back at the dead civilians, letting my light play over them. A child's face stared back at me, about the same age as I was when my mother had been killed.

Delp answered the question for me. He fired his plasma gun

through the front rank, killing a score of them with one shot. The Tahni screamed and tried to run, and the rest of the squad opened up on them without hesitation, plasma and grenade launchers lighting the dark warehouse up with a cacophonous firework show.

I should have stopped them, should have been yelling, screaming orders.

I turned and walked out, letting the thump of my footsteps on the concrete drown out the screams and the gunfire. Scotty met me in the doorway to the warehouse and somehow, the featureless face of his armor seemed disapproving.

"Sir," he said, hesitant, stuttering. "Were those Tahni trying to surrender?"

I stared at the bare metal and tried to imagine his face beneath it. Was there horror playing across those farmboy features? Disbelief?

"No," I told him, stepping past and heading back outside. "Tahni never surrender."

14

"You want another drink, sugar?"

I squinted up at the bartender and tried to remember what planet I was on.

The bar was no sort of evidence. It was the same sort of hand-built pressed wood and brick place you could find on any of a hundred colonies, easy to put up with local materials without investing in imported polymers or settling for ugly, cheap buildfoam with no sort of character to it. There might have once been art on the walls, or pictures of former patrons, or *something* to give the place some individuality, some identity, but they'd disappeared during the occupation. Even though the Tahni had been gone for three weeks now and the bar was open again, the memories hadn't returned, just left a gap, an empty hole in the heart of the world.

The woman was still staring at me expectantly, the bottle of crystal-clear vodka poised in her hand, the spout hovering over my empty glass. She was older, though she didn't look it, not even after ten months of Tahni occupation. The people here hadn't had it that bad, at least not compared to the colonists on Demeter or Vistula. They hadn't been starved, and before the

Fleet had jumped into the system, the Scout Service had managed to get a message to the civilians and most had evacuated the city and hid in a cave system outside their only major city, so they'd avoided the massacres others had experienced.

"Do you know," I said to her, my voice slurred ever so slightly, whether from the alcohol or the exhaustion I wasn't sure, "that something like ninety percent of everyone who lives on Earth will never travel more than five kilometers from the place they were born?"

The blond woman shrugged and the motion did interesting things to the low-cut blouse she wore.

"I was born here," she informed me. "And I ain't ever been farther than the coast for the weekend with my folks. But I guess that's more than five kilometers."

"Almost anyone could emigrate to one of the colonies, you know that?" I went on, hearing her answer but not really processing it. "All you gotta do is volunteer and someone would ship you out to a colony on a work contract, even if you couldn't afford to support yourself. But no one wants to go." I shook my head. "I never met a single motherfucker from the Underground, no matter how bad they had it who wanted to leave. They didn't want to have to work. They got a free place to live, free food, free entertainment, and if it meant living in a box three meters by three meters, well, it was a sure thing, you know? Hell," I scoffed, "I didn't *have* one of those three-meter-square boxes. I was living on the street, stealing, conning, sleeping in maintenance tunnels and if anyone had asked me if I would leave the planet and go live on a colony world, I would have said, 'fuck no,' because who wanted to go somewhere and work the rest of your life?"

"Well, there is the whole war thing, you know?" she reminded me, waiting patiently with the bottle. "Maybe they were onto something."

"Nobody in the Underground knew or cared about the Tahni before Mars," I assured her, my words gaining clarity and coherence with my own certainty. "I'd barely heard of them. They didn't want to go—I didn't want to go—because we belonged on Earth. That's what we all thought. There wasn't a damned thing for me on Earth, not a chance to be anything except another shuffling zombie, but I wouldn't have left if they hadn't made me go."

"Well, this is all just interesting as hell, sugar," she said, an indulgent tone to her voice, "but I *do* have other customers, so I still need an answer. Do you want another drink?"

I laughed softly and touched my 'link to the terminal in front of me on the bar.

"Keep 'em coming until I stop talking," I told her.

She poured me another two fingers of vodka and I frowned, wishing she would just fill the damned glass up. I sighed, picked it up and downed it without tasting it, just waiting for the vodka to do its fucking job and push the damned faces out of my head. The faces of the children...

"Alvarez."

I wasn't surprised, mostly because I was too drunk to be surprised, but I wasn't too drunk to recognize the voice from beside me at the bar. I turned and nodded to Captain Phillip Covington. He'd appeared like a camo-clad ghost beside me on the next barstool over, elbows leaning on the polished wood.

"Sir. What are you doing at the finest bar on...?" I frowned, and my eyes seemed to go slightly out of focus when I did. "Forgive me, I can't seem to remember the name of this place."

"Calliope," he supplied, what might have been amusement behind his cold eyes. "That's the planet. This...." He motioned around us. "...is the very imaginatively named Calliope City. Which is barely necessary, since there doesn't happen to be any other city on this planet. And this is the *only* open bar in the city, so far. Though I'm sure they'll get around to cleaning up the others in a few weeks."

Covington waved down the bartender and she walked back over from serving a local, a harried look on her face. The Skipper was right about this being the only bar, and it was getting busier the later I stayed. When I'd come in, just after local dusk, there'd only been a handful of patrons, Fleet techs from the uniforms. I hadn't noticed the others file in, but now there were at least a couple dozen Fleet spacers and even more Marines, gathered at high-tops and tables and squeezed around the bar, the buzz of their conversation a background static I'd been shutting out.

"Whiskey," Covington told the woman. "Whatever you have. Just fill it to the top."

He turned back to me while she hunted down the bottle of his preference.

"You usually drink alone, Alvarez?" he wondered.

"It's the *only* way I drink, lately," I confessed, feeling no shame in it. I probably shouldn't have been saying all this to Covington, but I just didn't care. "Can't drink with the platoon." I looked into the empty glass, wondering why the bartender hadn't come back to fill it yet.

"I see the other platoon leaders out here some nights," Covington said, his tone casual, conversational, but the question there and unstated.

"Yes, sir, I've seen them, too." I smacked my glass down on the bar, getting the attention of the friendly older lady and nodding toward it. "And I know they've seen me."

The bartender set a glass nearly overflowing with something amber and disgusting-looking in front of Covington, then went back to get the vodka again.

"I can understand," Covington told me, taking a sip of the whiskey and grimacing. It must have tasted as bad as it looked.

"You're OCS, they're all Academy grads. You're the oldest of them, the most experienced. They're all from Surface Dweller families and not a one of them has spent a day in the Underground or lived off free soy and spirulina. Has to be tough relating to them."

"The people I relate to," I told him, "have a nasty tendency to wind up dead. So, they're probably better off letting me drink alone."

He laughed at that and I had to remind myself he was my superior officer and probably quite capable of kicking my ass so I wouldn't take a swing at him.

"Son, do you know how long I've been a Marine?"

"Yes, sir."

"How many friends do you think I outlived?" He gulped down half the whiskey, licking his lips with an absent expression on his face, a thousand-meter stare in his eyes. "How many times do you think I sat where you're sitting?"

"Counting this one, sir?"

His eyes flickered toward me, coming back into focus, and I thought for a second he was going to bite my head off. Metaphorically, though literally was still a strong possibility.

"Point," he conceded. "I suppose the question you have to ask yourself is, what sort of life do you want after this war?"

"Are you really sure it'll ever end, sir?" I asked him.

"It will." He sounded confident.

"We fought them before," I reminded him. "We could have ended it then."

"Before, we'd barely had star travel for twenty years, the colonies were new, and there was a huge resource outlay establishing them. Fighting the first war nearly bankrupted the Commonwealth. The cease-fire seemed like a gift from God and we grabbed it with both hands and hoped it was all a huge mistake that we wouldn't make again. This time, too much has already been lost, too much invested. After the Tahni attacked Mars, no one in the Commonwealth government will be satisfied with less than an unconditional surrender."

"Tahni don't surrender, sir."

I hadn't meant to lace the words with quite that large a dose of invective. The bartender came to my rescue with a refill and I doused the images of my platoon executing the Tahni troops with another shot of vodka.

"Not easily," he agreed, like he was pretending not to notice my tone. "Things happen in war. In all wars. And I'm not going to lie and tell you that you'll ever be the same person you were before, but there's a clear choice to make about what you do once this is all over."

"You mean whether to stay in or not, sir?" I guessed.

"I'm not sure that's going to be an option." Breath hissed between his teeth, like speaking on the subject caused him physical pain. "If we do the right thing, if we take care of the Tahni threat, the government isn't going to keep paying for a military the size it is now. There will still be a Marine Corps, of course. Force Recon is cheap and I'm sure they'll keep a platoon of them on every Fleet ship for security. But Drop Troopers?" He shook his head. "Individually, we don't cost much, but the logistical support for us is damned expensive, and there's no reason for them to keep it up when the need isn't there. They might keep a battalion of us, a brigade at most, most of them on Inferno." He downed the last of his whiskey and the face he made might or might not have been from the taste. "And I'm not at all sure I want to spend the next ten years on Inferno."

"What would you do, sir?" I asked him, having to force my mouth closed first. The thought of the Skipper as anything but a Marine seemed like a violation of the natural order.

"Well, that's the real question, isn't it? For you and me. Me?" He shrugged. "There'll always be a place for people who do what I do. The Corporate Council has its own Security Force and I'm sure they'll be hiring after the war. Or I could use all that money I have saved up to buy a stake in a ship and travel to all the places I've always wanted to see. For you...." He jabbed a finger at me, the other four holding onto his glass. "... the question is, do you see yourself holding onto all this, all the memories, the things the war has done to you, the changes it's made in you, or do you plan on setting up on that farm you and Sgt. Sandoval have been talking about?"

I gaped at him in disbelief.

"How the fuck...?" I stopped myself and blinked to try to make my brain work again. "How did you know about that, sir?"

"About you and Sandoval?" He favored me with a thin, wry smile. "I'd have had to be blind and deaf to miss it. About the farm?" He shrugged. "Well, when someone like Vicky Sandoval begins asking Top questions about how to use the Veterans' Settlement Bonus and what planet she thinks would be the most favorable to settle on, it doesn't exactly require a quantum-core computer to add two and two together." Covington motioned for the bartender with his empty glass. "Have you heard from her?"

"No." I rested my elbows on the bar, my arms encircling my empty glass like I was guarding it from predators. I stared at the stacks of bottles and refrigerated kegs behind the bar, but my eyes were focusing light years away. "Not since she left. She's probably busy." I shrugged. "Or you know, some OCS platoon trainers are real hard-asses about comms, they won't let you send messages if anyone in the platoon fucks up...."

I trailed off. I was making excuses. She had other things to think about, and maybe that would include well after she got her commission. Maybe I was part of a life she was leaving behind at OCS. Maybe that last, frantic time we'd had together had really been goodbye. I'd told her I'd always be there for her, but she hadn't made any such promises.

"Sir," I told him, "I'm not sure I'm going to be the same man I was before when I see her again. The things I've seen, the things I've done...."

"Cameron, I am going to give you this advice like you were my own son."

I stared at Covington in expectation, wondering what words of wisdom he would bequeath to me.

"Pull your shit together. You're better than this, stronger than this. You've seen worse. I know you have. If I didn't think you could handle this, I wouldn't have sent you to OCS."

He touched his 'link to the payment terminal, then pushed his seat back and headed for the door without another word. I watched him go, trying to decide if his words had been as underwhelming as they seemed or if the vodka had dulled my senses enough that I just couldn't appreciate them.

I was still staring at the door when a local girl sauntered over from the other end of the bar, wearing a painted-on dress and a smile to match. She touched the back of the seat Covington had been using and looked a question at me.

"This taken?" she asked it aloud when I didn't respond.

"It's all yours," I assured her.

She was younger than me. Maybe twenty, but most likely closer to eighteen. Too young to be in here, but then again, this wasn't Earth and things were different in the colonies. Not really my type, but attractive for all that. Trying too hard with the short, red dress and too much makeup.

"Buy me a drink?" she wondered. The smile faltered. "The owners jacked the prices up for you guys so most of us can't even afford it right now." She shrugged. "Not that I'm complaining about you being here, given what y'all did for us."

"This one was easy," I assured her. I waved at the bartender, who had to be pretty fucking tired of me by now. "Whatever she wants," I said, tapping my 'link. I turned back to the girl. She was twisting a blond curl around her finger. Her nails were as red as her dress. "I don't even think we took a casualty here. Not like last time."

"Sure blew the shit out of the town, though," she said, snorting a humorless laugh. "Again, not complaining...."

I grinned.

"That's because you weren't in it," I assured her. "Since the Tahni didn't have any hostages, we got to hit them from the air, from orbit. All that was left was digging out some of the more stubborn types."

The bartender handed the blond a mixed drink and refilled my vodka.

This was gonna cost a lot, I realized. I hadn't been paying attention to the drink prices, but the girl said they'd jacked them up. Not that it mattered. I didn't have much else to spend my pay on, anyway.

"You can always rebuild a city," I reminded the girl.

"I guess you're right. I'm Breanna," she told me, extending a hand. I shook it. It was rougher than I'd thought it would be. She worked for a living.

"Cam," I returned. "Nice to meet you. What do you do here in Calliope City, Breanna?"

"Well, I *used* to work in the fabrication center," she said. Then she laughed, almost a giggle. "I'll probably have to find another job until they rebuild it, though. These last few months, though, I worked in the algae farms. Everyone did, that or the soy farms. It's all we got to eat. And there was nothing to do except work and sleep and eat, and I guess from what everyone is saying, we should be glad the Tahni even let us eat. But I don't feel grateful to them. I'm just glad they're all dead."

She'd gotten up a head of steam but it had run out and her

shoulders sagged as though it had taken too much energy to be so honest.

"It feels like it's been so long since I could just get dressed up and go somewhere," she said, taking a careful sip of the drink. "So long since I didn't have to look over my shoulder."

"Glad we could help," I said, raising my glass in salute.

She accepted the toast, taking a sip of her drink.

"You said 'this time' you didn't take casualties," she reminded me. "Did you last time?"

I hid behind my drink for a moment.

"Yeah," I said. "It was pretty ugly. I don't especially want to talk about it, if it's okay with you."

"Oh, sure," she said quickly, her face falling as if I'd slapped her.

"Everybody else wants me to talk about it," I explained. "But talking about it just makes me remember it's going to happen again. And I'd rather not think about that right now."

"I understand," she told me, and seemed to mean it. "That's why I came out tonight, you know? Because I didn't want to think about all that. I just wanted to...you know, have fun."

She caught my eye and I don't think there was any way, even three sheets to the wind, that I could mistake that look for anything else.

"Is that why you're out tonight, Cam? To have fun?"

"Yeah, I guess it is," I said, shrugging.

"Then why don't we stop paying too much for shitty drinks," she suggested, raising an eyebrow, her fingers resting on my bicep, "and go somewhere and have fun?"

"Somewhere" turned out to be a block of temporary apartments the Fleet Corps of Engineers had set up in some old offices, about a kilometer from the bar. Fall was settling into Calliope City and the night breeze was chilly, a wind stirring the high clouds, a few stars peeking through. A lot of the city was just gone, the wreckage bulldozed by the Engineers, leaving bare foundations ready for rebuilding, and it gave the walk a haunted, empty feeling.

Which matched the feeling in my stomach.

Breanna pulled me along by the hand, seemingly unaffected by the cold even though her dress was low-cut and exposed a lot of leg, but when we pushed through the door of her place and she wrapped her arms around my neck and kissed me, her skin was freezing to the touch.

Her lips tasted of alcohol and breath-freshener mint and she was skinnier than I'd thought, firm and soft against me, and dizziness washed over me, a combination of the vodka and the touch of her skin. She pulled the fasteners of my fatigue top loose and stripped it off of me, letting it fall to the bare floor just inside the front door, then began working at my pants. I was in a fevered rush, unthinking, uncaring, ready to let it happen.

You made a promise. You said you always keep your promises.

I pulled away from her, drawing in a breath, unsure whose voice I was hearing in my head. My thoughts were spinning out of control and it was hard to reach into the whirlpool and draw any single one out.

"What's wrong?" she asked me, grinning, reaching into my pants again. "You got the bed spins and we aren't even in bed yet?"

"Wait," I said, stepping back out of her reach and trying to catch my breath. I was still dizzy and I put out a hand to steady myself, feeling the rough surface of the newly-poured buildfoam wall beneath my palm. "Stop. I can't."

"What do you mean you can't?" she asked, hands on her hips. She'd pulled off her dress and I didn't even remember her doing it, and the sight of her sent my heart beating faster again, but I squeezed my eyes shut and concentrated on staying calm. "You looked like you were halfway there a second ago."

"I'm sorry, Breanna," I told her, bending down and grabbing my shirt and nearly keeling over from it. "I'm really sorry. I shouldn't have come here. I can't do this. I can't do this now...."

And I was out the door and back into the night, running away, not from her plaintive, insistent cries, but from myself.

15

I hesitated with my finger hovering over the call button, afraid.

What the hell are you afraid of?

What I might find out, maybe? Maybe I just didn't want to know what was wrong with me. Maybe she'd just tell me I was a shitty human being.

But would that be any worse than living with the guilt? The guilt of letting Carson and Delp kill the prisoners, the guilt of Valentine's death, the guilt of not being able to save those people on Demeter and Vistula...hell, I even felt guilty for ruining Breanna's first night out on the town since the invasion, as absurd as that seemed. I felt like I should go back and apologize to her, but I was too embarrassed.

I glanced around in the hallway of the makeshift headquarters of the temporary Fleet base on Calliope to make sure no one else was around, then I touched the button.

And waited.

"Come in."

I didn't know what the office had been before, but whatever previous identity it had possessed had been stripped bare down to white plaster walls and left that way, as if the current resident didn't believe she'd be here long enough to make them her own. She sat at an ancient, metal desk, the chair upholstered in what might have been faux leather or, given the fact we were out on one of the outer colonies near the ass-end of nowhere, it might have been real leather.

The woman sitting in the chair was as plain and severe as the office, her uniform unadorned by decoration or achievement, marked only by her Fleet rank as a Lt. Commander and the badge of her branch, medical corps.

"Dr. Atherton," I said, tentative and quiet, "I'm Lt. Alvarez. I'm one of the Marine Drop Troopers. Can I come in?"

"As I am currently between patients," Atherton said, the corner of her mouth curling upward in dry humor, "please. Be my guest. Close the door behind you."

I'd been planning on it. As much as I was hesitant to come in myself, I as even more worried about someone from my unit seeing me here.

"You don't have any other patients?" I asked, pushing the door closed. "Do people not...come to you for anything?"

"What you're asking," she said, eyeing me with shrewd discernment, "is whether any other Marines have been desperate enough to come see a Fleet psychological counselor. And the answer is yes, plenty have. But I honestly don't think anyone knows where my office is yet. I'm surprised you found it. Please have a seat."

The chair on this side of her desk was nowhere near as comfortable as the one she had, which was a surprise. I'd expected something soft and inviting. I settled into it anyway and it creaked beneath my weight.

"So, um, how do we do this?" I wondered. "Are there like alpha wave detectors or sonic stress analyzers built into the office or something?"

Her peal of laughter was genuine and loud, and warmth flooded my face.

"I'm not trying to interrogate you, Lieutenant," she said, the laugh cycling down into a chuckle before it died. "It's not my job to figure out if you're lying to me. I'm just here for you to talk to." She spread her hands. "So, talk. Tell me what brought you to this office today."

"Ma'am, it's just that...." I closed my mouth, not knowing how to go on. "I just made 2nd Lieutenant less than two months ago," I started again. "I went through OCS on Inferno. Before that, I was an E-5, a squad leader."

"Having trouble fitting in as an officer?" she wondered. "All those Academy ring-knockers shutting you out, don't want to talk to a lowly former NCO?"

"No...well, yeah, that too," I admitted. The fact she was familiar enough with the situation to guess told me I was hardly the first newly-minted L-T to run into this problem. "But that's only part of it. I mean, I guess that's why I'm here talking to you, because there's no one else I can talk to who would understand." I stopped. That didn't sound right. "I can't talk to any of my friends from before because they're still NCOs and I can't be out drinking with them, telling them my problems."

"And what problems are those, Lt. Alvarez?" she asked, steepling her fingers as she regarded me with a carefully neutral expression.

"I lost a Marine a few weeks ago," I told her. It was the easiest way to start, even though it was just a fraction of why I was there. "The first one since I became a platoon leader."

"And you feel guilty? Like you should have been able to save them?"

I resisted an urge to roll my eyes. I wasn't being fair. It was a reasonable assumption, but Marines don't like assumptions.

"No. It was a fluke. They weren't even on the front line of

the battle. That's the thing, though, this isn't the first person I've lost." I debated the best way to say it without sounding like I was complaining about the hand I'd been dealt.

"I've had most of my platoon killed out from under me when I was a team leader." I shrugged. "I was kind of a loner then and I didn't really feel a connection with them, and I guess it didn't bother me that much. I mean, I almost died, too, and that didn't even bother me back then. I didn't have much to live for, if I'm being honest."

I was rambling. I never talked this much and it didn't feel natural, but if I wasn't here to get it out in the open, then why had I bothered to come at all?

"But then, there were others...." An image of Maria flashed across my memory. I hadn't thought much about her lately. "I started to feel a part of the Marines, a part of my platoon, my company, started to make friends. It was hard, caring about anyone except myself, or believing anyone else could care about me. And a lot of them died." Henckel's face echoed back through time, earnest and cocky and always trying to prove himself to me. Lt. Ackley, so severe and businesslike, but always ready to teach, to pass on what it meant to be a leader. "I started feeling it. It hurt, bad. Bad enough I wished I had died instead of them.

"This one...it didn't. I felt bad, but it didn't last. We had the memorial and she was gone and that was it. I haven't really thought about her. I barely knew her. And I'm worried about that."

"You think you're getting detached again? The way you felt when you first joined?"

"Not like then. Then, I didn't feel a connection because I'd never belonged to anything before. Now, it's more like there was a part of me that could care, could be hurt by all this, and I feel like it's been burned away. That there's nothing left of that person and I'm changing into someone else."

I was babbling, not making sense, but Atherton wasn't stopping me. She'd been telling the truth, she was here to listen, no matter how much meaningless blather I threw at her.

"And that's it?" she asked me. "That's the main thing that's bothering you? That you're changing?" She leaned forward across her desk, smiling but with a tinge of sadness in her eyes. "Because I'll tell you straight-up, Alvarez, you *are*. That may not be what you want to hear, but it's inevitable. Death changes you. *War* changes you. Being an officer changes you, like it or not. You're responsible for more people, and the more lives under your command, the greater chance you're going to lose one. You aren't going to react to their deaths the same way you did to your friends getting killed."

She rubbed at her eyes, as if the whole conversation was exhausting her.

"Maybe if this was the Pirate Wars, where we rarely lost more than a few Marines or Fleet crew even in the big battles, officers could afford to get broken up over every casualty, but in *this* war? Total war with both sides throwing everything they have at each other? You'd go insane. I know it's not exactly comforting, but I will tell you this; the callus you're growing over your soul is necessary for now, but it doesn't have to last. You *can* go back to being a normal person after this is all over." She shrugged. "I should say, it's *possible* to go back. I hope you can do it. Not everyone can."

"The reason I'm worried," I said, finally drilling down to the meat of why I was there, "is that there's somebody who I...." I faltered. This wasn't something I was used to talking about. "There's a woman who I've known since I reported to my unit. She was an NCO and she just left for OCS a couple months ago, right when I reported to my platoon."

"You two are involved." Another assumption, but a good one.

"I love her." It sounded so juvenile when I came out and said it. "We've talked about settling down on one of the colonies after the war, about starting a family. But last night, I was at a bar here in Calliope, drinking pretty hard, and some local girl wanted to take me back to her place and I went with her and I didn't even *think* about Vicky until the last second. I mean, I was just going to go ahead and have sex with this girl and the thing is, it wasn't because I was lonely or horny. It was like I'd made this assumption that when Vicky went to OCS, it was goodbye. That when she came back, she'd see what I'd become and she wouldn't want to be with me anymore. I wasn't just afraid it *might* happen; I *knew* it was going to happen."

"It *might* happen," she acknowledged, spreading her hands as if in admission. "And not just because you've changed. What do you think will happen to her when *she* faces the same sort of pressures you've already encountered? When she finds out she *can't* look out for each of her Marines the same way she used to when she was a squad leader, that they're going to die and there's nothing she can do to change that? You think that won't change *her*?"

She sighed, eyes flickering downward as if she were considering her next words carefully.

"Lt. Alvarez, I'm going to come clean with you. I know who you are. I know your record. I suspected you might be coming to see me."

"How?" I asked her, shaking my head. "I didn't even know I was coming until this morning."

"Your company commander told me that you might be looking for some help." She smiled with what seemed like genuine fondness. "Phil is a tough old son of a bitch, but he does care about his people." The smile turned down and her eyes took on a deep sadness. "I don't know how he does it, when he's seen so many of them die." Her shoulders shifted as if she was shaking off the thought. "So, I know about your criminal record," she went on, "the reason you joined the Corps in the first place. I know about Brigantia, and Ambergris, and the medals. About Maria Shepherd, Private Henckel, and Lt. Ackley."

She settled back into her chair, her hands folded in her lap.

"I won't lie to you, Lieutenant, your career is not what I'm used to. Even most of the combat veterans I see in here who've been in the service their whole lives don't have the sort of resume you've built up in just the last three years. And I can't help but wonder if some of that is because of what you said, that you didn't really care if you lived or died. But I believe what you're really scared of is that you'll live through this. That you'll have to keep the promises you've made, get married to your Vicky, wind up on a farm on some backwater colony raising algae, and a brood of little Camerons and Vickys."

The laugh burst out on its own, the image flashing in my mind of the two of us dressed in coveralls and brimmed hats looking so ridiculous that I couldn't help it.

"I don't think I'm scared of it, ma'am," I told her, trying to be honest. "I just think I can't believe it'll ever really happen." The words tumbled out. I hadn't said them before, not to myself and certainly not to Vicky. "Everything the two of us are, who we've become as people, is so wrapped up in the Marine Corps, in the war...I just don't know how we're going to live without it."

"And maybe you won't. It won't be easy. You'll have to reinvent yourselves. You won't have any choice, because there won't be a war to fight. The question is, are you too afraid of the hard work of doing that to even try? Are you afraid of a problem you won't be able to shoot your way out of?"

I opened my mouth for an automatic denial, ready to tell her she was wrong, that I was willing to do anything to make it work with Vicky...and then I closed my mouth and forced myself to actually think about it.

It *was* scary. Scarier than a whole brigade of Tahni High Guard.

"So, what do I do?" I asked her.

"Talk to her."

"I've tried. She's at OCS and she's barely sent me any messages, and she never answers mine." I winced. I sounded like a fucking teenager...like the teenager I'd never had the chance to be.

"It's not important that she answers," Atherton said, "or even that she sees it. It's important that you *say* it. Write what you're feeling. And if you don't feel comfortable sending it to her, or think she has other things to think about right now, then just delete it. You don't have to be completely honest with me, Cam, or even with her. But you do have to be honest with yourself."

"Maybe I'll try that," I said, nodding slowly, staring at the blankness of the bare wall but seeing Vicky's face.

"You'll have plenty of time," she told me, then leaned forward as if we were conspiring. "Don't tell anyone you heard it from me, but I understand you're going to be pulling out of here in a few days. And you've got a long trip ahead of you."

[16]

I checked the hatch again just to make sure it was locked before I sat down on my bunk and touched a control on the tablet propped up facing me. A red indicator blinked, assuring me the message was recording.

"Hi Vicky," I said. "I know I haven't written lately. I've been going through some shit and I didn't want to try to talk to you about it until I'd wrapped my head around things. I think I've been a bit unrealistic about us." The words poured out, tumbling like a grenade tossed into the room. "I listened to you talk about living on a farm on a colony world and raising a family and I co-opted your dream of a better life just because I didn't have one of my own.

"The truth is, I don't have a dream for a life after the war. I don't have any idea what kind of person I want to be, much less what I want to do with myself. The question is, what *am* I if I'm not a Marine? If I'm not a Drop Trooper? I've never had to answer the question of what I am because other people have always answered that for me. I was an orphan. I was an outsider, a streetboy, a criminal, a grifter. A prisoner. And finally, a Marine

"And I've made myself fit into all those versions of Cameron Alvarez because I didn't have any choice. I was pushed into all of them. Being a Drop Trooper is the first thing I've done that I ever took any pride in, that ever made me feel like something more than what I am, than an orphan, an outsider, a streetboy. People's lives are in my hands. Victory or defeat, part of that is what *I* do." I shrugged. "There's bad sides to it, too, I know that. There's horror and death and sometimes I feel like it's all for nothing, that I'm not helping anyone. But I ran into someone on Calliope who told me otherwise. There are innocent people counting on us to do our jobs. But I know this won't last. Once the war's over, there's no way the Commonwealth is going to keep millions of men and women under arms. The Skipper told me once it takes a hundred noncombatant support troops to keep one Drop-Trooper in combat. That can't last.

"But when I think about a life after the Marines, I see us together, but I don't see what we're doing. I don't see me as a farmer. I've never been to a farm and I don't know a damned thing about it. I'm not sure you do, either, but I know it's something you've been telling yourself for a long time, and I would never tell you to give up your dream."

A sob welled up and I tried to keep it inside. Not because I didn't want Vicky to see it, but because I knew if I started now, I'd never finish this video.

"But I don't want to lose you. And I think that's why I made myself part of your dream. But I also don't want to lie to you, and, maybe more important, I don't want to keep lying to myself. If you come back from OCS and we have this talk and I tell you how I feel about this, and afterward, you still want to try to figure out a way we can be together, then that's what'll happen. But if things have changed, and maybe what we had has changed, I don't want you to think you're abandoning me or I'm abandoning you. What we had was incredible. It saved my life. But things don't last forever, no matter how much we love them.

"I do love you. And I love what we have together. And if it ends here, it'll still be beautiful when we remember it. And I'd rather it end while it still leaves us only good memories, not after it falls apart and the only thing we recall is how much we came to resent each other."

I had to clear my throat of the lump that had formed while I spoke and I wiped at my eyes.

"Anyway, that's what I had to say. I hope you don't hate me for it. And I hope I don't hate myself."

I touched the control to stop the recording and gasped in a shuddering breath. It had been a lot harder than I thought. I tried to imagine how Vicky would react when she heard it, wondering if she'd be hit as hard as I was or if she'd get cold and hard and freeze me out of her thoughts for good.

I flicked down the menu bar and examined the choices.

Edit.

Send Message.

Save File.

Delete.

My finger hovered over Send Message for a full three seconds before I stabbed it decisively into the Delete control. "Are you sure?" it asked me.

"Good question."

I touched yes, but I might have been lying.

After it assured me the file had been deleted, I composed myself, touched record again and sat back.

"Hey Vicky," I said, forcing a cheerful tone into my voice. "Sorry I haven't written lately, but I know you've been in the hardest part of OCS and I didn't want to distract you. Also, we've been insanely busy and well, you're never going to guess where we're heading..."

———

"I swear to God," Scotty said softly, pitched so that I was the only one in the shuttle who could hear him, "that I thought we wouldn't see this fucking place again until the war ended."

"There's an old saying," I told him, staring out the side viewscreen as the baked, dry plains of Inferno's northern continent passed by beneath us. "If you want God to laugh, tell him your plans."

Scotty eyed me sidelong, the corner of his mouth turning up.

"When did you get to be all old and wise?" he asked me.

"They pin it on along with the gold bar."

I glanced behind me, saw the other platoon leaders huddled with their platoon sergeants, not just from our company but from the entire battalion. Ahead of our position were the company commanders and first sergeants, all of us crammed into one shuttle while the rest of the troops waited on the *Iwo Jima*, sitting in orbit while we went to the oracle to bring back knowledge.

"Yeah, well, I wish they'd pinned on some dirt on why the hell we're here," Scotty said, leaning back against the headrest. "I've never heard of shit like this, hauling our whole battalion from Calliope all the way back ten fucking light-years to Inferno. I thought the whole idea was we were supposed to stay out there...." He motioned upward. "...and hop from system to system until we'd cleared all the Tahni occupation."

"The high command works in mysterious ways. And they generally don't share those ways with second lieutenants. I don't even think the Skipper knows. Maybe Colonel Voss knows, but I think she has orders not to tell anyone. She went down ahead of us, so she probably knows by now, anyway."

"And the Sgt.-Major probably knows, too," Scotty said, a

sour expression passing over his open, broad-featured face. "He's always lording it over everyone with how much top-secret shit he knows. Like the Tahni are so scared of him. Asshole."

I couldn't help laughing, even though Scotty should have known better than to badmouth a superior NCO in front of an officer. But I don't know if he'd quite got the part where I was an officer, yet. To him, I was the platoon leader, sure, but I was still just Cam. And maybe that was okay. I still needed someone who just thought of me as "Cam." And if I couldn't share everything with him anymore, at least he could share it with me.

"So," he said, a shrewd glint in his blue eyes, "you gonna sneak off and see Vicky at OCS while we're here?"

"Of course not," I said, frowning in disapproval. "That would be unprofessional and against regulations." I shrugged. "And the Skipper told me so in no uncertain terms when I asked him if he could arrange it. Plus, we aren't going to be here that long and Vicky's out on a field exercise like two hundred klicks out of Tartarus."

"Speaking of that shithole," Scotty said, nodding back at the viewscreen.

And there it was. A city designed for the military by the military and just as plain and ugly and unimaginative as that sounded. Everything was laid out in grids, every building squared off and squeezed together for maximum efficiency, none more than a few stories tall because it was easier and cheaper to build broad than high. And this being the military, everything was a muted earth tone, with not so much as a hint of color and the whole fucking place made me want to blow my brains out.

Just from our side of the planet I could count two dozen other shuttles and flyers buzzing around the city, either bypassing it to reach the spaceport at its edge or cutting through to take some admiral or general to one of those all-important face-to-face meetings without which flag officers and their staffs couldn't feel important. Like this one.

Whatever we were here for, I couldn't imagine it was something that couldn't have been handled remotely, even if it was top secret. And how top secret could it be when they were about to tell every junior officer and NCO in our battalion?

When we touched down and the belly ramp began to lower, a chorus of curses echoed through the shuttle, not all of them from the NCOs. No one missed Tartarus, and somehow, every time I came here, it seemed to be summer. Maybe it just always seemed like summer here and I was off on my estimate of the seasons. Seatbelts came off and everyone filed out as quickly as possible, climbing onto the vans to get back into air conditioning and out of the afternoon heat. Well, I *thought* it was afternoon. I'd gotten turned around on landing and forgot which way was east and west down here.

Since we were officers and senior NCOs, we didn't get crammed into the backs of cargo trucks the way I would have expected. Instead, passenger vans waited for us and the seats were actually padded. I suppose my look of wonder must have been too obvious, because Top cackled her amusement from the seat across the aisle to my right.

"Don't get used to it, Lieutenant," she warned me. "Air-conditioned vans are for captains and first sergeants."

If anyone knew, it would be Top. First Sergeant Ellen Campbell had been a Marine longer than there'd been a Commonwealth and she was possibly the oldest woman I'd ever met, though she didn't look it. Her face had an ageless look, like the mask of an idol carved out of ancient wood, and she kept her brown hair cut short, the sides of her head shaved bare to expose her interface jacks.

"Hey, Top," I asked her, long-held curiosity finally getting the better of my trepidation, "why did you choose Armored infantry over Force Recon?"

Covington raised an eyebrow, as if impressed I'd had the balls to ask Top about her past, but he didn't object, just leaned back to watch the show.

"Boy, we didn't *have* battlesuits when I joined the Marines!" She didn't seem angry about it, more amused. "We were all straight-leg Marines shooting bullets with gunpowder behind them. You do that shit long enough, you'd welcome some heavy armor between you and the enemy your own self!"

"You didn't mind the jacks?" I shrugged. "I mean, I didn't have any choice, not with the problems I used to have just being outdoors with no walls around me, but if I'd been given the option, sometimes I think I would have said no to the whole putting shit into my brain part."

I was talking a lot. I stopped, wondering why that was. Maybe the shrink had been right, maybe being honest with myself. I felt looser now than I had, like a knot had untied in my guts.

"You live as long as I have, junior," Top mused, "you just want to try something different, even if it means them digging into your head. You'll find out. You can't be any one thing forever."

"I'm starting to figure that out, Top."

The van took us through the center of Tartarus, parts of the base I'd rarely visited as a lowly trainee at NCO school or OCS. We pulled up at a huge office building, the Brigade Headquarters for the 187th Marine Expeditionary Force, a place I'd only been once before. The van didn't stop out front, waved through a covered entrance by an armed Force Recon Marine guard and down a ramp into an underground parking garage.

The driver, a junior NCO so silent he might as well have been an automated navigation system, guided us down a curving drive several stories below ground, finally stopping at a bank of elevators with no other vehicles around us.

"Anyone getting a real secret squirrel vibe about all this?" Cano said from the seat behind me. "What do you all think we're actually doing here?"

As if in answer, the driver touched a control and the van's side doors sprang open with the hum of servomotors, inviting us all to get the hell out without the NCO having to say a word. The elevator cars were huge, made for freight, I thought, and plenty big enough for the whole lot of us to squeeze into, though if we hadn't already been Drop Troopers and used to tight spaces, it might have inspired claustrophobia in some. The Skipper was at the front with the other company commanders and I wondered if one of them knew which floor to request or if the thing started up on its own when we were all on board. Either way, it moved once the doors slid shut, heading not up, as I'd expected, but down further into the sub-levels of the building.

"We heading into the planetary core or something?" Scotty murmured. He'd been fairly silent once we'd gotten into close quarters with Top, because she scared the shit out of him, but she was several rows away from us.

"I imagine a lot of the planning centers on the base are built pretty far underground," I told him. "I mean, it's *the* military base for the whole Commonwealth. They had to build shelters that could withstand nukes, even asteroid strikes."

"Hell, a fucking asteroid strike could only improve this place."

The car stopped and the doors finally hissed aside. I'd expected us to be in some hallway, some office suite like a thousand others I'd seen on a dozen different planets. Instead, it had deposited us at the rear of a large conference room, bigger than a normal situation room like I'd seen at company and battalion level, but not quite an auditorium. There were enough chairs for every officer and senior NCO not just in our battalion but in the whole brigade, and they were all there.

We were the last, I thought. Even Colonel Voss was here, seated near the front next to the Battalion Sgt. Major who Scotty hated so much. And sitting on the stage, front and center of the half-circle of seats arrayed around it, was a man I'd heard of, and seen recordings of but never encountered face-to-face, our brigade commander, General Terrence McCauley. He was short, almost ridiculously short in a day when such things could be adjusted genetically before birth, and his upper body was massive, his arms long enough I thought his knuckles might hang down past his knees if he let his arms sag. His uniform was neat and well-kept, but it didn't have quite the razor-sharp edge to it I would have expected from a general and I wondered if that meant he was sloppy or just insanely busy doing actual work and didn't have the time to worry about such piddly details.

"Good morning, ladies and gentlemen," he said, standing. His voice was rough and gravelly and his face was a collection of sandstone rocks glued into a loose formation. "I believe Fourth Battalion makes this little group complete, so we can get started."

They must, I thought, have scheduled the meeting around our arrival time, since we were the last. That was cutting it close. Our Battalion Sgt. Major guided us to a collection of luxuriously-upholstered chairs over to the right side of the stage and we filed in by company and sat, not a one of us making a sound, eager to hear what McCauley had to say.

"I know you've all come a long way," McCauley began, "and you're probably wondering why we've hauled you all the way back from where you were deployed at the front for a face-to-face briefing on Inferno. This operation I'm about to brief you on is the largest in the history of the Commonwealth military, and contrary to what you might think, the Tahni military *does* have a capable intelligence corps, and they *do* intercept our communications now and again. And this *cannot* leak. It's too big and too damn many things can go wrong between planning and execution."

He paced across the stage, hands clenching into fists like he didn't know what to do with them. Finally, he touched a control on his 'link and a hologram sprang to life overhead, a three-dimensional representation of a system I'd never visited but had heard so much about.

"This is our goal. We are going to retake Silvanus."

"72 Herculis," McCauley said, slipping into a didactic cadence, like my instructors at OCS, as he pointed at the representation of the star system in the projection, "is approximately forty-seven light-years from Earth, as close to the Sun in luminosity and mass as any of our colony systems. It has six planets as well as a major asteroid belt rich in minerals and water-ice. The second world from 72 Herculis, Silvanus, is one of our most heavily-populated worlds with over a million inhabitants spread over three major cities and a few smaller settlements. There are also thousands of civilians scattered throughout the asteroid belt and on the one semi-habitable moon of the fourth planet, a gas giant a bit smaller than Saturn."

"This system is a treasure trove of mineral and biological diversity, and due to its utility as a supply base and its distance from Earth and the core colonies, the Tahni have *not* given up on 72 Herculis or Silvanus the way they have some of the other human colonies they occupied. Their Imperial Navy has three destroyers and at least a dozen squadrons of corvettes spread out between Silvanus and Valius, the habitable moon, and through the asteroid belt between them."

"We estimate they have ten squadrons of dual-environment fighters on the planet, and a ground force of at least brigade strength, integrated infantry and High Guard armor. They do *not* want to lose this system and this nut will be a tough one to crack. But."

He smiled thinly.

"There had to be a 'but' in there somewhere, or we wouldn't have bothered with all this secrecy, would we? The but is an open secret of course, the propaganda horn we've been blowing since the beginning of the war. We still have forces in the system who haven't been evacuated and haven't been caught. The 'valiant resistance fighters of Silvanus' you keep hearing about in every special news documentary, the Marines and local militia who never gave up." He scanned the crowd and I thought he was looking me in the eye directly. "I know some of you must have wondered whether they were real or just a useful fiction the spooks and politicians dreamed up to boost morale. Well, not only are they real, but we've been keeping them supplied all throughout the war, as best we can. Scout Service drone ships jumping in during raids by the Attack Command missile cutters and launching stealth pods that coast in on Hohmann transfer orbits and drop on chutes. A lot are destroyed, but some get through."

Silvanus expanded to fill the projection.

"Because of the existence of a viable resistance, the Tahni have been forced to treat the civilians with more care than on other worlds they've occupied. If they were too harsh, they would just make the civilians so desperate that they would run and join the resistance. The Tahni have kept them well-fed and allowed them to live in their homes as long as they continue to operate the mines and farms for them."

Another smile, this one warmer.

"Now, another commander might have resorted to reprisals

against the people who work for the Tahni, might have tried to make the civilians more afraid of the resistance than they were of starving. But Colonel Daniel Oz did the opposite. He encouraged the civilians to keep on working...as long as they pass along food and, more importantly, intelligence to the military. Oz has sabotaged the Tahni effort quite effectively and they've spent much effort that might otherwise have gone toward extending their influence to other systems in the region to trying to catch him and his Marines and militia. He's been operating on his own for quite a while, but we've finally been able to promise him some backup."

Another tap on his 'link and the image zoomed into Silvanus, down to the capital city, the name of which I couldn't remember off the top of my head. Given how unoriginal and hackneyed most colony world city names were, I bet it was something like "Silvanus City" or maybe "Friendship Village." The original city was mostly intact but the Tahni military presence was a cancer that had metastasized through it, barracks, hangars, storage bays, and other air-defense installations surrounding the city and creeping into its streets, a rot we would have to excise.

"The Tahni have extensive anti-aircraft batteries and deflector dishes set up all around their bases, in the capital of Cairdeas as well as Aristaeus and Aegipan further west on the northern continent, and that's not counting the ground defense lasers *we* built for them before the war. Trying to take the planet back in any sort of conventional way would either require us to pound it into rubble from orbit or simply throw troops and shuttles at it by the thousands and accept the horrible losses it would take.

"Thankfully, Colonel Oz gives us a third option. His troops are going to take down the laser installations and do what they can to sabotage the anti-aircraft batteries. They won't be able to get them all, and they won't be able to do anything about the deflector dishes. Taking out those will be our job, and we're going to have to wade through the enemy ground troops to do it. But before we get the chance, we're going to have to make it through their outsystem defenses."

He hesitated, as if he were considering the best way to put what he had to say next.

"The 72 Herculis system is considered key to rebuilding the Commonwealth after the war. And for that reason, combined with the human civilians still being used as labor in those areas, we will not be able to simply bombard the asteroid mines, the gas scoops or the refineries on Valius. We're going to have to send in Drop Troops to take them back."

I winced. Around me, I heard rumblings of dissent at that, and not just from the platoon leaders.

"I know," McCauley acknowledged, raising a hand as if in an admission of guilt. "We're going to take casualties doing it that way, before we even get a chance to hit the planet. But this is the big one, ladies and gentlemen, the one we've been working toward. This is the last one, the last colony they hold aside from some tiny outposts that won't take a single company to retake. If we can push them off Silvanus, out of the system, they'll be back in their pre-war boundaries."

"Sir."

I didn't recognize the woman who'd raised her hand, but she was one of the other company commanders in the battalion.

"Yes, Captain Colton?"

"Sir, do you think this will be the end of the war, then?"

McCauley sucked in a deep breath, eyes clouding over in thought, though I wasn't sure he was deliberating how best to answer the question, or whether he should even attempt to.

"I have no firm information to back this up, so you'll have to take it as just my opinion and not policy, but I would say no. It's tempting to think we could just hit reset and take things back to the way they were before the war, then ask for another cease-fire and we could all go home to whatever we did before. But there's been too much death, too much cost. I don't think it would be politically expedient for the Commonwealth government to go back to the voters and say, 'we spent trillions of dollars prosecuting this war and all we've accomplished is to set everything up for the next one.' Because we have to know there'd be a next one. Fool me once and all that."

He clasped his hands behind his back and faced the center of the crowd around him, squared off like he was on a parade ground.

"No, this doesn't mean the end of the war, but it does mean a new phase of it. If we can do this, if we can pry their filthy, alien fingers off the last of our colonies, then we've stopped taking back what's ours...and stopped having to play with kid gloves. They know it, too. The Tahni aren't stupid. That's why they're holding on so tight here, trying to keep the last hostages they have."

McCauley tapped at his 'link and I felt mine vibrate at my side, heard the same staccato hum from across the room.

"I've just sent the op order for this mission to each of you. You are not to discuss this even amongst yourselves until your troop ships are back in Transition space. Is everyone clear on this?"

A chorus of affirmation echoed through the room and it seemed to satisfy him.

"Then get back to your ships and your people." He swept his hand across us like he was a priest delivering a blessing. "Get them ready, get yourselves ready. The time has come to take back what's ours."

The platoon stared at me expectantly, and I wondered if the eager, puppy-dog look on Carson's face was close to my expression when McCauley had delivered the briefing to us. It had been hard keeping everything from them until the *Iwo* had Transitioned, but McCauley had been very clear on the matter and, if he hadn't, Captain Covington had reinforced it during the shuttle flight back up and I'd made sure Scotty knew he was serious.

He was sitting at the back of the compartment, arms crossed over his chest, a cat-ate-the-canary look on his face as if he was reveling in their frustration.

"Okay, you may or may not have heard rumors about this," I said, "because even though we were all ordered to keep it quiet, you all know how effective that can be." A few chuckles. The only thing that could escape the gravity of a black hole was rumors, because nothing could stop them from getting out. "The target is 72 Herculis, which, for those of you who don't know, is the system Silvanus is in. We're taking it back from the Tahni and it's going to be a hard, dirty, bloody fight, I'm not going to lie to you."

"Shit," or some variation thereof seemed to be the most popular response to the news. It was a useful word, packed with all sorts of varying emotional content, from fear to excitement to disbelief.

"The planet has three major cities and our brigade is going to hit all three at once, but that's just the main event. Before that, we got an opening act, and like most opening acts, it's bound to be smaller, shorter and probably disappointing."

I didn't have a huge holographic projector like McCauley, so I settled on the tiny screen on the compartment wall showing them the star system. I centered the image on the gas giant and traced the moon around to the front of it. It was mostly white, covered in ice caps that stretched from the poles more than halfway to the equator and the rest was mostly ocean-blue with just narrow strips of green and brown.

"This is Valius, the largest moon of the gas giant Dionysus. And it is large, as big as Mars. The scientists think it used to be a planet in its own right, but some big game of cosmic shuffle-board happened and it was knocked free of its orbit and wound up being captured by Dionysus' gravity. Whatever, it's there now and it's at least partially habitable. The part that's not completely covered in ice. But habitable don't mean comfortable, and you're going to be damned glad you're wearing armor. The Force Recon guys we're following in aren't going to be nearly as comfortable."

I touched the screen again and brought up a computer simulation of two dropships.

"We're going in during a bombardment, which will be carefully calculated to be *just* enough for their deflector dishes to protect against, but this time we don't need to worry about taking out the deflectors. In fact, we want to keep them doing their thing as long as possible, to cover us doing ours."

I traced a line and the dropships followed a nap-of-the-earth course through a mountain range until they came to a pass and dropped dozens of tiny figures.

"We're going to cover the Force Recon infiltration team as they head through a mountain pass and down into the valley where the industrial facility is located and they're going in to bust free the civilian workers being held there."

"What kind of an industrial facility is it?" Kreis asked me.

"Some sort of chemical separation," I said. "It's in the detailed notes in the op order you'll all be getting via your 'links. There's not much of a human presence in the plant, about fifty of them at last report, but higher wants them all busted free and taken out on the dropships. Our job is to take out any High Guard presence, provide fire support for the Force Recon units when they bring out the civilians and guard the LZ when the dropships come in. If possible, we're to wipe out as much of the Tahni military presence at the facility as possible, but the main goal is to evac the civilians."

"This seems like a lot of trouble to go to for fifty people," one of the team leaders in Third squad, a corporal named Cronin said, scowling. "I mean, I know they're humans and we want to save them if we can, but isn't this a lot of risk for a handful of industrial workers?"

"It's all part of a clean sweep through the outer system," I explained. "We're just a small part of it, one platoon. The rest of the company will be hitting the orbital gas mines around Dionysus and believe me, we got the better end of that deal. At least here, if your armor takes a hit and you survive, you can breathe the atmosphere."

Cronin shuddered. He was young, younger than me, but he had a pale, sallow face like he was already middle-aged.

"Anyway, we pull this off, everyone else pulls off their part of things, while, at the same time, God willing, the Fleet is taking out the Tahni Imperial Navy destroyers and corvettes, and clearing out the inner system. Then we evac all the civilians and ride the troop carriers in close to Silvanus and get briefed along the way on our next target." I shrugged. "I've got a list of possible operations we might be running in the op order, but nothing is going to be decided until we get more intelligence from the planet. For now, we're going to be doing a few simulator runs that are programmed with the terrain and conditions we'll be facing." I checked the time. "It's an hour till lunch. Everyone meet up in Simulator Bay Three immediately after lunch. No later than two hours from now or we'll lose our spot to Fourth Platoon. You got me?"

"Yes, sir!" The response was spirited for all the doubts they'd shown earlier.

"Dismissed then."

"Get to the armory," Scotty snapped before they could start to disperse. "Run a maintenance check on your suits. Shouldn't take more than half an hour, so you'll have time before you head to eat." There was a chorus of moans and complaints but Scotty scoffed at them. "Yeah, yeah, what else were you gonna do? Go back to your racks and download porn? Get going!"

He watched them go, smiling fondly, like he was their schoolteacher. I wondered how he did it.

"They're not bad Marines," I said after the last of them was clear of the compartment and out of earshot. "But not a one of them is better than mediocre in a Vigilante except Delp, and he's no Henckel. I'm just not seeing any more Marines like Henckel coming to this company, Scotty."

He grinned with that same knowing, school-teacher expression.

"Or like you, you mean," he assumed.

"Me, Vicky, Top, the Skipper."

"What?" he asked, laughing. "Not me?"

"Scotty, you are one hell of a platoon sergeant," I told him, "and a great NCO. There's no one else I'd want as Gunny on my platoon."

"But I'm not a natural with the suit the way you are," he finished for me. "The way Henckel was. And you know what, Cam, if Henckel hadn't gotten himself killed, he'd probably be an officer himself right now, because he and you are just what the Corps is looking for to send to OCS. You don't see Marines like him because they all get kicked upward."

"I'm not sure that's a good idea." I shook my head and stared at the flat viewscreen on the bulkhead. It was turned off and all I could see in it was my reflection.

"Just because someone's good in a battlesuit doesn't mean they're going to be a good leader."

[18]

I was in the mess, eating alone at the officers' table when she ambushed me.

"You're Alvarez."

I twisted around in my chair and looked up at the woman... and then up some more. She was tall, a few centimeters taller than me, and didn't have the look of a low-gravity native either. There were muscles under her fatigues, and the combination of her build and something oddly girly about the cut of her red hair held a strange appeal. She was, I saw by her rank markings, a 2nd lieutenant.

"That's me," I admitted.

"I'm Palmer," she announced as if that explained everything, sticking out a long-fingered hand. "I'm the PL of the Force Recon platoon going in with you on Valius."

"Oh, yeah, nice to meet you." I stood quickly, shaking her hand. Her grip was firm, testing, and I tried to give it my best, although most of us Drop Troopers didn't spend quite the same amount of time in the ship's fitness center as the Force Recon types. There wasn't as much call for bulging muscles when you had a two-ton metal suit to do your dirty work. "Did you and your people want to schedule a joint walk-through before we drop?"

"Naw, it's pretty straight-forward," she said, slashing negation as if she were chopping the idea in the throat. "My boys and girls can handle it if yours can. We got the hard part anyways—all you got to do is stand around and look pretty." She grinned and I couldn't tell if it was friendly, mocking or a come-on. She looked me up and down in frank appraisal, and I still couldn't tell. "You ain't bad for a jackhead. We got twenty hours till Transition. Want to grab a drink? I brought the good stuff along, not the homemade hooch the enlisted smuggle aboard."

And I *did*. I did want to and it was maddening. It was as if God and Satan had got together one more time after deciding they'd had so much fun tormenting and tempting Job, and arranged an encore for me. I was *not* God's gift to women and rarely the target of anyone looking for a cheap thrill. The relationships I'd had in the Underground, if relationship wasn't too strong a word for them, had been fueled by a mutual and transitory need for protection and warmth and they'd only lasted until one or both of us got arrested.

There'd been Maria, of course. I tried not to think about the brief time we'd had together, not least because it hurt too badly to remember what had happened to her, but also because it hadn't felt real. We'd been wrapped in a bubble of unreality and we'd known it wouldn't last.

But now, when I had someone I'd tried to commit to, I couldn't turn around without someone propositioning me.

"Thanks," I said, "but I have duty after dinner. Maybe after the mission." And no, I didn't mean it, but I figured it was easier to lie than to try to explain the real reason.

"Maybe," she said with a shrug that seemed to be carefully calculated to be indifferent. "Or maybe not."

I watched her go and once she'd left, my meal didn't seem so appetizing. I tossed it into the recycler and stalked back to my compartment. Having a room to myself was one of the perks of being an officer, or maybe one of the downsides, because it forced even more isolation onto an isolating job. I don't know what I'd intended to do once I got there, but what I wound up doing was pulling out the tablet again, setting it up on its stand and priming it for another video message.

"Hey Vicky." I waved at the screen, unable to smile. "Okay, I've been doing some thinking since last time. I told you...well, I was *going* to tell you I thought we should end things in the last message, if I'd had the nerve to send it. I'd been so damned tempted to run off and have some fun with a local girl and I'd barely stopped myself. Today, just now, I had to turn down what might have been an innocent drink with a Force Recon platoon leader, because I thought it might have turned into something else and I felt like I couldn't say no if I went along with it."

I paced in front of the camera lens and I could see the dome-shaped ocular following me with each step.

"And I had to ask myself, why did I say no? If I really think we're not going to last, that you're not coming back after you get your platoon, why would I say no? I'm about to be part of the biggest military operation of the war and the odds are, I won't be coming back from it. Why would I turn down a little fun when it might be my last time, when it doesn't really mean anything?'

I stopped and sat down on the bunk in front of the tablet.

"And I think I know. You give me hope. Somehow, knowing you believe I could live through this makes me believe it, too. It's the only thing that does. I know the kids coming in now believe they're immortal, but I never thought that. I knew I was going to die, because everyone close to me had died in front of me. I was expecting it, welcoming it even. Until I met you. You didn't just give me something to want to live for, you gave me a reason to think I might actually survive. And I'm not ready to give that up.

"This job, being an officer, it's claustrophobic in a way being inside a Vigilante never was for me. You're more alone than you ever have been, with no real authority but shitloads of responsibility. You're a human shit-catching machine, that's what one of the NCOs at OCS told me. NCOs, she said, are the real backbone of the Corps, and when shit happens and things go wrong and everyone starts throwing the blame around, well, shit rolls downhill. But they can't let it roll down all the way to the NCOs because they need them." I grinned despite the gnawing feeling in my guts. "So that's why God made 2nd lieutenants, to block that shit before it can hit the NCOs." I snorted. "You should have heard Scotty laugh his ass off when I told him that one.

"Anyway, you're going to find out about that, but I hope when you do, I can be there for you, so you won't feel as isolated as I have. But right now, you're the only thing keeping me going. Maybe it's selfish, maybe it's stupid, but I can't let you go. I can't let *us* go. And I'm not going to. I love you. And I'll still be here if you come back to me."

I didn't hesitate this time, just deleted it. These messages weren't for her, I'd realized that. They were for me. I was going to work through this without dropping it all on her shoulders while she was trying to get through OCS, through the transition to being an officer.

I thought about recording another, more innocuous message like the others I'd sent, but decided against it. She'd be graduating soon and God knows if it would catch up with her before she left for whatever unit she was going to report to.

And I...I was going to get some sleep. Because we did Transition in twenty hours and there wouldn't be a spare minute for it after that.

———

"I don't mind Transition, I really don't," Scotty said, his voice a buzz in my ear. "But I really wish I didn't have to go through it every fucking time in the suit."

"You don't," I reminded him. "You just sleep through it every other time. I wish I could. Because I *do* mind Transition, even when we aren't jumping into the middle of a battle."

"Oh, sorry, sir," he chuckled. "I didn't mean to whine at my superior officer or anything."

He was right, though, it did suck riding out the Transition inside the guts of a dropship, wrapped in a battlesuit.

"Ten seconds to Transition," the crew chief told us.

I didn't try to count it down in my head because I always wound up psyching myself out. Instead, I just let my thoughts drift and when the universe twisted itself inside out and took me with it, it came as a surprise. I ground my teeth the way I always did, trying to wrest back a concept of self from a microscopically brief sense of being spread out through the entirety of creation.

I hoped the Attack Command pilots handled it better than I did, because they were truly in the shit. I'd tapped into the *Iwo's* tactical feed the minute we came out and playing out across the display of my helmet's HUD was what might have been the most hellish nightmare of a space battle I'd seen in my three years fighting this fucking war. Wave after wave of missile cutters boosted away from the Transition point, a new starfield made up of hundreds of fusion drives, diving into the teeth of the enemy.

"Here we go," Scotty said, an uncharacteristic excitement for the carnage in his tone. I glanced to my left, where I knew his suit was, even though I couldn't see him. I wasn't used to that sort of bloodthirsty voyeurism from the backwoods farmboy, but then he didn't usually get to watch the battles. I'd tapped his suit into the feed because he'd bugged me about it for the last three days.

The Tahni's primary interstellar interceptor was a bulbous, utilitarian craft they called something unpronounceable and we called, for some weird reason involving old water-navy terminology, a corvette. Unlike our missile cutters, the corvettes weren't meant to fly in an atmosphere and their lack of aerodynamics gave them an ungainly ugliness that only made them seem more dangerous. They were cheap and easy to produce and the Tahni turned them out by the thousands and threw them at us like the three-person crews were expendable, little better than living robots.

I'd never seen as many of the things in one place as I saw gathered around the orbit of Dionysus. The image seemed incredibly close, but I knew it was actually millions of kilometers away and minutes old, the feed from the external cameras of one of the missile cutters transmitted back to the *Iwo*. The Attack Command boats had come along tucked into three of their skeletal star carriers, and the kilometers-long vessels usually stayed out at the very edge of the system, lacking any armament and all but the barest hint of armor. Their only means of defense was escape, so it stayed far enough away that it could spot incoming threats and just jump out of the system if it needed to.

The carriers were vital, not because the missile cutters couldn't have come this far on their own but simply because the trip inside the tiny vessels would have worn on the flight crews without a chance to stretch their legs, exercise and breathe something beside their own body odor. And they were right behind us, just a million kilometers back, spitting distance in cosmic terms, tempting targets just hanging there in space.

Our cutter crews went in fresh and that was about the only obvious advantage we had. The numbers were on the Tahni side, anyone could see that just by the sensor readout, by the swarms of red avatars all over our blue ones. Tinier signatures separated from the red and blue, ejected outward like confetti before streaking out towards the enemy lines on high-g boosts from quick-burnout rocket motors.

Out there, beyond visual range even for the Attack Command cutter who was our eyes and ears in the battle, countermeasures warred with wave after wave of missiles, fighting a battle so evenly matched that I often wondered why our forces didn't make some sort of deal with theirs to just skip the missile launches altogether and save all that time and money. Here and there, a burst of gamma rays accompanied one of our ships popping into Transition space and coming out just a few million kilometers away, avoiding a missile that wouldn't be fooled by electrostatic chaff, or destroyed by oversized shotguns spreading out high-speed ball-bearings in the paths of the warheads.

And then the fight began in earnest, with squadrons of cutters jumping in unison, popping back into existence in beam range of globular formations of the Tahni corvettes and cutting loose with volley after volley of proton cannons. Lasers and coil guns responded and flares of sublimating metal winked in the night. It would have been fascinating to watch if I hadn't known men and women were dying with each of those sparks, like a ballet played out across tens of millions of kilometers, in and out, through another reality and back.

The missile cutters fascinated me. The larger ships like the *Iwo* or the star carriers couldn't make the short hops through Transition space, or so I'd been told by the Fleet pilots who I'd encountered at bars bragging about their rides. The power

195

requirements to create the rift into Transition space increased exponentially over a certain diameter, which was one of the reasons the Fleet hadn't deployed their massive star cruisers at the cutting edge of the war front. You didn't commit something that huge and expensive and packed with human crew to a knife-fight without the ability to jump back out if things got too hot.

The cutters could dance through T-space and normal space like boxers ducking punches, and stuck there in the belly of a dropship, a sitting duck in the docking bay of a lightly-armed troop carrier, that seemed like a pretty good deal. Sure, we lost a lot of the little boats in battle, but since there were only two or three crew in each cutter, it still worked out to a better percentage than the Drop Troopers. No OCS for pilots, they were all Academy grads, but if I'd joined on my own instead of being forced into the Marines by the government, I could have gone Fleet and become a crew chief, eventually.

A depressing number of blue avatars winked out while I watched, but even more red triangles went black, and the number seemed to cascade, dozens of them fading as the cutters jumped in closer to the military space station the Tahni had constructed in orbit around Dionysus. What happened next was predictable, and in fact, someone *had* predicted it.

The destroyers were giant wedges of crimson on the threat display, three of them in a loose formation, thousands of kilometers between them. They'd been in orbit around Dionysus, waiting for a threat deserving their ponderous attention, and the destruction of three quarters of their corvette force had proven us worthy. I'd seen a nature video once in one of the more entertaining lessons they'd taught on one of the rare occasions I'd attended regular school as a child, that showed hyenas harassing female lions off a kill. They nipped at them and yelped at them and chased them hundreds of meters and when the lionesses had tried to strike back, they darted away, just out of reach. Then the male lion, who'd been resting in the sun like the lazy son of a bitch he was, woke up, shook himself off, and took care of business.

I'd never forgotten the majestic fury of that massive cat sprinting across the savannah like he'd been shot out of a mass driver, and the look on the queen hyena's face when she realized she'd fucked with the wrong cat. The hyena ran as hard as she could, but the lion took her down with a single swipe of his paw, just snagging her rear leg and throwing her into the dust, helpless as he sank his fangs in and broke her neck.

The Tahni destroyers thought they were the lions, burning in on flares of annihilating matter and antimatter at six gravities of acceleration, closing the distance with our cutters by the second but really aiming at us, at the troop ships, the *Iwo Jima* and the Tripoli and the *Belleau Wood*, at the Fleet carriers, the *Bonaventure,* the *Intrepid* and the *Essex*. One swipe of the laser that ran up the center of each of the ships, fed directly from their reactor core, one strike through the core of one of the troop ships or the carriers, and they were gone, a short-lived supernova, and we were stuck here for the rest of our lives, which could probably be numbered in minutes.

But things weren't always what they seemed, as I'd found out at that top-secret meeting on Inferno. The Tahni destroyers were the hyenas, blustery, annoying, and overconfident, and the lions roared out of Transition space, massive grey monoliths a kilometer long and two hundred meters across, bristling with weapons, buried under centimeters of BiPhase Carbide and nickel-iron armor, their oversized fusion drives new suns lighting up the outer system.

The *Jutland* and the *Leyte Gulf* were two fifths of the remaining cruisers left in the Commonwealth Space Fleet, cautiously hoarded in the Sol system and the core colonies to prevent another sneak attack like the Battle for Mars that had ushered in this war. Had the Tahni gotten wind of the fact the Fleet was pulling the cruisers out of the 82 Eridani system, leaving Eden and Inferno with only static defenses and a few squadrons of slower-than-light patrol boats, it would have been a perfect opportunity for them to strike deep into our defenses. But the military had done something right, for once and by a miracle, not a word had slipped out.

"Holy shit," Scotty said, his voice an awed whisper. I couldn't help but agree.

The cutters faded back, content to let the cruisers take their share of the glory, but the remaining Tahni corvettes threw themselves at the giants in frantic desperation and were swatted aside by laser turrets, their destruction barely notable against the great bulk of the capital ships. The destroyers seemed almost frozen by the sight of the cruisers, and I had to think the crews were trying to switch targets, knowing their anti-ship missiles wouldn't be enough, trying to maneuver their spinal lasers into firing position.

They were too late.

The main gun of each of the cruisers, their *raison d'etre*, was a huge, spinal-mounted rail gun, using all the power of a dedicated fusion reactor and electromagnetic rails as long as the entire ship. I'd never seen them fired in person and wasn't close enough to see it now, but I'd watched video of it. It was visually impressive, unlike any other weapon we fired in space combat. Every energy weapon was invisible in a vacuum, every coil gun a dark streak against the stars, but the railguns...they did this trick, something Captain Covington had found so fascinating he'd actually played a video of it for the whole company once. The longer the conductive surface of the rails, the more velocity the shot had. So the engineers who'd built the cruiser's spinal guns had worked out a system where ionized gas was ejected from the muzzle of the railgun before each shot and ran an electrical charge through it. The charged cylinder of gas added velocity to the shot like an afterburner and, more importantly to us grunts watching the show, it was a yellow lance of flame extending out from the nose of the cruiser, a firework show in the vacuum.

The Tahni destroyers had electromagnetic deflectors, the same as the dishes they used to defend their ground-based installations and, theoretically, a powerful enough magnetic field could have sent the cargo-truck-sized projectiles careening off in another direction, but even the Tahni capital ships didn't have a big enough reactor for that. The tungsten slug was invisible to the naked eye, but the threat display showed us its passage as a streak of yellow against the stars. Its impact didn't need enhancement, didn't need special effects. The lead destroyer in the formation erupted in plumes of ionized gas, the antimatter contained in the electromagnetic storage at its heart merging with the matter around it catastrophically.

The second of the Tahni capital ships was struck amidships as it tried to turn away and the bow of the destroyer had time to tumble away into the black before the containment bottles failed and another supernova filled the ever-night.

"Kick their asses, you Fleet pukes," Scotty enthused. "Do something useful for once."

The last of the destroyers didn't even try to turn, just took counsel of desperation and jumped, retreating from the very universe in the face of the cruisers.

"Damn." Scotty sounded disappointed. "He got away."

"He won't be back soon," I predicted. "A ship that size, it takes them a while to build up the capacitor charge to Transition back and a while in T-space means tens of millions of klicks." I grinned. "And those cruisers aren't going anywhere."

"Dropships, prepare for launch." That wasn't the crew

chief, it was the *Iwo Jima*'s Tactical Operations Officer. I'd never heard the announcement when I'd been an NCO or enlisted; it went directly to the command net. "You are go in ten seconds."

"But we are." I switched from the private net with Scotty to the platoon frequency. "Third Platoon, launch in ten. The Fleet has done their job...now it's our turn."

[19]

Valius might have been habitable, but from where I sat, it looked pretty damned inhospitable. Snow-covered mountains harsher than anything on Earth climbed kilometers into the moon's atmosphere, jagged and threatening, and I didn't see how anything could live down there, much less humans. The drop-ship had deorbited on the other side of the moon from the target area and I assumed they'd used the cover of the Fleet attack to take down the satellite surveillance, but we had an assault shuttle running escort just in case the Tahni figured out we were here. The bird was behind us, a blip on the tactical board of the dropship, and an even smaller one in my helmet HUD.

Being an officer detached you from more than just the men. I was getting used to seeing things from orbit, from sensor screens, on mapping overlays. It turned battlefields into a chess-board and us into tiny, disposable pawns.

I'd rather think of myself as a rook.

The mountains were a barrier from north to south, cutting the primary continent in half, but we didn't cross them, instead following them southward. It was a good decision tactically, since it kept us off their sensor screens as we made our way down to the refineries at the southern tip of the continent, but the ride was a rough one, updrafts buffeting the dropship mercilessly. When I was a kid, I used to climb inside a rusty, old metal drum we found in an abandoned building and my big brother would roll me along in it until I got dizzy. Flying through those mountains in my suit, locked into the drop gantry, I felt like Anton had kicked that barrel down the tallest hill in the city with me in it and I began to long for the command to drop.

"Five minutes," the crew chief said an eternity later.

I echoed the announcement to the platoon, clearing my throat first so I wouldn't sound like I was about to puke inside my helmet. Five minutes...I tried to go over the op order in my head one last time, looked at the mapping overlay, re-hashed the order of march and the names and positions of the Force Recon platoon and still had two minutes left when I was finished. I started thinking about Vicky, wondering if she had made it to her platoon yet.

"One minute."

Would she be thinking about me, wherever she was? Or would I just be a background hum to the noise of her life?

Focus, Alvarez. Not the time for needy-boyfriend bullshit. You got along just fine for nineteen years mostly by yourself, you can do it a little while longer.

I didn't even hear the countdown, just the command to drop, and I echoed it out of rote habit, not even realizing what I was saying.

"Drop! Drop! Drop!"

How do you get used to falling out of the sky at four hundred meters up in a suit heavy enough to plow itself a few meters into the ground if the jets fail? How does that become an ordinary thing that doesn't register, doesn't provide an adrenaline spike anymore? Somehow, it had happened. I'd lost count of the training drops I'd done, and the combat drops were all running together in my memory. The only one that stood out was Brigantia because I'd nearly died about four times in one minute.

That didn't happen this time and I'd barely had time to get an IFF signal from the rest of the platoon when the ground rushed up to meet me and I was down. Just like that, barely a jostle. Dropping on a low-gravity world had its advantages, and my spine gave silent thanks for the lower impact.

I'd barely had time to look around on the way down, but I took a moment as I waited for Scotty to get the platoon in formation, waited for the Force Recon troops to land. They'd take quite a while longer, falling under the synthetic silk canopies of parachutes. There should, I thought, be something better, something higher-tech than a big piece of fabric designed watching spiders sail on the wind, conceived of by a Renaissance artist nearly a thousand years ago and actually tested over six hundred years ago. But jet packs were heavy and expensive and disposable, not to mention carrying a high thermal signature, and no one had been able to figure out anti-gravity yet, so men and women who'd travelled to another world through a different dimension on a starship powered by a fusion core as hot as the heart of a star glided slowly and anachronistically to the ground.

They fell in an orderly line up and down the same mountain pass where my platoon had landed, gentle slopes heading upward from either side of the broad path through the foothills, shrouded in shadows. My enhanced optics showed everything daylight bright, but with a hint of unreality that came from the veneer of computer interpolation, filling in gaps in visible and infrared light with a translation of thermal and sonic sensors to something I could see and understand more easily.

The road looked artificial, not a natural path, and I knew it had been blasted by the Corporate Council mining venture that had settled this moon, probably not long after the refineries were built. I didn't know where it led or why they'd wanted to leave the shore of the equatorial sea to head into the hills, but I was sure it had some sort of profit motive, because the Corporate Council didn't do anything unless there was a profit in it.

Something about the size of a weasel or a large rat popped its head up in the rocks beside the road, then darted from one side to the other before disappearing into a burrow. I blinked at the sight, surprised there was animal life here, though I don't suppose I should have been. It was probably something imported from Earth, originally, likely from somewhere high and cold.

"Alvarez," Lt. Palmer said, jogging up beside me, faceless inside her light armor, her helmet's visor too dark to see her face, even with my suit's optics. "We're all present and mobile."

"This your first combat jump, Palmer?" I don't know why I asked. Maybe I felt like a complete doofus for turning her down before. It was a fair question, though. Force Recon generally ran down the ramp of a dropship instead of throwing themselves out the back of it five hundred meters up.

"Second," she corrected me. "Are you jackheads ready to move?"

"Don't worry," I cracked, grinning even though she couldn't see it. "The big Drop Troopers will protect you and your tiny little Force Recon Marines."

Her laugh was low and seductive and I sighed at what might have been.

"Then by all means, you go first," she invited.

Delp and First squad led the way and I stepped in behind them. The march was going to be nearly five kilometers, and normally we could have made that in ten minutes, particularly on a low-grav world, but we had to slow down to accommodate the Recon troops. They were running, knowing the longer we were out here, the more chance we'd be spotted, but it would still be a twenty-minute slog.

We'd barely set out when I felt the first quake. I stopped and threw my suit's arms wide, maintaining balance as the ground shook beneath us.

"What the fuck was that?" Scotty blurted, though he'd still been composed enough to keep it on our private channel.

"Earthquake," I told him, grateful I'd spent so much time memorizing every section of the op order. "One of the main reasons this section of the moon is habitable is volcanic activity. They get a lot of them here." I switched over to Palmer's net. "Everything good to go, Lieutenant?"

"Just a little shaken up," she said, more of the same sarcastic humor in her tone. "Takes more than that to stop us. You tin soldiers can pick up the pace if you want. We're not the ones who let the machines do all the work...we can keep up."

"Anything you say." I switched to Carson's channel. "Pick up the pace just a bit. The Recon Straight-legs are getting bored."

"Roger that, sir."

The path climbed upward on a gradual slope, taking us through a narrower cut as the hills closed in on either side and it almost seemed as if the engineers had sliced through the cut with a laser instead of blasting it with explosives. The cut wound around the corner out of sight, but I noticed a few piles of slide rock near the sides of the walls.

I didn't think anything of it. I didn't know shit from geology and rocks were rocks, I thought. Maybe if I hadn't spent most of my life in the Trans-Angeles Underground, I might have put two and two together, earthquakes plus slide rocks. But we were jogging now, loping along with the Recon Marines keeping up at a good clip in a hopping, low-gravity run.

We'd hit the curve when the next quake came, and this one

was worse than the last, enough to throw me off my feet even with the suit's internal gyroscopes. My shoulder slammed into the padding and blackness billowed up around me, impenetrable even with thermal and sonics, just a solid wall of rock and dust. Something banged off my helmet, then my back, and the suit was rocked from one side to another and I couldn't talk, couldn't even think with the rattling inside and out.

I hadn't even noticed the constant background rumble and roar until it ceased and everything inside my helmet was silence.

"Scotty!" I yelled and my voice sounded obscenely loud. "Scotty, are you there?"

I saw his IFF signal in the display, blinking yellow. They were all blinking yellow except a few who had drifted into red, but thank God, none were black.

"Yeah, I'm here, Cam," he said, sounding a bit dazed. "Jesus Christ, what happened?"

"Get me a platoon damage report," I told him. "And see if you can move."

I tried, shifting first to the right, then to the left. I had no idea how much weight was resting on top of my suit, but it hadn't been enough to break it. To the right was a brick wall, unyielding, and I slammed into it without any result but a sore shoulder, so I tried the left. To the left, something gave, shifted, and I slammed back against it, feeling more than hearing shifting rock and dirt.

"Palmer," I called, strain in my voice. I wasn't using my own muscles to move the tons of rock, but I was throwing my effort into it to let the armor know how much force to use. "Palmer, are you there? Can you give me a status report?"

I had an IFF signal on all of the Force Recon Marines, but it wouldn't register damage, wouldn't show me if they were hurt or conscious. It would just turn black if their hearts stopped beating. I counted quickly, each black strip a punch in the gut.

There'd been forty-two of them, and now half were gone. Just like that.

"We're all alive," Scotty reported. "Miracle of miracles. First is all up, and Delp wasn't even buried. He's helping to dig out Carson. First has minor damage, nothing that would deadline their suits. Second is buried deepest and they're going to need help getting out. They have three suits running red, major joint damage and one with a deadlined plasma cannon, but no injuries. Third and Fourth took a beating, but they're nearly free now and only two have mobility issues. Delp says it was a landslide, a bad one. The whole side of the cliff just caved in and fell on us."

"What about the Recon platoon?" I asked him. "Does anyone have eyes on them?"

I gave another wrench to the left, digging my right foot into the dirt or rock or whatever it was wedged up against and finally I was free.

"Negative, sir," Scotty said. "There's too much dust in the air, no one can see shit."

I pushed my suit up to its feet, climbing up a pile of rocks nearly as tall as the Vigilante, almost falling again when part of the stack gave way and banged against the back of the right leg. Scotty was right, everything was a grey haze of dust, but it was thinning out and thermal imaging began to show me the isotope reactors of the battlesuits all around me, displaying distorted images of vaguely humanoid shapes struggling to dig themselves out of the rockslide.

I scanned farther back, trying to find the Recon Marines. They'd started out behind us, but some of them had move to the sides, trying to show us they could keep up with the suits. Rock and dirt were piled up nearly three meters deep across the trail for a good fifty meters on either side of our formation. Another aftershock hit while I was turning in a full circle, trying to find any sign of them, and I nearly went down again. Smaller swathes of dirt tumbled down off the hillside, but the largest rocks had already fallen and there weren't any left to add their weight to the pile.

"Palmer," I tried again. "Anyone in Force Recon, please reply."

She was right there, about thirty meters behind me. I could see her IFF transponder pinging. But where it said she would be, there was only a pile of granite and loose soil. I stepped carefully, trying not to lose my footing and trying not to step on anyone who might be trapped. She was at my feet. Somewhere.

What we really needed was a Search and Rescue team, but we weren't going to get one, not until we took out those Tahni. Hell, I couldn't even call for one without bringing down a missile strike on our heads. I dug into one of the larger rocks with the articulated claw at the end of my Vigilante's left hand and tossed it aside, the servomotors whining in protest at the weight. In standard gravity, it would have been a good 500 kilos, and even here it weighed well over 200. I had to be careful not to throw it on top of one of the other reported positions, and I wound up heaving it a good ten meters. It landed in a cloud of dust and fragments and I tried to look through the gap its absence had created, tried to find her beneath the ton of rocks and still saw nothing.

"Palmer, can you hear me?"

Her IFF signal went black.

Shit.

"Sir," Scotty asked me, "what do you want us to do?"

I thought hard and thought fast. If we tried to dig them out ourselves, we could wind up killing them. If they were still alive when we dug them out, we couldn't do a damned thing for them because we didn't have the medical supplies to treat internal injuries and multiple broken bones. And if we called for help, they were dead. There was only one choice and it sucked hard.

"We can't get them out ourselves," I decided. "We have to go take out the Tahni troops occupying the base and call for Search and Rescue once the area is clear."

"But Cam...sir," he corrected himself quickly, "what about the civilian workers? How're we gonna get them out from inside the barracks without the Force Recon troops? If we crash in there with our Vigilantes, they'll just as likely as not execute them all, and even if they don't, plasma guns and grenade launchers ain't very discriminating type of weapons, you know?"

"No, they aren't," I agreed. "But we each have a pulse carbine in our ditch kit."

Scotty didn't say anything for a second, just moaned in almost physical pain as he realized what I meant.

"Tell me you aren't saying what I think you're saying, LT."

"I am. It's what we're going to do because anything else I do sacrifices other people's lives."

"Sir, we ain't Recon Straight-legs. We ain't trained for busting in doors."

"We're not, Scotty." I swallowed hard and bared my soul for him. He deserved it straight. "Listen, this is beyond the op order and it's my call. But if you think it's stupid, tell me. I'm not perfect, I might be fucking up."

I heard the hiss of his breath, long and thoughtful.

"They won't be top of the line troops," he reasoned. "Likely they're just the REMFs left behind to guard the prisoners. They wouldn't waste Shocktroopers way out here, I don't think. We could do it. We're fucking Drop-Troopers."

"Ooh-rah. Get them moving. We'll split up at the rally point on the other side of the pass. And move fast." Something twitched in my cheek. "We don't have to hold back anymore."

20

The refinery was an ugly thing, built for maximum output on a world where the stress loads weren't as crucial, which meant struts and supports and overhangs everywhere you looked. From what I'd seen of Tahni military bases, the architects who'd designed this facility would have fit right in. It was also huge, at least fifty meters high and two hundred on a side, poured from raw buildfoam and then insulated by processed stone powder mined locally. Bulbous metal tanks rose high above the flattened metal roof at the rear of the place, where train tracks led from the refinery the short distance down to the coast to the spaceport.

I could see every detail lit up with a searing light brighter than any mid-day sunlight would ever shine on this moon, coruscating in polychromatic fury from the proton cannons raining down hell on the deflector dishes. Crackling blue and white energy forked off the electromagnetic dome of protection the dishes cast over the refineries, man-made lightning crackling out into the hills surrounding the hollow. I winced as a lance of rogue energy burst against a rocky outcropping only a hundred meters away from the crest of the hill where we were sheltered.

Below the dome of fire, it was eerily empty, with cargo trucks parked in front of the freight entrance to the refinery and not a soul wandering around outside. They didn't know *we* were coming, but they suspected someone was. Cruisers didn't hammer your shields with proton batteries just to send a message.

I shuddered as I backed down the rise out of sight, partially because of the deserted, haunted feeling I got from the industrial facility, and partially because I was freezing my ass off. I put a gloved hand up against the skin of my Vigilante, its chest yawning open like a clamshell where I'd climbed out, then pulled my fingers away again quickly when the painful cold radiated into my flesh.

"Third squad is ready, sir," Ernst Kreis told me, his square jaw set in determination, not giving into the biting wind coming down through the pass.

The NCO held his pulse carbine like someone who'd actually fired it, which was one reason I'd picked his squad to lead the dismounts. I'd discussed it briefly with Scotty in the privacy of our armor and after much verbal sparring, I'd made it clear to him I was going inside with the dismounts and he was staying with the armor and that was the end of it. It wasn't that I didn't trust Scotty, but of the two of us, I was the one who'd had *any* experience going up against the Tahni with just a rifle and my swinging cod. I'd actually killed a few with that rifle, which was more than anyone else in the platoon had done.

Third and Fourth were coming inside the crew barracks with me, while Scotty kept First and Second out for the distraction attack which would, hopefully, draw the Tahni troops' attention away from us and draw out any High Guard battle-suits they might have stationed here.

Would have stationed here. The Tahni had three destroyers in this system and I hadn't seen more than one during any battle I'd been present at for the last three years. They wanted to keep this system and they weren't fucking around.

The only question was, had they seen us yet? I didn't think so. There would be no reason for them to hide if they had. They wouldn't be able to run spy drones with all the electromagnetic static in the air from the load on the deflectors, and no one was going to stand outside to keep an eye out when a burn-through could send a fatal flash of radiation through and cook them where they stood.

The same thing, of course, could happen to us, so I hoped the gun crews on the cruiser knew what they were doing.

"Scotty," I said, grateful the laser-line-of-sight communications still worked despite the static charge in the air, "give us twenty minutes to get into position, then jet down there and hit the trucks in front of the cargo entrance with a missile launch. If the High Guard troops are hunkered down near the crew barracks, that should get their attention."

"Yeah, I remember the plan," Scotty said, still sounding a bit dubious about the whole thing. "Not crazy about it, but I remember it."

"Come on, Sgt. Kreis," I said to the Third squad leader. "Follow me."

And yes, I *was* walking point and *no*, Scotty hadn't much liked that, either.

I wasn't a trained Recon Marine, but I knew enough not to just walk straight down the trail to the center of the refinery courtyard in plain sight of God and radar. We hugged the rocks, making our way around the hill on the north side of the refinery, a slog with one arm and sometimes another foot braced against the rocks and dirt on the downhill slope. The dip in the trail where we'd halted was less than half a kilometer from the refinery, but it was a good two-kilometer hike around the edge until we descended the hill along a steep trail that came out on the western end of the complex.

My breath was a fog billowing out, the exertion freezing my lungs and threatening to make me cough uncontrollably, but I held it inside. Someone let out a soft, grunting hack ten meters behind me and I scowled but didn't say anything. It's not easy being stealthy when all you've trained for is smashing shit with a two-ton metal gorilla. I think having our faces bare to the elements might have helped. One of the biggest parts of the training for Force Recon is how to integrate input from their helmet sensors while they're moving at top speed and shooting on the run without allowing themselves to feel detached from their surroundings. It was a lot easier to avoid feeling detached with the wind slapping us in the face and every shadow at the corner of our vision or scrape of rock on dirt a possible enemy.

Not that I would have minded a helmet. Or just a hat. The field jacket in our armor's ditch kit had a hood, but it did nothing to keep my cheeks and nose from going numb in the face of the freezing wind. I felt totally naked, vulnerable not just because of the lack of armor but because of the strangeness of it. There were smells and tastes to a battlefield I never experienced inside my Vigilante. Ozone was strong in the air from the electricity arcing overhead, leaving a metallic taste in my mouth, warring with the grit in my teeth from the dirt carried on the breeze. I tried to spit it out, but I lacked the saliva for it.

I paused and hugged the cement block wall at the west end of the refinery, waving for the others to do the same as they scrambled down the dirt trail off the hill. Still no indication we'd been spotted, but I couldn't sit around and wait to make sure. I counted my little strike force, marking each with a finger on an imaginary slate in front of my face, paranoid as hell about losing track of one of them with no IFF transponders or thermal sensors to do the scut work for me.

Once I was sure I hadn't left someone up on the hill by accident, I circled around the back of the refinery at a swift jog, slightly bent over at the waist, more out of instinct than any sort of training. The web sling of my carbine yanked at my neck with each step, the spare magazines in the pouches of my tactical vest slapping against my ribs. There was probably a way to adjust or secure them better that would have prevented that, but I had no idea how to do it. I was lucky I had qualified with the damned gun just a couple months ago or I might have forgotten how to operate it.

Don't shoot me in the back, I thought hard at the Marines behind me. I wanted to say it out loud, but it would have just made them more nervous than they already were.

The giant cylindrical tanks loomed up tens of meters above us as we passed around to the rear of the building, and I idly wondered what was in them. I was sure there was some note in the op order about what this place actually made, but I'd seen so many mines just like this one that they all tended to blur together in my mind. It was something the Tahni wanted, either on principle or out of some pragmatic need and it was my job to deny it to them and free the workers.

Oh, come on, Alvarez, don't bullshit a bullshitter. You can tell Scotty it's just your job, but you know as well as I do that what you really should have done is taken the whole platoon back to the emergency rally point on the other side of the mountains and waited there for the dropship to make the low pass over the mountains and tried to signal them. It was right there in the op order under emergency procedures.

Yeah, and all I would have had to do was leave the trapped Recon Marines dozens of kilometers back with no hope at all of rescue, and abandon the civilians being held hostage. I tried to imagine going back to Brigantia after the war and telling Dak

Shepherd I'd done that and withering under the glare he would give me.

I was surprised by how quickly I'd grown used to the constant background crackling and the rolling peals of thunder overhead from one proton blast after another striking the shields, but they no longer registered, no longer wrung a flinch out of me with every distant boom. Nothing else made a sound on the storm-wracked night, at least no sound loud enough to be heard, and not even a transplanted weasel showed its face as we approached the crew barracks.

The building was large, a communal housing bloc three stories tall, about a hundred meters wide at the front and twice that in length, well insulated against the constant chill, its windows narrow and broadly-spaced. Through them, I could see a hint of light somewhere deep inside, leaking through closed doors, but no movement.

I turned back to the others and held up a fist, bringing them to a halt just before we cleared the back corner of the refinery. My hand was shaking and I tightened the fist, going down to one knee and then flat. I checked behind me and made sure the others had followed the signal, knowing most wouldn't have practiced dismounted hand signals since Boot Camp. Once I was satisfied everyone was down, I began high-crawling forward, my carbine cradled in my arms, scuttling on elbows and knees. There wouldn't be drones and probably not remote cameras, but a hardwired security system was possible, and some asshole standing by the window at just the wrong time was even more possible, as Murphy's Law attested.

The ground was hard, fusion-form pavement, created by the simple expedient of having a construction reactor dump plasma onto the ground before any of the other equipment had been flown in. It would have started out glass-smooth decades ago, but the wear and tear of winter after winter on this frigid moon had left it pocked and cratered and I didn't have the luxury of the body armor the Recon troops wore. I felt blood welling at my knees after fifty meters of the stuff and I heaved a sigh of relief when it gave way to a layer of dirt blown in by the winds and never cleared.

I reached the nearest wall of the barracks a few seconds later, cracked and patched and cracked again from expansion and contraction through the seasons, and turned right, keeping my left shoulder against it, staying below the windows. Light flickered down from the coronal discharge of the shields and threw shifting shadows in every direction, trying to draw my eyes away from the front with the promise of phantom enemies, but I just moved faster. The only way out of this was through it.

Another glance back and the others were still coming, a little strung out as some crawled faster than others, but everyone keeping their heads down and their asses out of the air, which was the best I could hope for. When I hit the side entrance to the building, I stopped, putting my back against the wall and waiting. Kreis scuttled up beside me, edging around his nominal point man, Private Meyer, and coming close to my ear.

"How do you want to do this, sir?" he wondered.

In other words, who's going through the door first? Honestly, I wanted to do it. It was still true that none of them was experienced at this and probably none were as good with a carbine, but I couldn't do it. Scotty would have yelled his head off at me and he would have been right. I might have been useful as a tactical asset on this operation, but someone had to lead it, and I didn't trust Kreis to be able to take up the slack if I went down.

"Send Meyer through first," I told him, having to speak up over the background hum. "The rest of his fire team right on his heels. I'm going in after them, and I want you to wait at the door until one of us comes back and tells you it's clear."

I was tempted to simply have them stack and pile in right behind us, but if I'd misread this and there was a trap on the other side of that door, someone had to survive and get the word to Scotty.

"If you hear gunfire," I spelled it out for him, "and none of us make it back out, pull everyone back behind the refinery and wait on Sgt. Hayes to hit the front, then try to head around the side and get back to your armor. Do *not* come in after us unless one of us comes back and signals you. Clear, Sergeant?"

"Clear, sir," he promised, and I believed him. Kreis wasn't a coward, but he was no fool, either.

"Get going, then. Get everyone ready and tell Sgt. Majid what I told you."

In thirty seconds, Meyer was in place, back against the door, carbine held at high port. He was a skinny, big-eyed younger man but he'd scored well in the last range work and shoot-house simulators we'd done with the carbines, which meant he was as qualified as any of the rest of them. Alpha team, led by Corporal Maggert, went to either side of the door, and at least they weren't sweeping each other with their muzzles.

And then we waited, because none of this would work without Scotty distracting them away from this entrance. I checked my 'link and swore softly. I'd thought I was cutting things too close when I'd ordered him to give us twenty minutes to get into position, but we still had four minutes left. It dragged out into forever and I found myself looking back and forth over and over, staring at the same shadows, my imagination trying to turn them into enemy assassins sneaking up on us through the piles upon piles of discarded cargo boxes cluttering the rear of the housing block. Probably food, I thought. No more would have been delivered during the occupation and I wondered if they'd run out, if I'd find more living skeletons inside like on Demeter.

A chest-deep concussion of sound shook the ground and jerked me out of a nightmare. One blast followed close on another, the light from the explosions flooding the night, reaching all the way into the alley between buildings where we were hiding.

It was Scotty. The attack had begun.

Now came the moment of truth. When I'd gone over the mission with Lt. Palmer, I'd asked her about getting through the side doors, whether they'd need some sort of cracking program to override the security locks and she'd laughed in my face. Why, she'd asked me, would anyone bother with computer locks or any other sort of lock on the outside of communal housing on a moon where no one lived except Corporate Council workers? And why would the Tahni bother to lock them in when the only place they could go was to work, which was exactly where the enemy wanted them? This was when we'd find out if she was right.

Maggert glanced back at me and I shot her a thumbs-up. The dark-eyed woman nodded to Meyer, then twisted the lever and pushed the door open, sending the point man rushing inside. Dim light shone from inside the door, but I didn't have time to note any details before Maggert led the rest of the team through and I followed. Loose dirt turned to a thick, cloth mat and then a bare, cement floor. The light I'd seen came through the crack beneath and interior door about five meters away. We'd come into some sort of utility room stacked with clothes washers and dryers, squatting in sullen disuse, some of the lids hanging open. A set of grey coveralls hung out of one of the washers, still dripping wet.

And it was warm, so wonderfully warm here inside, out of the wind. I took a moment just to breathe it in, just to let my lungs heat up to a temperature where every inhale didn't make them freeze solid.

Meyer was standing beside the door out of the washroom, pressing his ear to it, while Maggert and the others stood with their backs against the walls, looking tentative and uncertain. I grabbed Maggert by the shoulder and spoke quietly in her ear.

"Go tell Sgt. Kreis to bring the rest of Third squad in and stack on this door. Leave Fourth outside with Sgt. Majid and tell him not to come in unless I call for him or until he hears the shit kick off in here."

Mostly because there wasn't enough space for them inside the utility room.

A few seconds later, Kreis cat-footed inside with exaggerated care, Bravo team behind him. I chivvied them into the correct positions, or at least as close to a correct position as I could remember, spread around the walls beside the door. If I remembered the plans we'd been shown correctly, which was an iffy thing since they'd been part of Palmer's mission and not mine, the other side of that door would take us into a central rec room full of entertainment consoles, pool tables, poker tables and a wet bar. At the center would be a staircase leading to the top two floors, while leading right and left would be the hallways to the first-floor quarters and a few admin offices.

The rec room might be totally unoccupied, or crawling with Tahni or packed with hostages, but all I knew for sure was that there was a light on inside. I was going to have to go with my gut because there was no time for anything else, and my gut told me that the Tahni would stay on the ground floor because it was more secure against the bombardment, and I'd have been willing to bet they'd have the hostages close by.

If the Tahni were waiting there in the rec room, guns at human heads, then a lot of innocent people were about to die. But I also knew there'd be more humans than Tahni here, and the enemy, as overconfident and dense as they could be when it came to letting their religion and worldview get in the way of good tactics, wasn't stupid enough to think desperate people wouldn't try to swarm over them if they gathered them all in one place and basically dared them to. And while the outside door to the utility room didn't lock, the doors to the individual apartments would, because you didn't want fellow workers going through your shit while you were working and they were off.

My gut said the humans would be locked in their rooms and the Tahni would likely be gathered in the rec room, where they'd be able to keep an eye on all four entrances to the building. Heavy, crew-served weapons? Maybe, but I'd have been willing to bet they'd save those for the front entrance. If I was wrong on that, a lot of my people were going to die. Maybe me, too.

I slapped Meyer on the shoulder and he threw the door open.

21

I burst through just behind Meyer, every detail of the rec room crashing in on me like a wave. I had experience with sorting through an overwhelming flood of data and everything formed into a coherent picture in the back of my mind long before conscious thought could list the details in words. It was frozen like a Renaissance painting, each subject caught in mid-motion at a single moment.

There were fewer Tahni than I'd expected, probably the REMF's Scotty had thought they were, Rear Echelon Mother Fuckers, their supply clerks and cooks and repair techs and everyone whose job wasn't to point a weapon at the enemy. I could always tell them from the regular line soldiers by the poor fit of their armor, as if the Tahni military procurement system decided these guys weren't going to be fighting so they weren't going to bother tailoring their gear to their size. Their weapons were similar to ours, laser carbines, though ours fired pressure pulses from hyperexplosive cartridges feeding their thermal energy through a lasing rod, while theirs were a bit more compli- cated, using some sort of disposable charging crystal. Neither was ideally suited to ground combat, with high thermal signatures and poor penetration against heavy armor, but they had no recoil and were easy to aim and operate for personnel who weren't trained for it.

The difference between us was, we were ready to shoot and they weren't. There were forty or fifty of them that I could see, about half of them already crouched behind overturned furniture, more of the cargo crates, machinery I couldn't tell the purpose of, all of it hauled in and stacked across the front entrance hallway, blocking it off from the rec room. The rest had been covering the side entrances, but had abandoned them once the explosions had come from the front, scrambling across the room, heading for the barriers at the front hallway. Which was tactically unsound, but just what we'd been hoping for.

Meyer was ahead of me, but I grabbed at his shoulder and rushed past him, knowing what we had to do and having no way of communicating it to the others in time except to show them by example. Fifty bad guys against twenty of us was still high odds, and surprise would only count for so much. The safe thing would have been to duck down behind the cover the Tahni had left behind at the side entrance and use it as a fire base, but that would have left my guys firing across the room while the enemy was shooting at them and I just didn't have that sort of confidence in their marksmanship.

No one had turned our way, yet. No one seemed to know we were there. The Tahni were all dressed in dark grey uniforms, not that far from the color of our own ditch kit jackets, and in the dim lighting and panic of the moment, our buzzcuts would probably pass in peripheral vision for the close-cropped mohawks the Tahni wore.

I ran between the two forces, between the group that had been set up facing the front and the remainder trying to stream in from the sides, so close I could smell a peculiar, musky scent coming off them. I wondered if it was their natural odor if they all wore some sort of cologne or grease in their hair to make it twist into the queue down their back.

I didn't fire until they noticed me. It took a while, because viewed out of the corner of their eye, I could have been just another slightly-short Tahni soldier running for the barricades, and I was nearly two-thirds of the way across the room when the first of them turned his head my way, skin crinkling around his eyes as they opened wider in realization,

He grabbed at his laser carbine and I shot him. The laser didn't recoil, of course, but there was a vibration from the reaction chamber as a trio of hyperexplosive cartridges ignited in quick succession. The product of their sacrifice was a burst of invisible, infrared energy, the photons marching in lock-step like some ancient company of Swiss pikemen. The laser beam might have been invisible, but its effects were not. The air between us flashed to plasma at the extreme energy ripping through it, Zeus tossing a thunderbolt in the old myths, and whether it was the plasma or the laser that had birthed it, the Tahni soldier fell forward to his knees, clutching at the hole burned through his chest, not even able to cry out to the others.

Not that he had to.

The rest of Third squad opened up just after me, and I was gratified to see that at least most of them had actually followed my lead, weaving between the groups of Tahni and firing at the group running for the barricade at the front entrance.

The results were everything I could have hoped for. There were twenty Tahni soldiers in the group rushing from the side entrances to the front hallway and they went down like wheat before one of the huge automated threshers I'd seen in the fields on Brigantia, most of them not even realizing who we were until

225

it was too late. The few who actually got off a shot jerked the rounds high, the laser blasts impacting down the hallway toward the front entrance, setting wallboard afire and lighting up the darkened passage.

And the fog of war did the rest. I didn't realize this in the heat of the moment, of course—things just happened and I reacted. But in retrospect, it was clear as crystal. The Tahni rear-echelon soldiers weren't used to anyone shooting at them and the ones already manning the barricades were entirely focused forward. So, when their fellows behind them started screaming and dying and firing forward, well, those guys just assumed the threat was in front of them and they started firing down that hallway too...and if nothing fired back, that was just because there was too much smoke and too much fire to see it, wasn't it?

It almost went perfectly, would have if Majid hadn't burst through the side door with Fourth squad firing as he went. The laser bursts came perilously close to hitting us, and what didn't plow into the flooring did exactly the wrong thing and hit beside the Tahni troops who'd been facing forward. They turned, and laser fire turned with them like they were squirting it from a hose.

"Shoot them, Goddammit!" I snapped, practicing what I preached and spraying a long burst across the back of the line of Tahni soldiers.

Not long enough, though, because my magazine ran empty and it took me a good two seconds to realize it. I dropped to a knee and fumbled for a reload out of the pouch on my vest, then had to look down at the magazine well because it was narrow and I couldn't fit the damned thing in, and *damn it, this is taking too long!*

I was three long steps away from the front line of Tahni

troops and I went with a gut instinct that I was running out of time and just threw myself forward into the closest of them, swinging the carbine like a club. The Tahni are, on average, taller and heavier than a human, and one of their front-line soldiers could have probably kicked my ass on his worst day, but they gave the rear-echelon jobs to the older ones, the warriors gone to seed who couldn't make the cut anymore. This guy was old and out of shape and I slammed the carbine's stock into his face with an impact that travelled up through my shoulders, and he went down. I kicked him, kicked him over and over in the face, ignoring the shots flaring up in gouts of flame on either side of me until his hands went slack and his carbine slipped out of them.

And then everything went silent in the rec room, the sounds of the battle outside sounding distant and irrelevant, and the Tahni were down. I looked down and saw that I somehow still had the spare magazine in my left hand. I slid it home and chambered a fresh round before I quickly scanned the room. A Tahni soldier stirred, trying to crawl across the blood-stained, charred floor toward his laser. I shot him through the head.

"Are there any casualties?" I demanded, my voice sounding dry and raspy. "Squad leaders, report!"

"We're good!" Kreis reported, sounding confident.

Majid's head was whipping around like a mother trying to keep track of her children, but finally he nodded to me, swallowing hard.

"Yeah, we're good, sir. No casualties."

"Kreis," I ordered, "go check on the hostages. Check all three floors and make sure you get them all. Majid, your people set up a perimeter down here and make sure nothing comes in the damned doors but us. And Kreis, watch for any more Tahni hiding out in here!"

I made sure each of them acknowledged the order before I hobbled on a knee that I hadn't remembered hurting down the passage to the front entrance. More barricades had been set up to block the door there and I slung my carbine and hauled a couple of them out of the way enough to pull open the door.

A cold wind blasted through the gap and I gasped at the physical impact of it, taking a moment to blink my eyes shut at the sudden rush of tears. I squinted at the refinery and saw that the fight there was close to over.

Back on Ambergris, I'd witnessed a battlesuit fight from this vantage point, naked and helpless without my Vigilante, and I hadn't liked it much. This was slightly better, because the Tahni were the ones outnumbered and getting their asses kicked. I could see from the High Guard battlesuits burning fiercely in the center of the refinery courtyard that there hadn't been more than a squad of the enemy armor stationed here, which they probably thought was more than they needed. They'd been wrong, because when you assume, you make an ASS out of U and ME, as my old Drill Instructors used to say.

The last two of the High Guard troopers went down in the refinery entrance under a hail of plasma fire and the heat from the blast banished the chill of the wind for a good ten seconds. If they had a few battlesuits fighting each other with energy weapons here all the time, it might have been a comfortable place to live.

"Scotty!" I yelled into my 'link, hoping the laser line-of-sight would reach him through the smoke billowing off the burning suits and the wreckage of the two cargo trucks at the front entrance to the refinery. "Scotty, do you read?"

"Five by five, sir," he told me. "I think we've got things wrapped up out here." He pointed off to the left with the suit's one articulated claw. "There was an anti-aircraft defense turret off to the west, but I sent a fire team from First squad over to take it out."

He lumbered up to my position, steam rolling off his Vigilante, more than a meter taller than me and another meter wider. I felt the heat from his plasma gun at seven or eight meters away, the prickling-skin feeling of sitting too close to a fire.

"Any casualties inside?" he asked me.

"Not a one," I said, "which is nothing short of divine intervention. "Now, if the fucking cruiser would just stop with the...."

I stopped short and looked up at the sky. The constant glow of the deflector shield, the background crackling hum had become just something I accepted, part of the landscape. I hadn't even noticed it was gone.

"What the fuck?" I blurted.

"Hey LT." Kreis' voice was impossibly loud in my earpiece and I remembered I'd turned the volume up to overcome the background hiss of the deflectors. I cursed and touched a control on my 'link. "We found the civilians. They were locked in the quarters but we managed to find the central security control to override the locks."

"Get me a count," I told him. "And let me know how many are going to need medical attention."

"Roger that. There's...," he trailed off, a bit hesitant. "There's only about twenty of them left, sir."

Shit. Twenty out of fifty.

I heard Kreis talking to someone in the background, the voices mumbles in my ear.

"I got one of the foremen here if you wanna talk to him."

"I'll be back, Scotty," I promised, heading through the central hallway back to the rec room. "See if you can raise the dropship and get Search and Rescue down here for the Recon platoon."

I nearly stopped when I reached the end of the hallway and the smell hit me. I'd been too hyped up on adrenaline before and hadn't noticed it. The blood was pooling, rivers heading to the crimson sea at the center of the room, and the stench of it, the wafting, sickly-sweet odor of burnt flesh made me gag. I paused and swallowed the bile in my throat, passing through the nightmare landscape of corpses to a small cluster of humans near the rear of the building.

They seemed to be trying to keep as far away from the dead Tahni as possible, and I couldn't blame them for that, but the twenty civilians huddled together, shrinking away even from the squad of Marines trying to examine them, like abused dogs afraid to trust anyone. The man Kreis was standing beside was the boldest looking of the lot, his hair and beard long and unkempt, something feral behind his eyes.

"Sir, this is George Nakamura," Kreis said, motioning toward the older man. "This is my boss, Lt. Alvarez. Tell him what you told me."

"Are there any more of your people being kept somewhere else, Mr. Nakamura?" I asked him, glancing back at the little cluster of ragged scarecrows.

"No, Lieutenant," he told me, his voice verging on the manic side. "No, this is all of us." A muscle quivered in his cheek. "You want to know what happened to the rest of us?" I was about to say yes, I did, but he went on uninterrupted, as if the question had been rhetorical. The feral look in his eyes was replaced by despair gone nearly all the way to madness. "There was eighty of us when they came here, over a year ago. I knew every one of them, too. Eighty good men and women, good workers. Some died when the Tahni came, killed because they tried to fight. Twelve of us that died right away and another seven from

230

wounds they took, because the fucking bastards wouldn't let us use our auto-docs. Said that kind of technology was against the Will of the Emperor." He snorted a bitter laugh. "They worship their Emperor or something, I guess. I never could quite get it figured out even after a year with them here. Anyway, the rest of us, we did the work they wanted because we didn't figure we had any choice. And I didn't think the little bit of product we put out here would make no difference in who won the war."

Which was a good way to talk yourself into it, I guess. Not that I blamed a bunch of civilians for not putting up a fight, but...well, the resistance on Brigantia and Demeter had been civilians.

"Things seemed to go okay," he went on, memory haunting his sallow, gaunt face, "until a couple months ago. We'd been rationing our food, but eventually, everyone could see there just wouldn't be enough of it to last, so they elected me to go talk to the Tahni commander. He was one of them guys out there in the big metal suits." Something finally lit up behind those eyes. "Did you get him?"

"They're all dead," I confirmed. Unless some had run away, but I didn't go into that because he seemed gratified with the idea.

"Well, I went to the son of a bitch. Can't even pronounce his name right. It was something like Clint? Vrint? And I told him and asked if we could have some of their food, but he told me their food was sacred to them and to give it to humans was, well, as close as the translator could tell, sacrilege. And I got mad and told him if he wanted us to run the plant for them, he was going to have to feed us."

Nakamura sniffled, mouth working for a moment, but nothing coming out.

"So, this Vrint guy tells me that his technicians had figured out it only took twenty of us to operate the plant, and he'd looked up our records and found the best workers. And then he took the rest of us, the ones who weren't good enough for him, and he had them executed. And then he came and told me there should be enough food for all of us now."

The man was sobbing and all I could feel was a cold ball of rage in my gut. Just when I started to feel bad about slaughtering Tahni, like I'd turned into a killer and wasn't good for anything else, the Tahni would go and do something that just made me happy to keep pulling the trigger.

"Cam, we have a big fucking problem," Scotty told me, an insect buzz in my ear. I'd turned the volume down too low.

"What's wrong, Scotty?"

Nakamura wasn't paying attention anymore, still crying softly, one of the other workers folding him into a hug, but Kreis' eyes narrowed.

"I got a hold of the dropship," Scotty said. "The reason the bombardment let up was that the destroyer came back and a whole bunch of insystem patrol boats are coming with it. The cruiser had to withdraw to go deal with them, and without the cruisers to shield them, the carriers and the troop ships are pulling out. They told us to get to the backup LZ and prepare for dustoff."

"What?" I blurted, my face going slack. "What about the S&R crew? We can't just leave the Recon troops behind!"

"They ain't coming, boss," he said, sadness dragging down the words. "And we ain't got time to wait for them. The dropship is picking us up in a half-hour, hell or high water. They said it's an order."

"Shit." I felt as if I was going to collapse in on myself, imagining being one of those Marines, buried under dirt and rock, living off an on-board oxygen supply that wouldn't last more than another couple of hours, and no one coming to save me. Suffocating to death.

But what was the alternative?

"Sgt. Kreis," I said to the Third squad leader, the words an exhausted hiss, all the energy going out of me. "Escort the civilians outside and tell Gunny Hayes to take charge of them. Then get your Marines back in their Vigilantes and prepare to dust off." I looked around. "Where's Majid and Fourth squad?"

"Still checking out the upstairs rooms," he said. "We know we got all the civilians but he didn't want to leave before he checked them all out."

I sighed and touched a control on my 'link.

"Majid," I called, "you need to get your squad down here ASAP."

"Sir!" the man replied, breathless, as if I'd interrupted him during a workout. "We got one of them! We got one of them alive!"

"Got one of who?" I demanded, frowning.

"One of the Tahni, sir! He was hiding in a closet up here, little bitch!"

Oh, great. What the hell was I gonna do with a Tahni prisoner? They were notorious for being uncooperative and suicidal...on the other hand, this guy hadn't offed himself or thrown himself at our guns, as they'd been known to do.

"Is he one of the rear-guard soldiers, like the ones we took out down here?" I wondered. "Or a High Guard trooper?" Because considering how I felt about the High Guard troops here, I might just have him save us the trouble and put a round through the Tahni's head.

"Neither one, boss," Majid said. "I recognize his uniform insignia from the identification guide. He's flight crew. A pilot for one of those cargo shuttles down at the port."

My mouth had been open to give an order and I closed it. A pilot.

"Majid," I said, slowly and carefully, knowing full well what

I was about to do, "get him down here. Detail me two people to guard him and get the rest out of here and back into their suits."

I switched frequencies, my mind working a million kilometers an hour.

"Scotty," I said, "I've got an idea. But you're not going to like it."

22

"This is a horrible fucking idea," Scotty said, his words ringing in my ear for all the fact he was a dozen kilometers away. "You're going to get court-martialed, you know that, right?"

"Sitting in a brig for a while doesn't sound too bad to me right now," I assured him, the words distracted, distant.

My entire concentration was on digging. The Vigilante wasn't built for delicate precision, but it was all I had and, more importantly, it was all the Recon Marines had. I slammed my left hand into the dirt, pitching another rock away, and finally revealing the motionless form of Gunnery Sgt. Antonio Carver, Palmer's platoon sergeant. The man was unconscious, but not from blood loss or because he'd been concussed. His helmet's automated medical systems had put him out to prevent shock, because he had multiple broken bones at the least, maybe internal bleeding.

But he was alive, and so were the other nine we'd been able to dig out, the ones with their IFFs still showing life signs. I didn't know how long they had, but I knew how long they'd live without someone to get them off this moon.

"You see the dropship yet?" I asked Scotty.

I hadn't noticed it pass overhead, but then, I'd been busy and the backup LZ was quite a ways off. The spaceport, though, that was closer, much closer.

"It's landing now," he told me. "I've been telling the pilot what you're doing, begging the guy to give you a little more time, but he says there are Tahni patrol boats inbound and they don't have any sort of cover. He says he has orders to dust off immediately and he's going to follow them. You and Fourth squad are on your own."

"Roger that." It wasn't what I'd hoped for, but it was what I'd expected. "Get those civilians on board and get out of here." I hesitated. "And Scotty, if you see Vicky before I do, tell her I said I love her."

"Goddammit, Cam."

"Sir, I got the last one," Kreis told me.

After seeing him for the last couple hours out of his suit, it was strange to look his way and see the grinning skull of a Vigilante. He was gently tugging a Force Recon trooper out of a freshly-dug hole by the casualty-evac handle on the back of the woman's harness. She was limp and unconscious, just like the others, every one of them in a medical coma thanks to the drugs administered by their helmets. They looked dead, but the IFF transponders assured me they were still alive. Most of them weren't and it bothered the hell out of me to leave their bodies here. Marines didn't leave people behind, alive or dead.

"Get them up," I instructed. There were nine WIA and only seven of us, since I'd sent two of them along to the spaceport with the prisoner. "Kreis, you and I are carrying two of them. The rest of you pick one and be gentle. We still have to get them to the *Iwo*, and God knows how long that's going to take."

And I just dragged eight of my Marines into this. I hoped I wasn't dragging them down with me, but I knew in my heart that not a one of them would have voted to leave the Recon troops behind.

It was tricky finding a way to pick up two of the wounded, and I was worried I was doing more damage by draping them over the shoulder of my suit, but nothing would do more damage than staying here and dying, so I did it anyway. They were weightless to the byomer muscles of my Vigilante, limp rag dolls like the ones the little girls in Tijuana used to make from scraps of discarded material, and I gritted my teeth against the wrongness of it.

I led them out of the canyon, dreading the possibility of another quake while we were stuck in its confines, one that would finish them off and trap us for good. But the titans of Valius had gone back to sleep after unleashing their wrath on us so capriciously just hours earlier, and the only thing that disturbed our journey was the fear they'd left behind them.

Instead of following the dirt track back into the valley, we took it along the hillside, curving away from the refinery and out toward the seashore. This wasn't the shore I remembered from my youth, when my parents had taken us to the beach once a year to camp, no warm sand and sunny skies to be had. Ice-encrusted rocks lined the shore, and only the constant crashing of the violent surf kept the entire seaside from being a solid crust of ice. A freezing fog drifted out over the inland sea, frosting my battlesuit where it touched it, and God knows how cold it was inside the Recon troops' light body armor. We had to get them out of there fast or this was all going to be for nothing.

I picked up the pace, cognizant of the risk of compounding their injuries with each pounding step, each jolt, but not knowing what else to do. We cleared a steep, ice-shrouded cliff and finally, there was the beach...and the spaceport. Where there'd once been bare sand was fusion-form pavement, a landing pad for cargo shuttles and landers, and at the inland end of it a train station with a line of freight cars sitting beneath cargo cranes, ready to load containers of processed chemicals onto shuttles.

I didn't care about the train, didn't give a shit about the cargo, I just wanted more than anything to get on the damned shuttle. It was spherical, resting on heavy landing struts, its plasma engines shielded from the rest of the body by a ring of oval reaction mass tanks loaded down with pellets of metallic hydrogen. It was ugly and utilitarian, but if it had been a woman, I would have married it. The main freight ramp was down at the base of the landing gear, a steep climb up into the cargo hold.

Harsh work lights glowed inside the hold and, as I topped the ramp, I saw Corporal Steele and Private Richrath still in their field jackets, training their pulse carbines on the Tahni prisoner. He was sullen and withdrawn, his body language human enough that I almost forgot he was an alien, from a distance. The Tahni were frighteningly close to us, so close most xenobiologists thought they had to be related somehow, far back, though no one had any idea how that was possible.

I believed it. If they'd been just a bit more alien, a bit more different, we'd never have gone to war at all. They had to be enough like us to want what we had. And maybe enough like us for me to make this work.

"Gently," I warned the others as I set down the two Recon Marines I'd been carrying, setting them down as carefully as I could with the oversized muscles of the Vigilante doing the work.

I shut down the armor and cracked the chestplate, clambering out with practiced ease, grabbing my pulse carbine from the ditch kit because I didn't want to face the Tahni pilot without it.

"Kreis," I said, shouting the word instead of transmitting it because the squad leader was getting out of his suit on the other side of the cargo hold. "Have your squad start carrying them upstairs."

The shuttle was a hollow ball on the inside, most of it dedicated to the empty cargo hold, but a skeletal metal staircase ran along the inside of the hollow sphere, spiraling around it to the cockpit and crew stations at the top of the shuttle. It would take a while to haul the wounded all the way up there, but we'd have to do it if we wanted them strapped in.

"Yes, sir," Kreis said, not commenting on how hard a job it was going to be.

I scrolled through the menus on my 'link as I stepped up to the Tahni prisoner. We all had the translator program built into our issue datalinks, but I sure as hell had never thought I'd use it.

"What's your name?" I asked the pilot. The translator belted the words out in the Tahni language, the words sounding tinny from the small, external speaker.

The Tahni glanced up sharply, as if he hadn't expected us to try to talk to him. I thought, for a second, he would try to give me the silent treatment, but he grunted something that sounded almost human, like when you're too far away to hear what someone is saying and just hear the general patterns of speech. Too damned human.

"My name is Kah-Luwhen," the translator said, and I had to read the transcription off the screen before I was sure what I'd heard. "What do you want of me? Why have you not just killed me?"

"You're a pilot," I told him. "I want you to fly this ship out of here."

"Why would I help you?" he asked. The inflection of the translator was flat, no intonation, but my head inserted disbelief tinged with outrage. "You are the enemy. I am a soldier of the Imperium. It is my duty to kill you."

"It's your duty to die fighting us," I reminded him. Behind us, Third squad was carrying the wounded up the stairs, their boots clomping heavily on the metal grating. "Why didn't you? You hid. You surrendered. You want to live more than you want to fight. If you fly us out of here, you'll live. You have my word."

"What good is your word, human?" Scorn this time, if only inside my head. "What are you to me?"

"I am," I told him, "a warrior who has killed so many of your soldiers I've lost count. I've killed them with my battlesuit and with a rifle and with my bare hands." Well, using my carbine as a club anyway. "If I wanted you dead, I would kill you myself and not wait. I need you alive, and because I need you to do something that isn't your duty to do, I'll offer you your life in exchange. My people don't kill prisoners of war."

That was a lie, but we generally didn't kill them once we'd taken them on board our troop ships, so it was mostly true, and I hoped he couldn't read human faces well enough to tell the difference. I certainly couldn't figure out what was going on under those ridged brows, behind those beady, black eyes.

"I will do it," the pilot said.

I wanted to exhale in relief, but I knew it was premature. He could be lying, could be intent on destroying the ship with us in it. But I nodded, turned the translator program off.

"Corporal," I said to Steele, "take him up to the cockpit and get him strapped in. Let him get the ship powered up." I wanted to tell him to shoot the Tahni if he did anything suspicious, but how the hell would they know? How would *I* know? I wasn't any sort of pilot, even when the instruments weren't built for aliens and marked in a non-human language. "I'll be right up."

For all the good that would do.

There was one Recon Marine left on the floor of the cargo

hold and Kreis was tromping back down the stairs, looking winded. I didn't blame him. It had been a hell of a day.

"Help me with this one," I told him, sliding my hands under the armpits of the Marine. Kreis sucked in a breath and grabbed the man's legs.

I grunted with effort. They were a whole lot less weightless without the artificial muscles of the battlesuit, total deadweight and I was huffing and puffing as badly as Kreis by the time we reached the crew stations, just one level down from the cockpit. The other Recon wounded were already strapped into acceleration couches and the other members of Third squad were circulating among them, checking their straps. I would have told them to check their medical readouts, but the truth was, we didn't have any supplies to treat them with even if they'd been coding. Either the on-board diagnostics in their helmets would keep them alive, or they wouldn't.

Kreis and I lowered the last of the wounded into one of the rows of seats and began strapping her down when I heard the snap-bang sound of systems coming to life, of metal warming against the cold outside.

"Finish up," I told the squad leader, then jogged up to the cockpit.

The Tahni version of a pilot's seat wasn't all too different from the human one, except that there were four seats in a circular cluster, the viewscreens hanging above them, the controls built into the arms of the chairs instead of on a console. The prisoner was in the seat facing to my left, which was totally arbitrary in a round ship, and he was moving individual levers built into the ends of the arms of his chair with long, multijointed fingers. Their hands were the least human thing about them, with a pinky longer than the rest of their fingers, almost a second thumb, and an extra-joint to each of the digits, letting them curl into shapes that didn't seem natural to my human sensibilities.

Steele and Richrath were standing to either side of the male, their carbines pointed at him as if they expected him to announce it before he blew the ship up with us on it.

"Go ahead and strap in," I told them, waving at the three seats against the far bulkhead. "I'll take this."

I fell into one of the chairs in the command circle and strapped down, laying the carbine across my lap. The Tahni, Kah-Luwhen, ignored me as he'd ignored the two enlisted men who I'd left to guard him, and the whole shuttle began to vibrate at his systematic manipulation of the controls.

"Do you have crime on your worlds?" I asked him. The translator spat what sounded like chirping nonsense at him and he looked at me blankly, what I would have taken for incomprehension in a human. "People doing bad things," I expanded. "Things they're forbidden to do by your laws or customs?"

"Of course," he replied. "There would be no need for laws or customs if no one had ever behaved badly."

"On Earth," I told him, "we have people who break the law for profit, for gain," I told him. "They do it to survive because they can't find any other way, sometimes because they're lazy or often just because they're too smart to be living the unproductive life, just sitting around doing nothing like so many people enjoy. They lie, they cheat, they steal every day the way you would report for duty as a pilot every day, as a job, a calling."

"Why would you allow such people to live?" he asked, and my mind supplied the horrified tone that the translator wouldn't.

"Because there are just too many people living there to stop it. Our largest cities each hold hundreds of millions and policing them all would be impossible."

"Hundreds of millions in a single city?" he repeated. He didn't believe me, I could tell.

"I was one of those criminals," I said. "I stole food, stole clothes, stole luxury items. I stole from other criminals and sold their illegal goods for a profit. I was caught because I made too many enemies and given the choice of punishment or the military. I'm telling you this so you understand I have been in this position before, where my life depended on knowing whether or not someone was lying to me, whether they were playing me for a fool. Human, Tahni, it doesn't matter. You're a pilot. You fly this ship where I tell you to fly it, and if you try to lie to me, try to take me somewhere I don't want to go, try to signal your people, then I'll kill you and take the chance I can figure out how to fly it myself." I shrugged. "I just wanted you to know."

"Do not worry, human," the Tahni said, raising his voice to be heard over the roar of the engines. "Were I to try to deliver you to my people, they would simply kill all of us, including me. Tahni do not surrender to aliens. It is a dishonor worthy of death." His face twisted into an expression I didn't recognize, maybe a smile, maybe a sneer, maybe a grimace. "You may wish to prepare yourself."

I'd been twisted around in my seat to talk to him and I barely had time to turn around and tighten my harness before the fist of God slammed me back into the totally inadequate padding of the Tahni acceleration couch. The world vibrated around me with enough ferocity I couldn't focus my vision on the viewscreens mounted above my head, but I could see movement in them, the haze of fog and then the thicker grey of the clouds, and finally, blackness.

The agonizing press of high-g acceleration fell away and I sucked in a breath, as our boost ramped down to a single gravity. The lines on the overhead screens were clear now that physics had stopped trying to kill me, and a Tahni sensor screen was surprisingly similar to ours, although the colors were garish and the symbols impossibly complicated.

I loosened my restraints and pointed at a large icon shaped vaguely like the number nine if it had fallen over on its side.

"What's that?" I asked Kah-Luwhen.

"One of your ships," he said. "I am not certain, but I believe it is the kind which carries your ground troops to battle." The *Iwo*. It had to be the *Iwo*. "It is boosting away from us at one gravity."

"This thing has radio, right? Electromagnetic communications?"

"We do, though we prefer to use laser communication."

"Aim your transmission antenna at that ship and adjust to this frequency." I knew the frequency from the op order, one of those little details I didn't think I'd ever need, but had looked up on the way to the spaceport. "And patch the communications through my station."

I couldn't see what he was doing with the controls and wouldn't have understood if I did, but I watched him anyway, trying to make him believe I'd know if he was deceiving me. Hell, for all I knew, the ship in the sensor image was the Tahni destroyer and I was about to tell them I was a human on board their ship. At least it would be a quick death.

"Go ahead," the pilot told me. "Face front and speak clearly."

"CFS *Iwo Jima*, this is Lt. Alvarez, Third Platoon, Delta Company, Fourth Battalion of the 187th Marine Expeditionary Force. I am on board the Tahni shuttle at your six. I have wounded from the Recon platoon attached to our operation and I am declaring an emergency. Please respond."

Silence. On the sensor screen, the troop ship continued to boost away from us, and I wondered how long it would take before we ran out of reaction mass trying to catch up to her, or whether she'd just Transition back to the edge of the system with the carriers. And then what? Turn around and land again and hope the Tahni didn't try to retake the moon before the Fleet came back?

Of course, by then the wounded would have died.

"Attention unknown enemy spacecraft." The voice was human and I nearly cheered, wanted to hug Kah-Luwhen for being the equivalent of an honest politician, the kind that once bought, stays bought. "We are sending a patrol of assault shuttles to escort you in. Stay on the course we're transmitting and do not deviate or you will be destroyed. Do you understand?"

"Five by five, *Iwo Jima*," I assured him. "We will do backflips if you want, as long as you don't leave without us."

"Just stay on the beam." Whoever the guy was, he didn't have any sort of sense of humor. "And if you are Lt. Alvarez, well...you may wish you'd stayed on Valius."

[23]

The cell was three meters on a side of blank bulkhead, the only amenities a padded bunk built into one of walls and a toilet. No 'link, no tablets, no entertainment center, no news of the outside world at all. I'd lost track of how long I'd been inside because the first thing I'd done was sleep. I'd been so exhausted mentally, emotionally and physically, I hadn't even questioned the MPs who'd escorted me from the docking bay to the security holding cells.

Ironically, the last thing I'd seen before I stepped inside was Kah-Luwhen being shoved into a cell just down the hall.

I *had* been fed. I should, I realized, have kept some scrap of napkin or something to keep a record of how many meals I'd gotten, as some sort of counter of the hours, but that ship had sailed. And so had the *Iwo*. We'd jumped once and now we were in microgravity again and I was hooked under the restraint webbing of the bunk, wondering if I should try to go back to sleep.

Instead, I decided to dictate another letter to Vicky. True, I didn't have a tablet or a 'link, but I wasn't going to send it anyway, and the whole purpose was to be honest with myself, so it was just as good pretending to dictate.

Vicky, I bet you'll never guess where I'm sending this message from. Then again, you know where I'm from and how I wound up in the Marines, so maybe you wouldn't be too surprised.

I suppose I fucked up, but I can't feel too bad about it. I think if you had been in my position, you would have done the same thing. Maybe it's better this way. With the war, they're not going to throw me in prison or hibernation. The worst they'll do is bust me back to corporal and stick me in a fire team in a different company and honestly, I think I'd be fine with that. The only thing I've gotten from being a leader is the pain of watching people who trusted me die. I became an NCO and then an officer because people kept telling me it was the right thing to do, and maybe it was, but I won't miss it.

The only regret I have is that my platoon will have to drop on Silvanus without me. Scotty will lead them well, though. At least I hope they'll put him in charge instead of putting the platoon in the hands of some wet-behind-the-ears Academy grad.

I know I've said it before, but I truly believe you'll be a better officer than me. Hell, I can't check the date, but I think you're probably already with your unit now. I hope for your sake you won't have to see the things I've seen, won't have to make the decisions I've made. You deserve better. You deserve better than me.

I know you won't see this, but if you did, I'd tell you that I love you and I want you to be the best officer you can be and don't worry about me. I just wish I knew what day it was...

The magnetic lock on the hatch opened with an obnoxious clunk and I sat up so quickly I nearly floated free of the web restraints. Captain Covington walked through the hatchway, magnetic ship boots clicking and clacking as they released and re-anchored with each step. He seemed taller in free-fall and probably was. Something about the space between the vertebrae expanding without standard gravity to pull them together. I don't know, it was something like that—Vicky had explained it to me once but I'd forgotten the details.

I couldn't jump to attention and didn't try, but I did slide out from beneath the restraint web, holding onto it with one hand to steady myself.

"Morning, Alvarez," Covington said, his expression neutral, deliberately so I would have bet.

"Is it, sir?" I wondered. "I've kind of lost track of time."

The corner of his mouth quirked.

"I suppose you might. You've been in this cell fifty hours." He stepped inside and anchored himself to the center of the deck, arms crossed over his chest. "And Col. Voss would just as likely have left you in this cell until she could arrange a court-martial for you back on Inferno if she'd been the only one making the decision."

"Who else would, sir?" I wondered. Voss was the battalion commander and if she thought I should swing, then I was going to swing.

"Col. Arora of Force Recon." Now he did smile, the thin, cruel smile that was usually all he allowed himself. "Apparently, he was more impressed by the fact you risked your life and your career for his people than Col. Voss was. Then there was Gunnery Sgt. Hayes and every single one of your squad leaders, who all came to me and asked for a transfer if you weren't reinstated as their platoon leader."

I blinked. I guess I wasn't surprised to hear Scotty had done it. He was my friend and he took loyalty seriously. But the squad leaders...I had been pretty hard on them in training, hadn't been shy about correcting them, though I'd tried to keep it private.

"And I *still* had to call in every favor I've ever built up with both the Voss *and* the fucking *brigade* commander to get you out of this." The smile disappeared and he took a step closer, close enough I could almost feel the heat of his glare physically. "And don't fucking think it's going to happen again. You might have been able to get away with playing fast and loose with the rules as a squad leader, but you're an officer now. You don't just follow orders, you make sure everyone follows orders, and you represent the orders you get as if they were given *by* you. You do that because if you don't, people die."

"People were *going* to die," I reminded him. "Helpless people, wounded Marines. Marines who just needed another hour."

"If you want to follow your conscience instead of your orders," Covington snapped, "then I hope you're prepared to spend your next few decades in the Marines as nothing higher than a captain."

I blinked, wondering if I'd heard the tone I thought I had, a hint of bitterness and behind it a stubbornness that not even those decades of bucking the system could kill.

"I, uh...," I stuttered. "I didn't think I was going to stay in after the war, sir."

"Someone has to," he said, shrugging. "Someone has to teach the new batch of kids when the next war comes."

"You really think there's going to be another war, sir?" I asked, surprised.

"Son," he said, squeezing my shoulder, wistful sadness in those usually steel-hard grey eyes, "there's *always* another war."

———

"You get into trouble again," Scotty warned me, "and you're on your own."

I clomped into the platoon area on borrowed ship boots and extended a hand.

"Thanks, Scotty. I appreciate what you and the others did."

He shook it, grinning lopsidedly.

"Well, of course. I wasn't gonna let them put some fucking shave-tail fresh out of OCS in charge of my platoon!"

"Where are the squad leaders?" I asked him, glancing around the empty room. "I have to brief them now. We don't have much time."

"They're on their way," he assured me. "I got the notification while we were doing PMCS. They had to put the suits back together."

"Any word on the Force Recon troops we brought back?" I'd meant to ask Covington, but I'd been so gobsmacked by the news I wasn't going to be busted and sent to another unit, it had slipped my mind.

"They all lived," he said, shaking his head. "They were in pretty bad shape, but they're going to be okay after a couple more days in the auto-docs."

I blew out a breath. At least that had worked out.

"I gotta say, sir, that was reckless as shit. I would tell you that you can't do that sort of shit but you don't seem to listen when I say it." He snorted. "I wish Sandoval were here, she'd be able to talk some sense into you."

"I wish she was too, Scotty."

I hated zero gravity. I really wanted to sit down and you couldn't do it in zero-g. Not in any way that made a difference.

The hatch to the passage outside was hanging open from when I'd entered and I heard the buzz of voices approaching, knew who it had to be. Kreis was the first through and his eyes lit up when he saw me.

"Sir! Damn, it's good to see you back!" He looked as if he

wanted to rush up and give me a hug, but managed to restrain himself and just shook my hand. "Is everything good?"

"We're fine," I assured him. "All we have to worry about now is the mission."

"What's the op, sir?" Carson asked. She wasn't falling all over herself with relief like Kreis, but I thought I saw satisfaction somewhere behind her bland face.

The squad leaders formed a half-circle around me with Scotty at their center.

"This one takes straight to Silvanus," I told them, "and things there are a lot more uncertain than they were on Valius, and a lot more dangerous, too. We have limited intelligence because the situation on the ground there is so fluid. The Marines who were left on the planet have been striking at the Tahni, but they haven't been able to contact the Fleet because of the jamming and harassment by enemy air patrols and drones, especially since we jumped into the system. So, we don't know the realtime disposition of the Tahni forces onplanet or where they've massed to meet our invasion. The plan is to probe their defenses with landings in multiple areas and have more than half our forces held in reserve. Once the brass figures out where the main body of their ground troops is hiding out, they'll deploy the main part of our Drop Troops and Recon Marines."

I tapped a control on my 'link and the image of a city snapped to life in the room's holographic projector, anachronistic in its architectural lines. I wasn't up on mid-Twentieth Century designs, but whoever had written this part of the op order apparently had been, because they'd included an aside about how the whole place had been built along the lines of 1950s Italy, which I recognized as being somewhere in Europe.

"This is Dolabella, the second-largest city on Silvanus."

I scrolled past the main part of the city and into a collection of squared-off boxes, utilitarian and ugly in stark contrast to the quaint if kitschy beauty of the town.

"This is our target, the industrial park just outside town. We're supposed to secure it for a staging area for the next wave of troops. It shouldn't be too complicated, but we don't know what sort of opposition we're going to be facing, so anything can happen. The plan is for our platoon to drop between the town and the industrial park, run a perimeter patrol around the whole thing, check for opposition and clear it out, then stay and hold the area until relieved."

"Do we have any air support if things go bad?" Majid wondered.

"Maybe," I told him. "Depends on how well our signal can penetrate the jamming. We'll have ECM drones up trying to deactivate theirs, but you know how that kind of thing goes. We might have clear signals the whole time or it could be nothing but static. If we don't, then we just have to handle it. As always. But our orders are to try avoid being decisively engaged." I smiled thinly. "Which is officer talk for, we need to try to avoid getting in over our heads and *needing* air support."

I waved at the image.

"Any questions?"

"Yes, sir," Carson said. "I haven't been a Marine that long, and I've been a squad leader even shorter, but I gotta say, I've been noticing that things always go ways the plans didn't account for."

"No battle plan ever survives contact with the enemy, Sgt. Carson," I told her. "It's a reality of war. Is that a question?"

"I guess my question is, sir, well...." She squeezed her eyes shut like she was trying to think about how to say it. "You had something happen that no one expected, and you didn't have anyone higher than you on the ground to tell you what to do. And when you tried to do what you thought was right, what made sense, they threw you into a cell. What do they expect us to do when things happen that aren't in the plan?"

I understood the question, but I wasn't sure how to answer it. What did she think I was, the Skipper? Top? I was barely twenty-three now, barely a staff sergeant before I'd gone to OCS and now barely a lieutenant.

And yet, to her, I was the Old Man. That was a shock to the system. I was the representative of all the combat wisdom in the Marine Corps. And I began to understand what the Skipper had been trying to tell me about presenting orders as if they were my own.

"Carson, for right now, you let me be the one to make the decision. That's why I'm here, because someone has to be responsible." Which sounded better than "shit collector." "I'll make the decisions and try to do what's right for the Marines, for the mission, and for you. And if anything happens to me, you still have the Gunny." I nodded toward Scotty. "But if the time ever comes when you're the one in the position to make those decisions, all you can do is try to do the right thing and accept the consequences that come with it." I met each of their eyes. "If there's nothing else, we jump in-system in an hour and we drop in three. The op order is on your 'links. Go brief your squads and get ready to go. This is the big one. Don't let me down."

"Ooh-rah, sir!" Kreis said, and the others echoed it as they left the compartment.

"Scary, isn't it?" Scotty said to me after they'd gone. I didn't have to ask what he meant.

"Yeah. I'm not ready for this."

He laughed and headed for the hatch.

"No one ever is."

[24]

Dolabella had looked quaint and picturesque in the op order images, a throwback to a simpler time. Seen in the stark light of day from the industrial road circling the city, it looked more like a ghost town.

"Where the hell *is* everybody?" Scotty wondered, seeing the same images I was on the long-range optics.

Deep green shingles baked in the mid-day glare and what looked like real glass windows winked reflections at us, but not a soul walked the streets and no thermal signatures shown from inside. Audio sensors that could pick up a voice from a kilometer away registered nothing but the creaking of hinges from open doors swinging in the warm, summer wind.

We'd dropped near the edge of the entertainment district on the main road out through the industrial district. It eventually led to the spaceport about a hundred klicks away, centrally located between the two largest cities, but there could have been a pitched battle happening there and I never would have seen it. Or heard anything about it.

"You picking up anything, sir?" Scotty asked me. I suppressed an urge to snap that he would have heard any signals coming through at the same time I would. He was nervous, and if Scotty was nervous it was because there was a good reason to be.

"No communications relay drones or dropships overhead right now for line of sight comms," I told him. "And the jamming is shutting down all indirect EM signals still."

The Tahni transmitters were out there, somewhere, bouncing their jamming signals off automated drones. If we found them, we could take them out ourselves, but how often had that happened on any mission I'd ever been on? They hid the things well.

The drop, at least, had been uneventful. The pilots had told me that the Tahni air defenses had been concentrated around Van Trak, the larger of the two cities, and there was a hell of a dogfight happening over there between our assault shuttles and the Tahni dual-environment fighters that the flight crew was quite happy to be missing. We hadn't seen a missile, hadn't detected a single incoming round from launch to drop and I was starting to entertain hopes we could keep up the streak through the whole mission.

I couldn't remember the last time I'd dropped into a combat zone without firing a shot, and I wouldn't have minded giving up the chance at more war stories to tell for some down time. But I wasn't going to hold my breath waiting for it.

"First squad," I said. "Lead off."

Delp was getting better, I thought. Maybe there was just some things the simulator couldn't teach, because with each combat mission, it seemed as if he was picking up the tricks of walking point, things I'd tried to pass on to him that just hadn't seemed to take. There was a certain intuition you had to have to walk point, not just an intellectual knowledge of the terrain features and how they related to tactical movement, but a sense of how the rest of the platoon would have to move behind you if you went along a certain route.

The industrial park was a good three kilometers from the edge of town, far enough away that the purists who had moved to Dolabella for the architecture wouldn't be forced to bear the pragmatic plainness of fabrication centers, warehouses, and automated assembly bays while they basked in vaguely European anachronisms. The city was built in the gently-rolling hill country to the south of the largest continent, and the tree-dotted rises between the city and the industrial areas assured their visual isolation, and assured we would have to move through the perfect place for an ambush along the way.

I felt an itch between my shoulder blades with each step and almost ordered Delp to hit the jets and get us an overhead view, but refrained for the same reason I didn't want to try to launch an aerial drone. The enemy knew we were in the area, but they didn't know which way we were coming, and I felt like it would be a bad idea to advertise our avenue of approach.

We were bypassing a rise, moving through the saddles between two hills, ripping up chunks of shrubbery with each step, when the line suddenly stopped.

"Sir," Delp said, urgency in his words, "I spotted something."

Instinct urged me to run up to his position and see it with my own eyes, but training kept me rooted at the end of First squad, letting the laser line-of-sight relay from around the curve of the hill feed the images from his suit cameras to my Heads-Up Display. The industrial park was visible past the next hill, stretched along both sides of the main road, the one we'd been studiously avoiding on our approach. Stark white sheet metal walls glowed painfully bright in the mid-day light, almost drowning out the details of cargo trucks parked in lots beside loading bays and a flatbed train car sitting in desultory isolation on an otherwise empty track running behind the line of buildings on the right-hand side of the road.

I scanned through the images, both visual and sensor, and was about to ask him what he was talking about when I saw it, too. Just a flicker of an image on thermal, almost invisible against the heat collected in the sheet metal from a full day under the summer glare of the system primary, but I noticed it nonetheless. Bipedal, less than two meters tall, the suit's analytics informed me. And, after a moment's consideration to build a larger data set, they also informed me it was likely human rather than Tahni.

"Everyone else stay in place," I ordered. "Delp, go up and investigate. It could just be some frightened industrial worker the Tahni have kept out here until the last minutes, trying to work his way home, so try not to look threatening."

"I'm in a big, black, metal suit bristling with weapons, sir," Delp reminded me. "I don't know how to look anything but threatening."

Good point.

"Just keep your plasma gun pointed down, okay?"

"Yes, sir."

At least Delp was getting the smart mouth of a point man down pat. That was something else you could only learn by doing.

I tapped into Carson's view and watched Delp approach the building slowly, arms at his sides, and I worried for a moment that it might be a trap until the man stepped out into the open. I switched back to Delp and saw immediately that the man was dressed in the armor of a Force Recon Marine, a Gauss rifle tucked under his arm. He pulled off his helmet to reveal a weathered, lined face with skin the color of café au lait and dark hair cut within a centimeter of his scalp.

"I'm Colonel Daniel Oz," the man said. "I need to speak to your commander."

———

"I've heard a lot about you, sir," I said, shaking the colonel's hand. His grip was firm through his glove, and I had the feeling he was a hard man even before he'd spent a year fighting a Tahni invasion from the inside. "After we lost comms with you and the resistance, I was afraid maybe the Tahni had finally managed to pin you down."

"That'll be the day," he said with a snort of dark amusement that was echoed by the other men and women gathered around the small, folding table.

It was hard to make out their faces in the dim light of the single, glowing strip-light on the wall. No daylight made it past the blackout curtains hung on the windows of the business office built deep in the bowels of a fabrication plant, and from the thermal blankets piled against the walls, no heat or sound would escape it.

Not all of the people at the table were Marines, I could have told that even without the difference in equipment. The Recon troops who'd come here with Oz were a rough group, a hollow, gaunt cut to their faces, something dark and nameless in their eyes, but their gear had been kept in tip-top shape, and if there were some patches holding together the junctions of the armor, they were made carefully and neatly. Their weapons were as uniform as their armor, the standard-issue Gauss rifle of the Recon Marines, and I was a little surprised they'd managed to keep them supplied with ammunition after all this time.

The civilians, though, were a more motley lot, wearing stolen Tahni body armor, some taken from conventional infantry or rear-echelon troops, some salvaged from Shock-trooper powered exoskeletons and repurposed. Their hair was long, the beards on the men shaggy, and there was a feral glow to their faces, one I'd seen before on the resistance on Demeter. There was something that happened to a civilian, someone who'd never even considered joining the military or going to war when they were forced into a situation where they had to fight or die. A flip got switched and it was like they went from victim to victimizer without the benefit of a military trainer to break down their old life and ease them into the new one. I wondered if they'd ever be the same again.

I glanced over at the door, as if I could see what was on the other side. The platoon was out there, hunkered down under thermal blankets, except for Delp, who was still outside on watch. The rest of Oz's force was out there, too, and when I'd come in, I'd estimated there had to be at least two civilians for every Marine.

"Is this all you've got left?" I wondered. I felt naked, sitting there without my suit, but it hadn't seemed politic to refuse a colonel's request to un-ass my armor and talk face-to-face.

"No, I left most of my people back at Van Trak to coordinate with the main effort there." He scowled. "That was when I realized something was wrong. Those Tahni bastards pulled a fast one on me."

"Where are they?" I asked him. "We haven't detected a damned thing, not even from orbit. And where are all the people?"

The place didn't have a holographic display and even the old-style flatscreen monitors in the office looked broken and useless, but one of the civilians had set up some sort of makeshift projector screen on the table by virtue of leaning a meter-wide piece of wallboard against a cement block. Oz took out his 'link and set it on the table, then pushed a control on it and an image projected out onto the wallboard, an aerial view of the road we were on.

"This is where we are," he said, pointing at a rectangular building near the edge of the industrial district, on the side closest to the town. "It used to be a tractor assembly building where they'd take the parts the fabrication plants spat out and put them together into auto-harvesters for the farms."

Which seemed a useless bit of trivia to include, but the guy had been here on his own for a year, so I wasn't going to throw the first stone. He traced a line down the road, past rows of nearly identical buildings, to...something. A dome, but I couldn't tell if it was buildfoam or local concrete, and a really big one. Judging by the size of the building we were in, I estimated the dome had to be at least two hundred meters across. And I didn't remember seeing it in the layout we'd been shown of the place before the drop.

"The bastards built this dome a couple months ago," he said, "right on top of a bunker system left over from the first war with the Tahni. It was built for the civilians to hunker down if the enemy started bombarding the planet from orbit, but the first war never reached this far and most people forgot it existed. But the Tahni garrison commander found out about it a few months ago."

"How many of them are down there?" I asked.

"*All* of them." The disbelief washing over my thoughts must have been plain to see on my face, because he expounded. "Oh, they left their REMF troops along with a couple battalions of Shock-Troopers back in Calliria to distract us, slow us down. But every single one of their High Guard battlesuits is in that complex. Two full battalions, and there's plenty of room for them."

"How big *is* this place?" I demanded, perhaps forgetting a bit of military decorum since he was a colonel, but still...

261

He grinned, not seeming to blame me for it.

"Big enough. It was designed to hold the whole city and then some, ten thousand people. There's enough storage space for supplies to hold a fucking brigade of High Guard in there."

"What's the point, though? How long do they think they can hold up in there? Even a bunker system like that can't stand up to railgun shots from orbit, and it's far enough from town that the Fleet boys wouldn't be worried about hitting the...." I trailed off, the reality of the situation smacking me square in the face. "The civilians," I realized, squeezing my eyes shut, resting my head in my hands, elbows on the table. "They have the civilians there."

"The whole fucking town." That was one of the civilians, a woman with long, blond hair tied into braids. Her words were harsh, but her expression was harsher. "All the ones who've survived this long, who weren't smart enough to get out while the getting was good."

"We estimate it at four thousand people," Oz supplied. "The Tahni built pens inside the dome and they have some of their conventional infantry up there, maybe a few Shock-troopers just to keep a handle on things."

"And if you hadn't been here to warn us," I guessed, "we would have seen the thermal signatures inside the dome and gone in to free the civilians, encountered light resistance and called in Force Recon units."

"And the Tahni would have slaughtered them and whatever armored troops you'd brought along for overwatch. And there'd be no air support, no orbital fires because of the civilians."

"What's their endgame though? What do they think they can do beyond killing a bunch of us?"

"They're aliens," Oz reminded me. "Don't assume they think like we do. But my best guess is that the garrison comman-der, this royal prick named Kan-Ten, thinks he can hold off the ground forces and cause enough casualties for the Fleet to pull back until the Imperium can resupply the system, reinforce their Navy here." He shrugged. "It might even work."

"It won't," I assured him. "The Fleet brought two of the cruisers with them and they're not going to risk those on an extended mission out here. If it becomes clear we're not going to be able to free the civilians, they'll bombard the bunker from orbit and consider the residents of Dolabella an acceptable loss."

I don't know how bleak and cynical I sounded, but even the hardened resistance leader blanched at my statement.

"Jesus, kid," he said, "what the hell have you been seeing?"

"Too much." I stood up, pacing around the room, trying to think. "I have orders not to get decisively engaged. What I *should* do is withdraw and try to get a direct beam signal through this jamming, let my company commander know what's going on. The rest of the landing force is due in just a couple hours and they'll notice the heat sources inside that dome eventually. We have to make sure they don't send anyone in there without knowing what's waiting for them."

"If you're right about what the Fleet's gonna do," the woman who'd spoken before piped in, "then the minute you tell them what's going on under that dome, those people are dead."

"There's not much else I can do about it," I told her. "I got one platoon here, and while I'd be willing to try my hand at getting the civilians out, there's no way we can take on two battalions."

"You might not have to," Oz said. He shared a look with the others in his little command council. "If we're going to use it, this is the perfect time."

"Use what?" I asked. "Sir."

"Follow me."

We ducked quickly out of the door to the office, trotting down a short set of metal-grating steps. None of the others came with us and I assumed they already knew what I was about to see. He led me beneath the hood of an assembly line housing over to what looked a lot like a dome tent, formed from thermal blankets and pieces of wall board. Oz pushed aside a flap and motioned for me to precede him inside.

"What's that supposed to be?" I asked.

It was squat and cylindrical, obviously metal and just as obviously Tahni. All of their tech had a character to it, above and beyond the whole form-follows-function effects that made a spaceship look like a spaceship. Whatever this thing's functions were wasn't obvious from its form, other than it was about a meter long and another meter in diameter and it looked heavy as shit.

"Back during the initial invasion," Oz told me, "there was a pretty honkin' big space battle in orbit, as you can imagine. One of their corvettes took a hit and got knocked into a reentry burn. Those things aren't designed to enter atmosphere, you know. But I guess they were desperate, because they did their damnedest to bring that thing down. And they *nearly* made it, but not quite. But they crashed intact enough for my Marines to salvage this out of the wreckage."

I thought about all the things you could pull out of a Tahni corvette and which of them would be the size of the cylinder at my feet...and which of those a man like Colonel Oz would think was pertinent to the situation. I didn't like what I came up with at all.

"That's a nuke," I said, not one shred of doubt in my heart.

Oz smiled and nodded.

"At least they didn't send me a dumbass. It's the fusion warhead off one of the corvette's anti-ship missiles. The only one we could get off of it, really the only useful thing left." He gestured at the warhead. "There's a single entrance from the bunker into the dome. If you can hold the High Guard troopers at that choke point long enough for my people to get the civilians out, we shove this damned thing right down their throats and set it off."

"That dome won't contain the blast," I said, not even knowing if I was right but willing to take the guess.

"No," Oz admitted. "But the bunker's blast shield will. We just have to get it into the entrance, down the ramp into the storage area and close the damned door."

"Oh, *that's* all," I said, rolling my eyes at him and the hell with his rank. "This is a fucking suicide mission, sir."

"Son, you're talking to a guy who's spent the last year fighting a whole brigade of Tahni troops with a company of Marines and a few hundred half-trained civilians. You want talk to *me* about suicide missions?"

"I got orders," I insisted, "to avoid becoming decisively engaged. This, sir...." I jabbed a finger at the bomb, "...is pretty fucking decisively engaged. You could put a video of this in the fucking dictionary right next to the term 'decisively engaged' and use it in a military textbook."

He started to say something and I waved it off.

"Look, sir, if there were communications open, I wouldn't even listen to this shit. You're not in my chain of command, you know that, right? But it all comes down to this: I can't even think about doing this unless you can get word to the rest of the invasion force. Because if this shit goes sideways and we get wiped out, we're leaving them with two fucking *battalions* of High Guard sitting there ready to bite their ass."

The lines around his mouth hardened and I thought for a second he was going to try to punch me in the face, but he sucked in a breath and nodded.

"I understand. We do have a one-man flyer, homemade job someone used to take out as a hobby back before the war. I could send one of my people back to Van Trak to carry a recorded message from you." He shrugged. "I can't promise he'll make it through. There's a lot of anti-aircraft between here and Van Trak. But he'll get there faster than any of your people."

The man's expression shifted, as if he'd given as much ground as he intended.

"And I'm gonna be straight with you, kid," Oz told me, "I'm carrying off this assault with or without your help. You may not be in my chain of command, but I'm in solid command of my people, and we move out in an hour. It's your call whether you're part of the plan or not."

I stared at Colonel Oz, wondering if spending a year leading the resistance here had left him as desperate and unbalanced as those civilians back at the table, as the ones on Demeter. Was I letting a madman talk me into a suicide mission? Or was I just as crazy as he was?

What the hell was Scotty going to think about all this?

"All right, sir," I said. "Send the messenger. And then get your people ready. We have to do this now."

Before I come to my senses.

[25]

"You have got to be shitting me."

It was, I thought, about the fourth time Scotty had said the same thing in the last hour, and I couldn't honestly blame him for it.

"They're just gonna charge 'em right out in the open?" he demanded.

"That's the idea."

I could see him, but just barely. The platoon was spread out behind two warehouses less than a half a kilometer from the dome, way too close for my comfort, but Oz had assured me that they'd tapped into the hardwired cameras days earlier and were running a looped image from an hour ago, and the jamming would prevent any drones from transmitting a signal back. I wasn't sure whether I believed him or not, but we didn't have time for anything more complicated, so I pretended I did.

The plan was simple. The militia was going to distract the troops guarding the civilians with a frontal attack, draw them out while Oz's Force Recon Marines snuck in behind them and freed the hostages. And like most simple plans, it was also going to be insanely difficult, because getting four thousand people out of that building was going to take time, and the enemy was going to notice. That was where we came in, and that was going to be cutting it awfully Goddamned close.

The part that had offended Scotty this particular time was the frontal assault, because as distractions went, it was pretty damned blatant. The civilian militia was driving up-armored cargo trucks straight down the road, jury-rigged with splinter shields and crew-served KE guns stolen from the Tahni forces over the course of the last year of raids and insurgency. The engines were old-fashioned internal combustion, fabricated from patterns two centuries old and running on home-distilled alcohol, growling with effort as their knobbed tires threw up clouds of dust and clods of dirt behind them. There were seven of them, running with a lead vehicle about fifty meters ahead of the next two, then two by two after that, spread out at intervals so each had a clear field of fire.

In the beds of the trucks, huddled behind the improvised armor shields, the civilian militia clutched stolen KE rifles and laser carbines just slightly oversized for human arms, in armor adapted to their smaller frames from the Tahni. It made them look like children playing dress-up in their parents' clothes, if their parents happened to be genocidal alien religious fanatics.

And while the militia rumbled down the street and we waited behind the factory buildings, Oz and his people were on foot, double-timing around the far perimeter of the industrial district, just inside the tree line of the nearby woods, and with them, on a motorized all-terrain cart, was the bomb.

"Any second now," I said, still on the private channel with Scotty.

The lead truck was a hundred meters from the semicircular freight entrance at the front of the dome, looking as if it might reach the building unopposed, when the double doors slid aside. The Tahni hadn't built bunkers around the outside of the dome to guard it because it was bait and they *wanted* the enemy to walk into the trap, but neither was it undefended. Portable turrets, protected by heavy shielding and mounted on round wheels like powered casters, rolled into position as the doors parted, and heavy, crew-served KE guns opened up on the lead truck.

Sparks rang off the snowplow-style armor across the engine compartment of the truck as tantalum slugs dug craters into plating four centimeters thick. The armor even covered the cab windshield, the drivers steering using external cameras hard-wired into the monitors mounted above the steering wheel, which was rare foresight for which I credited Colonel Oz. The gunner in the back of the truck returned fire, the hum-snap-crack of the electromagnetic weapon audible even from five hundred meters away, like a mosquito buzzing around inside my armor.

"He ain't gonna make it," Scotty opined, something more than disdain but not quite despair in his voice.

And it looked as if he was right. The armor at the front of the truck was being chewed away and the gunner was missing more than he was hitting since aiming from the back of a moving truck was harder than aiming from a fixed position. But the truck wasn't alone, and the formation they'd chosen hadn't been by accident. The two makeshift armored personnel carriers on either side of the lead truck were firing as well, walking streams of penetrator darts up from puffs of dirt to sprays of concrete as they touched the paved courtyard at the front of the dome, and then to sparks of metal on metal.

The Tahni gunner was single-minded and concentrated his fire on the lead truck, and it paid off for him when the vehicle's turret went up in a globe of fire that had to be the gun's power cell catching a round and discharging catastrophically. The truck swerved but pulled back into line with the entrance and my fists clenched when I realized what he was about to do. Militia fighters dived out the back of the vehicle, rolling out of control as they hit the ground at sixty kilometers an hour, ditching at the very last second before the driver slammed the truck straight into the mobile turret.

I hadn't been part of the planning session, hadn't heard how the trucks were equipped or what the plans were, so I didn't know if the explosives had been his idea or something the militia had come up with on their own. But the second the truck hit the turret, it went up in a blast that could only have come from at least a kilo of hyper-explosives.

It was a huge risk. The explosion could have killed hostages, could have brought down the whole front wall of the building, but the armor of the turret seemed to contain it at the front entrance, the concussion reflecting backwards to blow the doors off their tracks and send them crashing to the ground.

Billows of smoke poured up into a mushroom cloud and like cockroaches streaming out from a nest, Tahni Shock-troopers charged out through the gap where the doors had been, pouring streams of KE gun fire at the trucks still approaching the entrance. The powered exoskeletons were an old design, predating the High Guard battlesuits, almost obsolete on a modern battlefield against front-line Commonwealth troops, but still effective against the ragtag militia. Hitting a stationary target from a moving vehicle had been hard for a half-trained resistance fighter; hitting a man-sized figure running through smoke with servomotor-assisted speed was near impossible.

The trucks skidded to a halt and the militia fighters jumped out under fire, trying to use their own vehicles for cover while the turret gunners hunted through the black smoke for the Shock-troopers. Enemy KE guns answered and the fight began to bog down outside the entrance. Normally, I would have been concerned, but this had been the plan. Not *my* plan, but the one

I'd been handed. More troops were pouring out the front, dozens, maybe over a hundred, and the whining hum of KE guns merged with the constant crack of their rounds breaking the sound barrier to create an insistent background static I wished I could shut out.

"Damn it," Carson snapped, "they're going to get slaughtered! Should we help them, sir?"

"Negative," I told her, though the urge was strong for me, as well. "This is a distraction to give Colonel Oz time to free the hostages. If we charge in now, their own battlesuits will come after us and the civilians will be caught in the middle. Maintain position and wait for orders."

Which was exactly what I should have been doing, but I didn't point that out and Scotty had the good grace to keep his mouth shut. At least in front of the platoon, he did. He'd given me an earful when I'd briefed him on what we were doing, particularly the part about the nuke.

"Didn't you come close enough to a court-martial on Valius?" he'd asked, almost yelled at me. "And don't think you'll get off with just being busted in rank and reassigned! If we fuck this up and live through it, you'll spend the rest of the war in a cell! And that's if they don't just stick you in punitive hibernation and misplace your damned file!"

"You're one hundred percent right," I'd told him. "And we're doing it anyway, because everything else I can think of to do is so much worse. And because Oz will do it by himself, whether we help him or not."

That had brought him around, and I knew it would because the same line of thinking had convinced me.

"They're moving in," Scotty said, like the announcer in a soccer game.

It took me a second to spot Oz and his Marines through the smoke and fire and death and chaos playing out in the street.

The stealth coating on their body armor was still intact even after a year cut off from the supply chain, which reduced their thermal signature to close to the background heat, but the furtive hints of motion between the trees gave them away, showed me where to look. They darted out from the concealment of the woods, not becoming embroiled in the pitched battle outside the entrance, simply slipping past it under the shroud of the drifting smoke.

"Get ready," I warned the squad leaders. "Right now, the Tahni think they're winning. But once you see the civilians heading out, the High Guard is going to notice and intervene. If they let those people get away, they're giving up the only asset they have and the Fleet can drop a salvo of railgun shots on them at their leisure."

I was repeating myself, because I'd explained all that before, but that was what you did right before a fight. You reminded the troops of things they should have already known because when the adrenaline started flowing, people forgot the things they were supposed to remember.

It couldn't have taken more than a minute, but a minute was forever during a fight and dozens of the civilian militia had to have died in that time, throwing down their lives to buy it, sacrificing themselves for the ones who hadn't had the chance to fight.

Would there be memorials for *them* after the war? For the ones who didn't pull the final trigger but were willing to die rather than give their world up? For people like Dak and Maria? They were the ones who deserved it. We were just doing our jobs; jobs we volunteered for knowing the risk. All these people had wanted was a simple life on a colony world without Earth holding their hand, and when bad things had happened, they took their defense into their own hands. *That* was admirable. That was worthy of a statue.

"There they are." Scotty spotted them first, probably because he was watching closer than anyone, nervous as a mother hen. "Coming out of the west side."

The entrance on the north was for freight, equipment and the High Guard battlesuits to pass through, but the Tahni had built a smaller, personnel exit on the west, a very human thing, I thought. No human would want to keep opening and closing the ponderous cargo doors just to go in and out of the bunker and it seemed the Tahni were just as impatient and concerned with convenience as we were. Which was also convenient for us.

People streamed out of the western door in clusters of five and six at first, then by the dozens, and I zoomed in with the suit's optics to get a better look at them. They weren't hungry, weren't ragged, showed no signs of deprivation, but they did look desperate and for that, I didn't blame them. Fear was written across their faces, lips drawn back from clenched teeth as if they expected a shot in the back at any second. Oz's Marines escorted them, herding the lot of them toward the woods, possibly to safety but even more importantly, to a place where they couldn't be used as human shields. Dozens, then hundreds of them, and then more of the Marines were coming out behind them and joining in the fight on the side of the civilian militia and I knew any second....

I flinched, even though I knew it was coming, the crackling thunder of the electron blast lighting up the interior of the dome, static discharge sending forks of electricity into the metal tracks of the sliding doors. I couldn't see where the shot hit, but I knew what it had to be from.

"Move out!" I ordered. "Jump, now!"

Delp must have been waiting with the jump controls half-pressed because he burst out from behind the factory like he'd been shot out of a cannon before I could finish saying the words.

The rest of Carson's squad followed him a half-second behind, arcing over the roof of the fabrication center, the superheated exhaust of their jump-jets quivering in the air below them. I waited a full second before hitting my own jets, the boost pushing my chin down into my chest.

Data crashed into my Heads-Up Display, IFF transponders, thermal readouts, targeting symbols, threatening to overload my senses, and I was forced to shed it like water off a duck's back, ignoring the Christmas-tree lights and focusing on what was inside that building. The unmistakable thermal signatures were popping into existence as if by magic, emerging from a shielded tunnel somewhere beneath the dome, just as desperate to stop the exodus of civilians as the hostages were to leave.

Delp reached the freight entrance at the same time as the first of the High Guard battlesuits, the discharge of their primary weapons so close they merged into a single, coruscating globe of white light, so blinding on optical and thermal sensors, I couldn't make either of them out through its glow. It faded in the two seconds it took me to touch the ground only fifty meters from the entrance to the dome, and Delp's Vigilante staggered backward, smoke pouring off charred BiPhase Carbide armor and the suit's left arm burned away at the elbow.

The enemy battlesuit had collapsed forward, the heat pouring off it from the plasma strike making the metal around the hole in its destroyed chest glow white. Carson and the rest of First squad thundered across cracking pavement, disappearing into the shadowed recesses of the dome, leaving Delp leaning against the wall beside the entrance. I wanted to check on him, but his IFF signal said he was stable and the suit diagnostics were flashing yellow, which meant he was still up and running, and I couldn't hold up at the door, not with what was going on inside.

"Scotty, check on Delp!" I called, and then the madness under the dome swallowed me up.

It reminded me of the Shoot-house simulation, a special challenge round we ran sometimes in the pods. The computer just threw everything at you: Shock-troopers, infantry, High Guard suits, civilians, friendly troops and every distraction you could think of. You didn't play to complete the mission because it wasn't possible; the computer just kept sending more and more enemy troops at you until you finally went down. The competition was to see who could survive the longest.

It helped me to think of it like that, to see the shredded bodies of the militia members as a collection of zeros and ones in a computer simulation rather than real men and women who were leaving behind grieving husbands or wives, parents, children. It helped me to ignore the scintillating electron beams crisscrossing the smoke-filled interior of the dome and the sun-bright plasmoids answering them, to think of the triphammer beat of tantalum darts from the Shock-troopers' heavy KE guns as just the computer fucking with me, trying to distract me.

I restricted my focus to only two things: the hostages and the High Guard suits. The Force Recon Marines had the pens open and they were standing in there despite the blistering heat of the beam weapons discharging and the capricious death on the hunt, shepherding the civilians out of the broad, high-ceilinged dome and taking casualties to do it.

The High Guard troopers were pouring out of a hole in the concrete floor, a ramp heading downward to the bunker, huge, shielded double-doors hanging open. The sheer size and weight of them explained why the response had taken so long. Just opening the damned things must have taken nearly a minute all by itself. But they were yawning wide now, and the High Guard suits were pounding up the ramp three abreast, all of them trying to get at the hostages, to stop the Marines from freeing them by the simple and ruthless expedient of killing enough of the ones trying to escape to frighten the others back into their pens.

Scores were already dead, scorch marks on the concrete floor and scattered bits hardly identifiable as having once been part of a human body the only hint they'd ever existed. That wasn't going to happen while I was here. I hit the jets and angled forward, the roar of the turbines painfully loud even inside the suit, reverberating back at me from the walls and ceiling, and shot across the interior of the building, ignoring the fact that I was making myself a target.

Three High Guard troopers were stepping off the top of the ramp and one of them swung his electron beamer toward me. There was no way I could get my plasma gun up in time, but I was in a perfect position to fire a missile. It couldn't get target lock this close, less than fifty meters away, but I didn't have to. He was so close, I couldn't miss. The warhead had just enough time to arm, and the detonation ripped the Tahni trooper into twisted, charred chunks of metal with enough force to knock the two suits beside him off their feet.

Someone, I wasn't sure who with the chaos and bedlam all around me, killed one of the two with a plasma shot and I pulled up and swung my suit around upright three meters over the other downed High Guard suit and then cut the jets. I pistoned my legs downward, smashing my spiked footpads into the suit's chest with a concussion that traveled up my legs and rattled my teeth. The armor over the enemy suit's chest was tough, but force always equals mass times acceleration and my Vigilante had a shitload of both. The High Guard suit's chest plate caved in and crushed the trooper inside and I barely registered his death in a desperate attempt to avoid my own.

Twin bursts of actinic ions sought me out from lower down the ramp and the only reason I wasn't killed instantly was the angle—they'd had to aim high to clear the downed battlesuits and their electron beams flared off the ceiling in coronas of vaporized metal. I barely had time to get my feet under me and was trying to shuffle back around the cover of the door frame, knowing even as I did that I wouldn't be in time, when a barrage of plasma blasts set the very air on fire.

I jerked backwards, convinced at first, that the starfire was another attack from enemy troopers behind me, but the fusillade pounded into the next rank of High Guard suits instead, forcing back the ones it didn't destroy outright. I risked a glance backwards as I shuffled behind cover and saw the IFF transponders lighting up on the Vigilantes of Sgt. Kreis and Third squad clustered around the bunker hatch, the emitters of their plasma guns glowing red.

"Thanks for the save, Kreis," I told him, then took the moment's respite to check on the rest of the battle.

First squad was still engaged with two of the enemy battlesuits just outside the cargo doors to the dome, and Sgt. Carson and Private Jha's transponders were already blinking yellow from damage. Only a few hundred civilians were left inside the building, and Oz's Recon Marines were escorting some of them out the side exit while others simply ran in panic through the chaos of the combat at the freight doors. There were more bodies on the floor than I wanted to try to count, scores of them, maybe hundreds, and quite a few were wearing Recon armor.

"Scotty!" I said, noticing his transponder just outside the cargo entrance. "What's going on out there? How's Delp?"

"He'll be okay," Scotty told me, his voice calm despite everything, "but he got a pretty bad burn and the suit has him too doped up for combat. I sent him into the woods to cover the civilians. There...," he trailed off, sucking a breath in past his teeth. "There aren't many of the Recon troops left to go with them. And the militia is down to about a squad of effectives."

"If you have a line-of-sight, tell that crew with the bomb to get their asses in here while we still control this door!"

"Roger that. They're heading your way now."

Well, what took them so fucking long? I wanted to ask but didn't. I knew they'd been waiting until they had a clear shot through the main entrance and that made sense. They were our one shot at ending this. A flicker of motion caught my eye from the edge of my display and I saw the team escorting the cart past the burning wreckage littering the cargo doorway, their Gauss rifles held at their shoulders, looking for something they could actually hurt with the popguns. Colonel Oz was at the head of them. I'd been surprised when he told me he would be taking the bomb into the bunker instead of out leading his people in the assault.

But I suppose it would have been hard to ask anyone else to do it.

"Shit, here they come again!" Kreis said.

I received the warning from my targeting sensors almost at the same time as the one the Third squad leader shouted, just a mass of reactor signatures coming up from the bottom of the ramp. I tried to line my plasma gun up for where I thought they'd come clear of the overhanging roof and was about to order volley fire when the world exploded.

Or at least that was what it felt like to me when more missiles than I could count blasted up from the bottom of the ramp, fifty meters below, and shot past us with a physical concussion of superheated air, strong enough to make even my Vigilante stagger backward. They didn't hit me, didn't detonate near the entrance, just kept soaring upward until they hit the roof of the dome just to the left of the cargo entrance.

A chain-fire detonation splashed gouts of flame through the building and the shockwave slammed downward like the hand of God, just ahead of several tons of debris.

[26]

I had a flashback to the collapse of the cliffside on Valius, but this artificial landslide didn't bury me or Third squad. It cascaded onto the flooring just inside the entrance, the closest chunk of reinforced concrete twenty meters away from the line we'd taken up at the bunker entrance, sending up huge clouds of white dust to join the smoke billowing outward from the massive new hole in the ceiling.

Second and Fourth squad, though...where were they? IFF transponders were flashing red in scatter patterns to either side of the door, and what I'd thought were lumps of concrete on the floor were my troops, their Vigilantes covered by grey dust. Some were moving, and I was pretty sure most of them were alive.

But the bomb...

The cart had overturned, one of its wheels smashed by falling debris, but the warhead itself was intact, though the once-shiny surface of the cylinder was scratched and gouged. The Recon Marines who'd been escorting it were buried under chunks of rubble, unmoving.

Shit, Colonel Oz was with them.

And suddenly, I had more important things to worry about, because all those missiles had come from High Guard suits, and all those Tahni troopers were rushing up the ramp, covering their assault with a salvo of electron beam fire. Kreis took the first hit, a subatomic scalpel slicing through his right arm at the shoulder, his scream warbling inside my helmet, and I couldn't even take the time to check if he was still alive.

"Fire, Goddammit!" I snapped, throwing my Vigilante onto its side, shooting from the prone. "Scotty, Carson, get in here!"

Someone was listening to me, because when the Tahni thundered up the ramp, they were met by a volley of shots, but not enough, and there were just too damn many of them.

"Break contact!" The order was bitter in my mouth, an admission of failure, and yet I had to give it. If we stayed here and slugged it out with them, we'd be overwhelmed. There was half a brigade down there and we'd started out as a platoon. "Pull back past the entrance!"

We could still make it. The civilians were gone, that part of the mission was accomplished, I just had to go get that bomb. Scotty and I had the communications code to activate it programmed into our 'links as a failsafe. I could get the bomb and take it down that ramp and if I didn't make it out, well... maybe I knew how Oz had felt. Who the hell else would I order to go kill themselves?

"Scotty, Oz is dead. I'm taking the bomb into the hatch."

He was yelling something at me, but I couldn't hear him over the cacophony of battle and the roaring inside my head. I pushed to my feet, fired one last round at the High Guard suits pushing past the burning hulks of their brothers-in-arms and began falling back. The bomb was fifteen meters away, and I kicked the Vigilante in the ass with a burst from the jump-jets, boosting myself the distance in a second.

I grabbed at the bomb blindly, feeling around with my left

hand while I kept my eyes on the High Guard troops coming up the ramp. I still had missiles and God alone knew whether I could accurately target anything with them at this range, but they weren't going to dock my pay for using them, so I fired them off, one after another, not aiming at anything in particular, just sending them through that hatch.

More explosions shook the foundations of the dome, more debris rained down, trailing fairy-dust sprinkles of plaster lit up by the sunlight through the shattered roof. People were dying. I saw two transponders go black and didn't want to read the names beside them. I didn't want to take their names with me to the afterlife, if there was one.

"Get those doors shut behind me, Scotty!" I yelled, taking a step onto the ramp.

I didn't see the shot that hit me. It was lost in a haze of dazzling afterimages, overwhelming the filters of my helmet optics, turning everything into a white blanket of static and I couldn't even separate our fire from theirs until a lance of pure, unadulterated agony speared into my left leg at the hip.

I'd experienced pain before and I thought I knew it, thought we were old acquaintances on speaking terms, that I knew its ins and outs like a veteran. But I hadn't known pain until now. Fire clawed at my body with talons of pure, white-hot metal and I was falling, unable to put a single coherent thought together other than "they're coming."

And they were. I could see them, even though my addled brain couldn't make sense of the images. Three...six...ten...I couldn't count any higher, just one after another of the dull grey golems stalking upward from hell, wielding swords of fire.

The pain fell away and my brain began working for the space of a few seconds before it began to go numb again under the influence of the drugs the suit was injecting into my veins. Some of the Tahni troopers had made it out the front doors, while others were going down, tumbling across the legs of our own dead and wounded, and the rush stalled for just a moment. That was when I saw Scotty.

I knew it was him, not just from the IFF transponder display. I knew it was him because he was prying the bomb out of my suit's clawed hand, grabbing it in his own, firing his plasma gun so close to me the heat was stultifying and I nearly passed out.

"Majid," Scotty said, "get the LT out of here. Portnoy, Bodhi, get on those doors and shut them when I tell you."

"Scotty, no!" I was surprised I could say anything coherent. The words came out slurred and I wasn't sure if he understood, so I repeated them. "Fall back," I told him. "That's an order!"

"There's too many," he said, dismissing both my authority and my estimate of the situation, loping down the ramp. "Portnoy, Bodhi, get your shoulders into those doors!"

"No, damn it!" I screamed the words, but they seemed to be tiny, far away, and I realized I was farther away as well. Sgt. Majid had hold of my suit by the evacuation handle on the backpack and he was pulling me toward the entrance. "Scotty, don't do it!"

"Get that hatch closed, then get the hell out of here," were his last orders, as he ignored mine.

Scotty kept moving, firing his plasma gun as he disappeared into the hatchway. I don't know if Portnoy and Bodhi understood what they were being told to do, but they were both privates and didn't question their platoon sergeant. They slammed the doors shut and even through the explosions and the thunderclaps of energy weapons going off in the enclosed space of the dome, and the beat of my own pulse in my ears, I could hear the massive thump, like the lid of the universe's largest coffin closing.

"No...," someone was sobbing, and I was pretty sure it was me.

We were outside, though it took me a moment to register because the sunlight had disappeared behind grey clouds roiling in from the horizon, as if called in by the smoke pouring off our battlefield in some sort of ancient, pagan ritual. It was raining. Somehow, amidst the chaos, the lightning-strike flare of electron beamers and the supernova blasts from our plasma guns, I noticed the rain.

Majid had let go of my casualty handle and was standing over me like a guardian angel, his plasma gun sending a shot out every few seconds as if on a timer, his last missile popping out of the launcher on his back and streaking off to find a target I couldn't even see. There was at least a company's worth of High Guard troopers who had made it out of the bunker and against the remains of my platoon, those numbers were no contest. We were all dead.

The ground shifted beneath me, rolling like a wave, as if the very planet had rebelled against our war and was trying to shake us off. The dome collapsed in on itself, crumbling like a sandcastle, and the warehouses and fabrication centers around it began to shake themselves to pieces. Majid stumbled to the side, throwing out his arms for balance, like a surfer riding a swell, but the shaking was too much and he was thrown off his feet, crashing to the ground beside me.

The nuke was low-yield, designed to funnel energy through a lasing module and pierce spaceship armor with a single-use laser because nukes were an inefficient weapon for space combat, since there was no atmosphere to propagate the shockwave. The lasing module had been left behind with the wreckage of the corvette, but the nuke was plenty big enough to bring the whole bunker complex down, and maybe us with it.

I was flattened out on the ground, strangely disconnected

from reality, understanding what I was seeing but somehow not afraid. The ground was caving in beneath the wreckage of the dome, swallowing up the remains of the dead, memorializing them under columns of black dirt and dust. The crumbling edge extended outward, ten meters, twenty, seeking me out, trying to bury me with the dead. I welcomed it, knowing my family would be there waiting.

The collapse ceased at the edges and instead, the crater deepened, caving in at the middle again as the bunker's underpinnings gave way, flattening out, opening up a hole dozens of meters deep.

Scotty's down there. But I had to correct myself. *No, Scotty was atomized. There's nothing left of him.*

My head swam, my thoughts scattering away with every gust of the wind. The Tahni High Guard troops had been knocked off their feet just like my platoon, but they were getting up, rolling to the side and pushing themselves off the ground like turtles flipped over onto their backs. I wanted to tell the others, tell Majid, yell at them to get on their feet and fight, but I couldn't put together the thought, couldn't make myself speak over a whisper.

There was still a roaring in my ears, but it sounded different, like it was coming from outside my helmet. Something buzzed distantly and I thought maybe someone was trying to talk to me. I concentrated, narrowed my eyes and forced them into focus.

Aircraft. The sensors were warning me there were aircraft incoming.

Majid was up, shooting, spinning to the side to avoid an electron beam and I wanted to help, wanted at least to pay attention, but I just lay on my back and watched the black dots growing into massive lifting body shapes, kept in the air by sheer power.

Dropships.

Those were our dropships. The flyer had gotten through.

A swathe of scintillating laser pulses chopped into the ground and slewed across a cluster of High Guard suits, sparking halos of sublimated metal disguising the fiery, horrible deaths of the Tahni troops inside. I watched them die without exultation, without relief for myself, only grateful that I hadn't gotten my whole platoon killed.

I felt so damned tired, ready to just sleep, and I knew it was the suit. It had hit me with another dose of painkillers and I wasn't going to be able to keep myself from passing out.

"Majid," I hissed, my voice barely audible. Somehow, though, he heard me.

"Just stay still, sir," the squad leader said, raw emotion tearing at his voice as he stood over me. "You're going to be okay."

How badly hurt was I? The suit simply showed a solid red glow over my hip, critical damage to me and the mechanism, but it didn't tell me whether I had a leg left below the hip. I wasn't sure if Majid was broken up over how mangled I looked or because he knew what had happened to Scotty.

"Take care of the platoon, Christian," I told him, blackness creeping up on me, ready to smother me like a blanket. "You're in charge."

I laid my head against the cushioning in the back of my helmet and surrendered to the darkness. I knew it wasn't permanent, wasn't death coming to claim me. But I wasn't afraid of death. I was afraid of what I would face when I opened my eyes again.

[27]

My eyes fluttered open and the round, pleasant face of an older man wearing white Medical Corps scrubs cohered into sharp relief in the harsh lights overhead.

"Welcome back to the land of the living, Lieutenant," he said, tapping something into the tablet he held down at waist level. "I'm Major Hollingsworth."

I tested myself, tensing one muscle after another from my neck down to my feet before I tried to move. There was a slight tension to my right leg at the hip and I felt like my foot had been asleep and was just waking up. Nothing hurt, though, and I sat up in bed. I was, no surprise, in a sick bay. I wasn't sure *which* sick bay, but there was gravity. I took a deep breath and tasted just a bit of the tang of a living atmosphere, subtly different from shipboard air even inside an air-conditioned building.

"I'm still on Silvanus."

"Very good," Hollingsworth said, miming applause. "I guess I can skip the cognitive tests since you obviously seem to have your faculties about you. Yes, you are still on Silvanus and to answer the question that *always* comes next, you've been kept under for the last one hundred and ten hours."

I blinked, trying to do division in my head.

"That's like four and a half days, right?" I said. I looked down at my right leg. I was dressed in a short hospital gown and my legs were bare, so I could see that there was something...*off* about the right one. It took me a moment to realize it was that there was no hair on my right thigh. "How bad was it?"

"Let's just say," Hollingsworth told me, quirking an eyebrow, "that you have a brand-new warranty on everything between your hip and your knee. There wasn't much left and we had to grow the replacements in a cloning vat." He shrugged. "Well, most of it. The skin and muscle. We replaced the nerves with superconductive fibers and hooked them through to your natural nerves with a small implant computer, and we replaced some of your ligaments and tendons with byomer, which is, I understand, the same thing you use for the motivators in your battlesuit."

He snorted as if he found it amusing.

"It'll be more durable than the original setup, so don't worry about that. The nerves are still synching up with the superconductive fibers, which is why you may be feeling some pins-and-needles below the knee. It'll go away in a day or two."

"Am I good to go, then?" I wondered. I looked around, but didn't see any clothes.

"You are," Hollingsworth said, with something of a craftsman's pride in his smile. "But you're going to have to wait here. We sent for someone from your unit to bring you some clothes and escort you back. They should be here shortly."

I nodded, setting back on the bunk.

"I got the room to myself," I said, looking around at the three other empty beds in the room. "Did we not have many casualties?"

"There were a few." He shrugged. "Mostly civilians from their militia. But you're one of the last to recover. I don't keep up too much with that end of things, but from what I've been told, there wasn't much opposition on the ground, once the Fleet got past the air defenses."

"No, I suppose there wouldn't have been." At least that was some comfort. "Thanks for taking care of me, sir."

"It's my job, son."

He left the room, nose buried in the tablet and I discovered that I had to relieve myself. The door to the head was open and I was ambulatory and not burdened by a catheter, so I did it the old-fashioned way. When I came out, Captain Covington was waiting for me, arms full of a uniform and pair of boots.

"Skipper," I said, trying not to flinch. I felt like I was six years old again, waiting in my room for my father to decide on a punishment for some mischief I'd been caught at.

He said nothing, just took the clothes over to the bunk and set them down, placing the boots beside them as if in some sort of sacred ritual, a memorial for the dead.

"I'm not here to lecture you about what you did wrong, Cameron," he told me. "Partially because I don't think you need me to, but mostly because you did a lot of other things right. You took a huge risk and went against express orders, and if things had gone differently, you'd be facing the court-martial you avoided just a few days ago. But that's not what happened. The actions of your platoon saved the lives of thousands of civilians and probably prevented hundreds of casualties for our own troops, so instead, you're probably looking at a medal."

I walked over to the clothes, grabbing the pants and pulling them on, unable to meet his eyes.

"Scotty deserves a medal," I told him, "not me."

"There'll be plenty to go around," he assured me. "In fact, I wouldn't be surprised if Gunnery Sergeant Hayes was awarded *the* Medal."

Now I did look up into his grey gaze. The Medal meant the

Medal of Valor, the highest decoration in the Commonwealth military. It was usually awarded posthumously.

"Colonel Oz should get one, too," I judged. I hesitated, knowing the question I should ask and yet dreading it. "What was the butcher's bill, sir?"

"Along with Gunnery Sgt. Hayes, you also lost Sgt. Joanna Carson, Corporal Andre Levoie, and Privates Nicholas Coffee and Cece Nemmens."

Each name was a kick to the gut. Five dead, including Carson. I hadn't even seen her fall. Levoie was a team leader from Third squad, and Coffee and Nemmens were both from Second. They'd probably died when the roof caved in on us.

"As for WIAs, well, that was nearly everyone." He raised an eyebrow. "But you were the most seriously wounded and the last to get kicked out of sick bay. We have temporary barracks set up in downtown Dolabella, and they're waiting for you there."

I stripped off the hospital gown and replaced it with a T-shirt and a fatigue blouse, then knelt down and pulled on the boots, taking my time strapping them tight. My shoulders shuddered as I clenched my jaw against a sob.

"How can I face them?" I asked him, choking the words out. "How can I walk in there after what I did to them?"

"This is what being an officer is about," Covington told me, his voice soft, the way my father's had been when he gently explained to me what I'd done before laying down whatever punishment he thought was justified. "These decisions. There's a price you're going to have to pay for them, not just today but for the rest of your life. And it's going to be worse than anything a court-martial could throw at you, son."

He offered me a hand up and I took it, letting him help me back to my feet.

"But that's a judgement you're going to make on yourself.

Your people won't hate you for the ones who died as long as you don't throw their lives away. They'll love you for winning, for leading them into the guns of the enemy. And as much as you may hate yourself for it, you have to let them."

I didn't know how to respond to that, so I changed the subject.

"What are we doing now, sir? Do you know? Are we staying here?"

"For a while. Nothing official has been announced, but everyone knows this was the last domino to fall. We've taken back our worlds, now it's time to take down the Imperium. I'm sure that'll require a bit of reshuffling, reinforcing, restocking. You know how it goes."

The ghost of a smile tugged at the corner of his mouth.

"In fact, while you've been on the mend, we've been getting reinforcements in. Fresh battalions of Drop-Troopers, with Vigilantes right off the production floor, and officers straight out of OCS. Once you've checked in on your people, you might want to take a transport buggy over to First Platoon, Alpha Company, Fourth Battalion. There's someone there who wanted to say hi."

———

Dolabella had come back to life in the last four days, the remnants of the population moving back into their houses and pulling down the boards from their businesses, already trying to restart their lives without a break.

I'd tried to catch one of the transport buggies, the automated, open-topped cars making their way back and forth from one end of the town to the other, but the first two had filled up quickly and I'd finally just decided to walk. It was, I'd discovered, mid-morning, and the sky was blue and beautiful. It might have been a spring day in any city where thousands of people hadn't died in a war. It was educational.

There were no haunted looks in the eyes of these civilians, no resentment, only gratitude. More than one rushed out from their shop or their restaurant or café to shake my hand and try to give me free food as I walked across the downtown to the Marine encampment on the opposite side from the industrial district. They had no way of knowing who I was, that I'd been there when they'd been freed from the pens, but they knew *what* I was, and that was enough.

It almost made the losses worthwhile. Almost.

I took a breakfast sandwich when it was offered to me by an older lady wearing a stained apron and a huge smile, both because she'd insisted and because I was starving, and I ate it on the way.

I found her in a makeshift, outdoor platoon area, a ring marked off by empty cargo containers between temporary shelters thrown up from buildfoam. Folding seats were gathered in a circle around a sand table and four very young-looking squad leaders listened while a seasoned gunnery sergeant stood off to the side, arms crossed, scowling in general disapproval, as if he began the day pissed off and then went looking for privates to justify it.

"This will be our patrol area," the young platoon leader told her people, pointing at the north side of the city-in-miniature as represented on the sand table by empty ration wrappers and a few stray rocks. "We've been tasked with making sure the Tahni didn't leave any troops behind for sabotage or insurgency operations. We'll be running two patrols a day, one at dawn and one just before dusk. Second Platoon will take the night shift for the first two days, then we'll switch unless they've pulled us off it by then. This isn't rocket surgery, just basic tactics. I want you to go over the tactics and movement techniques involved with your squad, so get a lesson plan ready before lunch and present it to Gunny Bruell for approval. Are we clear?"

"Ooh-rah, ma'am!" the junior NCOs chorused.

"Then get going!" the Gunny snapped. "Get your asses in gear!"

The squad leaders scattered to the wind and the Gunny grumbled after them, leaving just Second Lieutenant Victoria Sandoval. Vicky's hair was cut shorter than I remembered from her last video and she'd lost some weight, thinning out her face, leaving edges sharper. I stayed where I was, partially concealed behind a maintenance rack and the Vigilante suit resting upright in its grasp.

I stepped out from behind the battlesuit. Her eyes flickered toward me, not truly seeing who I was at first, then snapping back up and locking on mine. Then she was flying across the distance between us and throwing herself into my arms, kissing me fiercely. I held her tight, not wanting to ever let go, reveling in the feel of her, in the warmth against my body.

It wasn't exactly model military decorum, and someone might have been watching but neither of us much cared. It lasted forever, and once forever was over, she hugged me around the neck, burying her face in my chest and sobbing softly.

"The Skipper told me about Scotty," Vicky said, the words muffled against my chest. "I'm so sorry, Cam. I can't believe he's gone."

"It should have been me," I said, pulling away from her, bitter anger rising in my gut. I'd been unconscious for days and feelings I hadn't yet had time to deal with welled up unbidden. My fists clenched and I squeezed my eyes shut, not wanting to let the tears come because I knew they wouldn't stop anytime soon. "It was my command. No one else should have had to do it."

"Scotty was a good man," she said, stopping me with a hand

on my chest. "And he was a good Marine. He knew what he was doing, and he knew you would have done it if you could." She gave me a stern look. "Don't second-guess him. It was his choice."

"I'm going to have to record a message to his family," I realized, horrified. My legs felt as if they were going to give way, and I collapsed into one of the folding chairs. "What the hell am I going to say to them?"

Vicky sat down beside me, grabbing my hand in hers and squeezing it.

"Tell them the truth. He gave his life to save his friends." She shook her head. "It's more meaningful a death than most of us are going to get."

"I've been thinking about that a little since you left," I confessed. She was still holding my hand and I felt her fingers tighten reflexively.

"What?" she wondered, forehead creasing in confusion, or perhaps concern. "Dying?"

"That, too." I shrugged. "I mean, how could you not? But mostly what happens if I don't. If *we* don't."

"I thought we'd already decided on that. Remember? The farm, the shared nightmares, the kids we would freak out with our war stories?" She was trying to make light of it, but there was a stress behind the words.

"We did," I acknowledged. All those videos I'd recorded and deleted, everything I had told myself she didn't need to hear I just blurted out anyway. "But we both keep changing, Vicky. The war keeps forcing us apart, and it's nobody's fault, it's just the way things keep happening. Every time we come back together, we're different people. Shit, sometimes I feel like I've aged a million years. And I'm just afraid that one of these times when I see you again, that new version of you isn't going to love the new me anymore."

I thought she might be angry. I could understand her being angry. Instead, she kept hold of my hand and kept her voice steady and calm.

"Let me tell you something, Lt. Alvarez. You are my anchor. However much either of us might change, because of this...." She ran a finger over her lieutenant's bar. "...or because of what we go through, no matter how much we get tossed around by the waves in this shitstorm of a war, you are the one thing that holds me to a center point. Without you, I'm just drifting."

"That was almost exactly what I said to you in a video message I recorded," I told her, laughing softly. "I didn't send it because I was dealing with some stuff and...well, you had OCS and I didn't want to lay it all on you right then."

She leaned over from her chair and pressed her forehead against mine.

"Things are going to get crazy pretty soon," she warned. "We're going to be invading Imperium worlds. I can't wrap my mind around that shit unless I know we're going to be there at the end. So how about this? We don't have to promise we'll love each other after all this is over. We don't even have to promise we'll like each other. We just have to promise we'll give it a chance." She drew back and offered a hand to shake. "Deal?"

"Lt. Sandoval," I told her solemnly, "you've got yourself a deal."

WHAT'S NEXT IN THE SERIES?

CONTACT FRONT
KINETIC STRIKE
DANGER CLOSE
DIRECT FIRE

ABOUT RICK PARTLOW

RICK PARTLOW is that rarest of species, a native Floridian. Born in Tampa, he attended Florida Southern College and graduated with a degree in History and a commission in the US Army as an Infantry officer.

His lifelong love of science fiction began with Have Space Suit---Will Travel and the other Heinlein juveniles and traveled through Clifford Simak, Asimov, Clarke and on to William Gibson, Walter Jon Williams and Peter F Hamilton. And somewhere, submerged in the worlds of others, Rick began to create his own worlds.

He has written a ton of books in many different series, and his short stories have been included in seven different anthologies.

He currently lives in central Florida with his wife, two children and a willful mutt of a dog. Besides writing and reading science fiction and fantasy, he enjoys outdoor photography, hiking and camping.

www.rickpartlow.com

Printed in Dunstable, United Kingdom